W9-CCX-584

AUG 18

BRASS

This Large Print Book carries the
Seal of Approval of N.A.V.H.

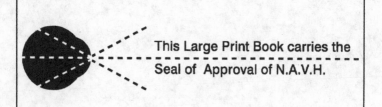

This Large Print Book carries the
Seal of Approval of N.A.V.H.

MT. PLEASANT PUBLIC LIBRARY
MT. PLEASANT, IOWA

DISCARD

BRASS

XHENET ALIU

THORNDIKE PRESS
A part of Gale, a Cengage Company

Farmington Hills, Mich • San Francisco • New York • Waterville, Maine
Meriden, Conn • Mason, Ohio • Chicago

Copyright © 2018 by Xhenet Aliu.
Thorndike Press, a part of Gale, a Cengage Company.

ALL RIGHTS RESERVED
Brass is a work of fiction. Names, characters, places, and incidents either are the product of the author's imagination or are used fictitiously. Any resemblance to actual persons, living or dead, events, or locales is entirely coincidental.

Thorndike Press® Large Print Peer Picks.
The text of this Large Print edition is unabridged.
Other aspects of the book may vary from the original edition.
Set in 16 pt. Plantin.

LIBRARY OF CONGRESS CIP DATA ON FILE.
CATALOGUING IN PUBLICATION FOR THIS BOOK
IS AVAILABLE FROM THE LIBRARY OF CONGRESS

ISBN-13: 978-1-4328-5082-1 (hardcover)

Published in 2018 by arrangement with Random House, an imprint and division of Penguin Random House LLC

Printed in Mexico
1 2 3 4 5 6 7 22 21 20 19 18

TO MY MOTHER:
THIS BOOK IS FOR YOU,
NOT ABOUT YOU, I PROMISE

CHAPTER ONE:
ELSIE

When the last of the brass mills locked up their doors and hauled ass out of town once and for all, it seemed all they left behind were blocks of abandoned factories that poked out from behind high stone gates like caskets floated to the surface after the Great Flood of '55.

But that wasn't true. They also left my father's hands with nothing to callus them, those poor idle bastards that once upon a time abandoned a Korean Stratocaster knockoff in favor of a Bridgeport milling machine, and just like most love triangles, it turned out he chose wrong. It left my mother slumping over the assembly line at the Peter Paul Mounds and Almond Joy factory down the street in Naugatuck, where she sometimes felt like a nut but more often she felt like a highball. It left my sister, Greta, younger than me by two years but with test scores that painted me a remedial toddler by comparison, with a tic that made her pull out her hair until the white bald patches of her scalp shone through like flags of surrender.

And when the last of the brass mills locked up their doors and hauled ass out of town once and for all, they left me with a change jar that hadn't even gotten me close to the wicked coupe that was going to drive me out of Waterbury so fast I wouldn't even bother to burn the skid marks that would mark my goodbye.

What I got instead was a job at the Betsy Ross Diner, slinging poutine fries and spanakopita to third-shifters headed to or coming back from their jobs as hospital guards, machinists, small-time drug dealers. And I got Bashkim, an Albanian line cook at a Greek diner named after an American patriot.

I swear to Allah, you are the most beautiful girl I have ever seen. That's what Bashkim said to me after three weeks, when he finally looked up at me in the kitchen window for the first time. It was 1996, the middle of March, a brutal part of the year when spring was supposed to hit but didn't, when I'd given up on ever being warm again.

My being beautiful was about as likely as me ever wrapping my fingers around the leather steering wheel of a souped-up six, but for the first time since I'd started working there, clocking in seemed worth the sweatbox polyester uniform and jingle-change tips. My mother had warned me when I took the job to watch out for the Albanians who worked at the Ross, because she heard they treated their women like sacks and that their tempers ran hotter than the deep fryers in the kitchen, while the nice Lithuanian boys I should've been dating had the decency to ignore their women altogether and drink themselves silently to death in their garages. *These Albanians,* she'd say, shaking her head, *they just speak Albanian to each other all the time.* Her own parents barely spoke English but also didn't want their kids to learn Lithuanian, lest they be accused by their neighbors of being pinko bastards, so to her, open communication in any language was offensive and weird. But I was never one to take advice, and anyway, I figured she was talking about the teenage Albanians who jumped kids in the movie theater parking lot, or the middle-aged ones who choked me out of the dining room with the Marlboro Red smoke that leaked out of their mouths like cartoon thought bubbles. My mother wasn't talking about Bashkim. He was way worse than she could ever have known about, or she never would've lent me the money to buy the uniform.

I swear to Allah, you are the most beautiful girl I have ever seen.

Well hallelujah! or whatever the hell Muslims had to say about that. I might've had an Our Lady of Sorrows prayer card tucked into my wallet where the dollar bills were supposed to go, but I believed in Allah right then, because Allah believed in me. I'd been holding out hope that I wasn't really ugly, just a type of pretty that common people didn't get, and what was I surrounded by if not the common? But Bashkim, no way, he wasn't common. He'd lived halfway across the world, as far away from Waterbury as my grandparents once had. Albania. Europe. So it was Eastern Europe, with its dictators and Communism and plastic sandals worn with mismatched tube socks. No geography teacher ever taught us that Eastern Europe and Europe are not one place, not one people, not one neighbor lending sugar to the other. Anyway, the way my mother told it, Albanians were basically Arabs with a European mailing address, while we Lithuanians had had the good sense to be conquered by nice righteous Christian crusaders. Still, I was thinking

10

that maybe Bashkim saw something familiar in me, something Old World and refined, despite the thousands of years of peasant stock that had culminated in the second-generation American plainness that was Elsie Kuzavinas. I thought maybe some of my grandparents' European blood still somehow coursed through my veins, despite forty-something years in Waterbury, Connecticut: Brass Manufacturing Capital of the World.

I swear to Allah, you are the most beautiful girl I have ever seen.

Those weren't the first words he said to me, actually. Before that there was: How do they want that burger cooked? Why are you throwing away those creamers that aren't even used? How old are you?

Almost nineteen, I told him.

What's your name?

Elsie.

I swear to Allah, you are the most beautiful girl I have ever seen.

Bashkim's accent was even worse than my grandparents', who mostly let their twenty-six-inch Panasonic do the talking for them anyway. His voice started so far back in his throat that every word smacked of laryngitis, almost hurt to listen to. And Bashkim wasn't pretty, either, at least not in the bland way that girls like me were supposed to like. His nose and cheeks were as harsh as his voice, all angles and sharp points ready to pierce right through you if you looked him straight on. But his eyes, god-damn. So blue they were almost black, as if the grills in the kitchen had singed a perma-nent reflection of the butane-blue flame forever licking up under his chin.

"I swear to Allah, you are the most beauti-ful girl I have ever seen." He bore right into me with that stare, didn't look down while he sliced tomatoes into lopsided wedges that oozed green guts onto his apron.

"Shut up," I said.

"What reason to shut up? Don't you want to be a beautiful girl?"

"I don't care."

"You should care. You should feel lucky you are so pretty. Most people are not so pretty. Most people I don't like to look at so much."

Adem and Fatmir ignored him. The only English they understood was cussing, and anyway, I'd already figured out that the cooks at the Betsy Ross all had their favorite waitresses, wide-hipped single mothers of one or a couple, girls so desperate they heard compliments in the calls of *fat ass* that followed them out the kitchen doors.

12

Compliments like that earned the cooks blushes, giggly slaps on the wrist, blow jobs in the employees' bathroom before the ten to two o'clock rush. So I guess Adem and Fatmir figured it was finally Bashkim's turn, that it was either shyness or the wife the waitresses told me he'd left back in the old country that had stopped him from calling out before. But what he said, it wasn't *fat ass* and it wasn't a compliment, not really. It was something more like a threat, at least with those eyes sharpening it into something that jabbed my gut like a switchblade.

"Unless you are ungrateful," he said. "Unless you are a bitch."

He got me on that one, man. Even my mother, Catholic to her core even if she hadn't said a Hail Mary since getting knocked up with me by a Holy Cross High School dropout, would agree it was something close to sin to be ungrateful.

Then Bashkim ignored me for the next three nights, even though I still walked slowly through the kitchen on my way to the employee exit to see if he'd look over. But he said nothing, so I just stepped outside to wait for my mother to pick me up, since I'd broken up with my last ride, Franky, three nights before, the timing not at all coincidental. I didn't know if I could pronounce Bashkim's name right, but even if I got the accents all wrong, it still sounded like a symphony to me compared to *Franky*. And Franky, not Frank, was his honest given Christian name, which was funny to me before it was embarrassing, although really, what did I have to be embarrassed about? One look at my stringy White Rain hair and yeah right I'd ever be the girlfriend of a boy named Laird or Lawrence or Anything the III. Those boys lived down in Westport or Fairfield and maybe, *maybe* the worst off of them got sent to Taft, the boarding school fifteen minutes away in Watertown. I bet it was the rich boys with disciplinary problems who got sent there: the rich parents thought their sons would watch the poor bastards who maintained their dorms pull off in dry-rotted Datsuns, and that they would imagine the poor bastards going home to their second-floor apartments on the East End of Waterbury, to their crinkly-eyed twenty-three-year-old common-law wives and their scraggly toddlers with chronic drips of Fudgsicle on their yellow tank tops even though Fudgsicles were too expensive to have in the house, and the troubled rich sons would think, Could that happen to me? though in

14

fact, no, it could not happen to them.

So fine, I'd gotten rid of Franky, because it was true he was no knight in shining armor. But I wondered for a minute if that hunk of Toyota steel he used to drive me around in was close enough to it, because I didn't feel a single one of the eight degrees the bank's digital thermometer had said it was while I waited ten, then fifteen minutes for my mother, who had a history of leaving me stranded while she napped. And even if I found a dime to call from the pay-phone lobby, and even if she didn't sleep through the ringer, it would be ten minutes minimum before her LTD could even begin to climb out of first gear and keep pace with our neighbor Jimmy riding his daughter's pink ten-speed to some strip-mall pub after having sold his ancient Chevy for scrap metal. So I stomped my Buster Browns on the pavement, partly to keep the blood circulating but mostly just because — because the skid marks Franky's tires had made a week before were still frozen into a blackened patch of ice that I could shatter if I kicked down hard enough, because to hell with my mother and to hell with Franky and to hell with the waitresses who were inside and warm and giving head to the cooks in exchange for baskets of hot cheese fries.

Then I heard, from behind me: *What are you doing, ding-dong?*

It was enough of a shock to scare the steady out of my legs and send me ass-down to the ground. "Huh?" I said and scrambled to get back to my feet.

"I said, 'What are you doing, ding-dong?' " Footsteps crunched over the gravel, and then Bashkim stood in front of me, fists gripping the red ties of a half dozen weeping trash bags.

I must've looked like someone who knew a thing or two about trash herself, down on the tar with my legs splayed, showing off the cotton briefs bunched underneath my pantyhose, the ugly, shiny pantyhose that only fat dance-line girls and diner waitresses wore. And I was the most beautiful girl Bashkim had ever seen, right? Obviously he didn't understand what the word meant in English, or else he'd gotten fluent enough to lie straight-faced in a second language.

"I fell down, jerk. Thanks for asking," I said.

Bashkim offered his hand to help me up, and his skin was as cold as the air, so his touch felt like needles. And he didn't let go when I was back on my feet, and I swore even with everything else out there frosted over I was somehow sweating, that a fever I

16

didn't know I had was breaking.

Still, I managed to say, "And don't call me ding-dong. Nobody says that. Just call me an asshole if that's what you mean."

Instead he called my name.

"Elsie. Elsie," he said.

Where it came from, what it meant, I didn't know. But I knew where it went. Straight from the tips of my toes, which I thought had been frostbitten to permanent numbness, but no, I was wrong, because a feather-tickle started there and then danced on up those shiny tights, which were suddenly warm as fur. Franky had never said my name twice like that, as if it sounded so good he had to hear it again. Rocco before him had never said it, or Joe Pelletier before him. Especially not Joe Pelletier before him, who instead had just shrieked when he tore what was left of my virginity, crying because he thought the blood on his thighs was his own.

"What are you doing out here? It's too cold for you out here," Bashkim said.

"It's too cold for anyone out here."

"It feels good to me. The grill is hot. Even in winter it feels like hell back there."

"Maybe hell froze over," I said. "And that explains why it's so cold in this town."

Bashkim finally let go of my hand and

squinted at me, as if he'd lost a contact lens and had confused me for someone else this whole time.

"It's an expression," I said. " 'When hell freezes over.' "

"I know that. I know the expression. You think this is hell here?"

Across the street, one sign remained lit in a plaza with a half dozen storefronts, a rent-to-own center that had managed to stick around a couple of years, even though the refrigerators people rented to own must've been hard to fill after the grocery store in the plaza had gone out of business. Next door to the Ross a floodlight shone from the garage where people brought their Dodge K-cars that had broken down on the way to the rent-to-own center, where they were shopping in the first place because they couldn't afford to buy refrigerators outright after putting their paychecks into last month's car repairs. And next door to the garage was a dingy twenty-four-hour laundromat, where people washed their linens while waiting for the estimates from the mechanic, bleaching the brown halos left behind on their pillowcases after sweaty, sleepless nights worrying about where the next rent-to-own payment would come from if they couldn't get to work without their K-cars.

And then they came into the Ross for bottomless cups of Maxwell House, and left behind thin dimes for me.

"I think this is maybe the crappiest place on earth," I said.

Bashkim laughed and pulled a cigarette from behind his ear. "How much of earth have you seen?"

"Enough," I said, but I didn't mention that it'd all been in my grandfather's *National Geographic*s. "Can I have a cigarette?"

"You haven't seen nothing," he answered for me and pulled a soft pack from his front pocket, the Marlboro he shook from it curved from the shape of his thigh. The cigarette was still warm when it reached my lips, and it sent heat through the rest of my flesh before he even flicked his Bic to light it for me.

We both stood for a minute, exhaling, our white breath thick in the air between us like a chaperone.

"I'll be out of here when I get a car. And finish school. But mostly when I get a car," I said. My mother liked to remind me that I'd barely put away enough for a pine air freshener after three years of my big talk, but she was a woman who went by Mamie because she didn't like the sound of Mommy, said it reminded her of creepy skinny guys who pay money to be bossed around by ladies in leather. And she couldn't use Mom, because that was for women with tennis bracelets and husbands. I'd ride a Power Wheels down I-84 just to prove that lady wrong.

"I lived in three countries without a car. Now I have a car, and I don't leave to go anywhere anymore," Bashkim said.

"Don't tell me it's because you reached your destination."

Bashkim ashed his cigarette, then pulled the one from my lips and ashed that one, too. I decided to interpret that as a weird Albanian act of chivalry, though really, any act of chivalry would have been just as foreign to me.

"You're freezing," he said. "Hell froze over. Your boyfriend is picking you up?"

"My mother. I don't have a boyfriend."

"Yes you do. I am your boyfriend."

"I don't know if your wife will like that," I said.

"You don't say anything about my wife. That's rule number one."

Rule number one. It was settled, then. We had our first rule before we had our first kiss, but for damn sure that was what made him my boyfriend. And it hurt me to face that kind of truth, like seeing my ugly face on the video cameras on display in the front entrance at Sears, but I couldn't wait for rule number two.

The next night, Gjonni, on duty for what must've been his twenty-seventh straight hour, argued with Bashkim in words that sounded like a Zeppelin record played backward. I never could understand who at the Ross was actually related to each other, since everybody called each other Cousin, except for Gjonni, the boss, who went by Uncle, and Yllka, his wife, who people were too afraid of to call anything but her proper name. But I knew Gjonni and Yllka were real family to Bashkim, because the three of them fought the hardest, and because Bashkim and Yllka, who the waitresses told me shared actual blood, had matching deep creases scored across their foreheads and mouths, Yllka's just a little deeper set with middle age. She'd already gone home for the night, though, so this bout was strictly man-to-man.

Gjonni said to me, "You can use our phone to call your mother. You don't have to spend your money on the pay phone, princess."

Bashkim answered for me. "It's late, xhaxha, this is when regular people sleep. It's not busy. I will drive her home, I will come back."

Gjonni shook his head and spoke louder, talking so fast that I didn't think even Bashkim could catch it all in his native tongue. But even though Gjonni's voice overpowered Bashkim's, apparently Bashkim still won, because a few seconds later he was unknotting the apron strings around his waist.

"Let's go," he said.

He wadded the apron into a tight ball that tumbled apart when he threw it onto the counter behind him. Inside my intestines were doing the same, streaming into my legs like unspooled thread from a bobbin.

Bashkim led me to a Fiero in the parking lot, a white coupe in fresh-off-the-lot condition even though Pontiac had booted that model from the assembly line years before. It was the kind of sports car that Franky and the rest of the auto-shop meatheads in my school used to drive, since it implied muscle and always needed to be worked on, but it apparently also appealed to Eastern Europeans who were pretending to be James Dean without ever having seen a James Dean movie. Bashkim thumbed at a scratch that didn't exist before he unlocked the door for me.

"This is what you're saving for, huh?" he asked.

"Kind of," I said.

"You know how to drive something like this?" His pointer and middle fingers wrapped over the stick shift, those two digits thick enough to span the entire eight ball that, naturally, was the shifter's knob. Big thick fingers like that reminded me of the overfed amaretto-soaked shift bosses who always volunteered to play Santa at my mother's Christmas parties back when the factories would spring for Christmas parties, but somehow on Bashkim they didn't gross me out. They seemed right, like he needed strong hands for more than just fondling preadolescents after a fistful of rum balls.

"Not really," I said.

"Your father did not teach you?"

"Last thing my father taught me how to drive had training wheels," I said.

"That's reverse."

"What? Where's reverse?" I asked, but he just wiggled the shifter somewhere else.

I tried to pay attention to what his clutch foot and shifting arm were doing as he lurched forward and pulled out onto Wol-

23

cott Road, but mostly I fiddled with the radio, rolling the knob from the AM talk radio station it was set on through a half dozen FM classic rock stations, all of them playing songs more worn-out than classic. Bashkim pressed harder on the gas, and the engine revved into the same shrill pitch as the Billy Squier pumping through the speakers.

"Aren't you supposed to shift it?" I asked.

"I know how to make this car move, ding-dong. You just pay attention."

The car was moving. Moving and bucking and growling like a rabid junkyard dog.

"Okay. You have to take a left up here at Stillson," I said, but he drove right past it and instead banged a last-minute right onto Long Hill, a road that lived up to its name, lined on both sides with woods dense enough to bury the victims of the kinds of things that took place in the neighborhood where Long Hill ended.

"Where are we going?" I asked.

Bashkim shrugged. If he was taking me somewhere to slay me, I hoped the newspaper would get it right when my body was discovered and some local crime reporter had to come up with three hundred words about it: that I was happier to have died Bashkim's victim than his nothing-at-all.

24

Instead he pulled the car into the parking lot of an L-shaped warehouse tucked behind a gate of overgrown shrubbery and parked it nose-out at the farthest corner from the road. "Get in this seat," he said. I moved my hand to open the door but he grabbed my wrist. "Just crawl over me."

I swung my leg over to the driver's side and slid across his lap. He grasped my hips between his hands and held me on top of him for a few seconds. His lap was so warm a million tiny beads of sweat sprouted from my skin and I felt greasy and disgusting, exposed for what I was.

He let go.

"Tight squeeze," he said.

I nodded, pulled myself the rest of the way over to the driver's side, and gripped the steering wheel tight while he settled into the passenger seat.

"What are you doing, ding-dong?" he said. "You have to turn the car on if you want to drive it."

I turned the key in the ignition. The car turned over and retched and stalled out.

"You have to push the clutch in to start it," he said.

I pressed the clutch down and tried again. The car turned over and the engine kept running this time.

"Hey, I did it," I said.

"You have to move before you can say that." He pulled my hand onto the shifter and draped his over it. "You start in this gear. Push in the gas a little bit and let out the clutch a little bit at the same time."

The car choked like an asthmatic and puttered out.

"Little more gas," he said. "Let the clutch out slow. Very slow."

I tried it again. This time the car sneezed but kept rolling forward.

"Now we're going," he said. "Let the clutch go all the way. Now go faster. No, keep steering, too, ding-dong. Just drive around the whole outside of the parking lot. Hear how the engine is so loud now? Now you have to go to the next gear. Here," he said, and he guided my hand to second. "When the engine gets loud like that, you have to shift to a higher gear. There are five gears. You get to fifth gear on the highway only, usually. Here is too small to get higher than second, maybe third. You see, there's a picture on the knob there of where the different gears are, but you can feel it. In between the gears you are in neutral. It's the same as when you press the clutch, that's neutral. Get it?"

I nodded, even though I only kind of got it.

"Good. Now pull out onto the street. Make sure you're in first. Always start in first."

It wasn't graceful, but I managed to do what he said. For the first few minutes, he had to direct every move that each of my limbs made: *left leg over the clutch, now press down onto it, relax your right hand, now pull the shifter to the right, now push it to the left, slower now, faster now,* all acting and reacting and going against instinct. My left hand had to steer the car alone, and my bicep ached after only a few minutes of guiding it without the help of power steering. Driving the Fiero was nothing like driving my mother's LTD, which felt passive, like it was the road that was moving while I sat still. Bashkim navigated me through streets that I'd never driven down even though I'd spent my whole life in Waterbury.

"This is so awesome," I said, once I'd gotten used enough to the movements that Bashkim didn't have to prompt them step by step.

"Yes, and it will be more awesome when you can drive it over twenty-five miles per hour. Always it was my dream to have an American sports car."

I didn't tell him that no American had ever dreamed of owning a Fiero, that at best they'd settled for it.

"Now pull into that parking lot up there on the right," he said, guiding me to another tucked-away warehouse. "Put the shifter in neutral and turn the car off."

After a minute he still hadn't given me the next direction, so I turned to him and asked silently for it. The glow from the nearest streetlamp barely lit the car, but even so, I could make out the lines around Bashkim's eyes, radiating like the beams of a sun in a child's drawing. He smiled, and it filled in the creases around his lips. Before that night I wondered how those lines had even gotten there, when I'd never once seen him smile.

"Now come over here." He patted his lap. "I want to teach you something else."

I obeyed. After all, he'd gotten me this far.

For weeks Bashkim and I dated in the front seat of that Fiero. He never let me drive it again, and I took that for another act of chivalry, that he wanted to chauffeur me around, because why would I want to take it for anything else?

But eventually I started complaining

about the stick shift leaving a dent in my lower back, and that I was starting to feel like one of those two-dollar whores we sometimes cruised past on Cherry Street on our way to the Burger King. Finally he caved one night, negotiated with Gjonni to work a single instead of a double, and drove us to the dozen-room Queen Anne he shared with two dozen other people. The house was like most of them at the top of Hillside Avenue, all clapboards and gables and places for Rapunzel to let down her hair, but nobody thought to call them mansions anymore, not since the brass executives who used to live there fled down to Georgia and the maids moved into the places they used to clean.

"Like *90210*, right?" Bashkim said.

"Yeah, it's, you know, big," I said. And it was, only those epic ceilings you couldn't reach even with a step stool just made extra room for all the sadness, all those lace curtains draped over foyer windows like widows' veils. It was a house built for pipe tobacco that reeked instead of Marlboro Reds.

"It needs soap and water," Bashkim said, looking at the three women leaning against a banister. It was obvious they didn't speak English, but they knew they were being accused of something, and they stared at me like I was the one who'd tattled. They scattered when we walked past but came back together when we closed the door to Bashkim's room behind us. Even if I didn't understand any of the words they used, I understood perfectly well what they were saying. Other than their outdated denim and the babushka that the oldest one among them wore, they were just the same as the girls back at Crosby High.

"They don't like me," I said to Bashkim.

"They don't like nobody, not even their husbands," he said.

"Do you like me?"

"I love you," he said, and it was a good thing there was a doorframe to lean against, because hearing him say that almost took me down. Bashkim had misused words with me before, like *blow work* when he meant *blow job,* but then again, I had been promoted from car girlfriend to bedroom girlfriend, so I thought: Well, maybe he means it?

So I said to him — whispered, really — "I love you, too," and he answered in Albanian, a word I never learned the meaning of but now assume meant something along the lines of *oops.*

There were tiny thumbtack holes all over

the walls in Bashkim's room, little scars where the snapshots of his wife had obviously been the day before. I probably should've chosen to think of it as courtesy that Bashkim had shoved them all into a drawer with his underwear and tube socks, but instead it made me feel like one of those two-dollar whores down on Cherry Street all over again, which even my skank stretch jeans with the lace panels up and down the legs didn't make me do. Having something to hide made it seem like we were doing something wrong, when up until that point I was feeling like everything was pretty damn right.

"What was up here?" I asked.

"Up where?"

"On the wall. What was hanging? All the holes. Looks like you had pictures tacked up."

"There is nothing," he said and went back to work on me, which took so much effort on the air mattress that we finally just finished off on the floor.

But once he was done, I went back to thinking about the pictures that should've been hanging. A lady in a babushka and no smile, like the lady outside Bashkim's door. A lady dressed in gray even on her wedding day.

31

"What's the matter with you today?" Bashkim asked, after I passed on a cigarette and ignored him jabbing his thumb into my armpit. He flirted like a kindergartner, jabbing and poking and running away.

"Nothing's the matter," I said.

"Liar," he said.

"It's just."

Another thumb in the pit. "Spit it out, dum-dum," he said.

"It's just what's the story with your wife?"

"Ach," Bashkim said. He swung around and pulled up his BVDs, but I grabbed on to his arm before he could put on his trousers. I planted my face into his back, which was hot and full of pimples that I had never noticed before.

"I didn't mean it like that," I said.

"I told you not to ask about my wife."

"We have to talk about it sometime," I said.

"Why?"

"Because I'm lying here naked in your room and you're telling me that you love me and you're going to have to leave me someday."

"I am not leaving anything ever anymore," he said. He pulled away, but he dropped his pants back on the floor and sat down on the mattress, and we sat there looking at our own useless limbs.

"Don't worry about Agnes," he said, finally. It was the first time he'd spoken her name aloud to me, and even though I was the one who brought it up, I wanted him to take it back.

"I can't help it," I said. "I know how this is going to end."

"You don't know nothing. She is not leaving Albania and I am not going back. What does that sound like to you?"

"It doesn't sound like anything. It sounds like exactly how things are right now."

"And that is not enough? You want more?"

"I don't know," I said, but I did know: of course it wasn't enough. I still needed a car and a ticket out of my mother's house and an epic sort of love you can get tattooed across your forearm without thinking twice about it.

"You want more?" he asked again, this time a little disgusted, and I was about to change my mind and tell him, *No, of course not, this is all I need,* because I was afraid that he would take even that away. But then he said, "She does not want more. She wants nothing," and I saw that the disgust wasn't directed at me, and I felt so much relief that I had to smile, even though I knew that wasn't appropriate, like laughing at a funeral.

"Sorry," I said, but he wasn't looking at me anyway. He was looking at the holes in the wall like he was trying to make a pattern out of them, a constellation or something, but he couldn't read an astrology map any better than he could read English.

"That place, everything it did to us, to our families. She would be happy to die there like our fathers. Born in a camp, a prison, and she wants me to die there. It's sick. It's not the way things should be."

"Camp?"

"Yes, the camp, the labor camp," he said, like the phrase was supposed to jog my memory, but to me camp was just a place where practicing Catholics sent their kids to study the saints and where they usually instead popped their cherries. Bashkim saw my blank face and shook his head like a special ed teacher talking to his most hopeless student. "The work camps, they were places where enemies of the state were sent. Disgusting places. You would not even want to raise animals in there."

"And your father was in one?"

"My whole family. I was born in one," he said. "It was home until I was fourteen."

"Jesus," I said.

He shook his head. "There was no Jesus,

no Allah. No god at all there."

The Albanians at the Ross, sometimes they talked about stuff like *the Party* and *the Prisons,* but I never really thought about what those words meant to them, because they were just line cooks and dishwashers, and every line cook and dishwasher I knew came from the kind of terrible third-world place that made Waterbury look like Daytona Beach or some other mystical paradise. I didn't want those people to try to convince me that I really didn't have it so bad here, the way my grandparents, fifty years after landing in Waterbury, still said things to me like *You think cleaning a toilet is hard? Try living under the Bolsheviks.* I didn't want to think about how it was unfair that some people had it so much worse when I'd already committed to fixating on people who had it so much better. But Bashkim wasn't just a line cook from a land that it seemed like *Time* invented for a cover story. He was the person who taught me to drive a stick and give a proper hand job and make everything taste better with feta cheese. He was the first person I knew who was willing to go thousands of miles to upgrade a crap life for a better one, when my own people seemed to have landed in Waterbury only to take the first offer that was handed to them.

35

He was perfect, an inch shorter than I thought I would've liked, but with an extra few inches around the biceps. That was the wrong thing to be thinking at that moment, but I was thinking it anyway. It took both of my hands to circle one of his arms.

"Why were you there?" I asked. "What did your father do?"

His muscles grew stiffer under my palms, and he shrugged. "He owned cows," he said.

I waited for him to continue, and when he didn't, I said, "And?"

He looked at me. "And nothing. That is enough. He had cows that he didn't report. He wanted to sell them, but the state found them and took the cows and took our property, and my parents were sent to dig in the fields."

"But that can't be it," I said. "You weren't allowed to have cows?"

"What do you mean, it can't be it? Of course it's it. You could not have anything that the Party didn't want you to have. That meat was for Hoxha. Everything was for Hoxha. That is all there was. You were either friend or enemy of the Party."

"What's Hoxha?"

"Not what, who. A dictator. I would not even call him a man."

"One man? How can one person eat all of

that meat?"

Bashkim and I looked at each other, each of us shocked by how confused the other was. "One person could not. That was not the point. The point was that nothing was for you, everything was for him."

"But that's *it*? Really it? Just cows?"

"That's it? You do not understand at all. That was a big, dangerous thing. That was not just *it*."

"So it was like Russia? It was that bad?"

"Russia. I would have liked to escape to Russia."

"My grandparents escaped the Russians in Lithuania. They talk about it like it was the worst thing in the world, like half their school-teachers got sent to Siberia," I said.

"The worst thing is when your own people are the ones torturing you. No Russian knows how to hurt you the way your own people do."

"God," I said. "Really?"

"And this is what she wants, to stay there and remember," he said, kind of quiet, like he was talking to himself.

"That's stupid," I said, and it was supposed to sound encouraging, but he wasn't listening to me anyway, or at least he wasn't looking at me. He was still reading those walls, a little more intently even. Maybe they were starting to make sense after all.

"The problem with Albanians now, it's Albania this, Albania that. Albania has most beautiful mountains, Albania has most beautiful seas. But what do they know about mountains or seas? They lived in a prison. Even the ones not in the camps, they lived in a prison. Then Hoxha dies and the Party falls and they go to Austria or U.K. and work in kitchens all day and night. They don't know nothing about any world outside of Albania. They just close their eyes so they don't have to find out. Me, no, I know better. I come here and I won't go back. Never."

"I'm glad you're here," I said, like an idiot.

"When I get my money back, I will divorce her, and then the last of me is gone from there."

"Money?" I asked.

He smiled a little, and I could almost see that yellow canary feather stuck between his teeth. "Yes, money. Good money. An investment I made. One good thing about Albania, it's, what do you say, the ground floor now. You put a little money in now, it comes back soon four and five times more. This money I made at the Ross this month, already it's twice as much." He shook his head. "I will be paid back. It's too late for my father, but I will be paid back."

Investment, he said. A year in America and he already understood better than I did what this country was built on. As far as I was concerned, an investment was some kind of cheap ploy to make you give someone your money in exchange for promises that are impossible to fulfill, the way the billboard for Western Connecticut State University on I-84 said INVEST IN YOUR FUTURE, and showed a smiling nurse-to-be checking the pulse of an old lady who'd soon not even be alive. It was a scam, the billboard. I went to an information session and they told me there was a two-year waiting list to even be accepted to the nursing program, but in the meantime I could take core classes like English and Sociology, which would give me the kind of solid foundation it takes to be unhirable for life. When Bashkim said the word *investment,* though, it didn't sound quite so hopeless. He had a light in his eyes that the recruiters for WCSU most certainly did not. And he was also talking divorce, which was the whipped cream and cherry on top of it all. Never mind that I'd seen enough prime-time TV to know never to believe it when your boyfriend talks about leaving his wife. But Bashkim wasn't a soap opera villain, some conniving *90210* hunk, he was for real, and I knew it because he was talking about leaving Aggie not for my sake but for his. The way he said it, all bitter and disgusted. And the opposite way he said *investment,* all hopeful and smug, he obviously understood something about it that I did not, even though the word was in my native tongue.

So I asked him what he meant, and he just laughed.

"It's not something to explain to a woman. All you have to know is I won't be flipping hamburgers forever. Soon I buy my own place, you know? Gjonni can be my cook."

"And what will I do?"

"You will do nothing. You will just enjoy. You will drive your own sports car that I buy for you."

"A Jetta," I said. "Not a sports car. A new Jetta."

"What else?"

"An apartment in Manhattan."

"What else?"

"Um, a fancy dog. A poodle or something."

"Okay," he said. "Whatever you want." He wasn't even smiling like it was part of a joke. He was for real, this plan he had was for real, and I was lucky enough to be invited

40

along. Maybe everything he was talking about was just a hypnotist's pocket watch swinging before my eyes, but even if there was a little piece of me that thought I should know better, there was no way I'd refuse the offer. An impossible dream was better than no dream at all.

Some people won't be surprised at the fuckery of which you're about to prove yourself capable. These would be the people who see you as a case file: latest in a line of fatherless daughters, lifelong recipient of free school lunches, attractor of stares since puberty came on fast and hard six years before, when you were more interested in Saturday morning cartoons than Saturday evening rec room parties. But those that look deeper into the file will also see a lifetime of honor roll recognition, an IQ well above average but safely shy of genius, not a single behavioral demerit from K all the way through twelve. And those that know you outside of the file will recall how you quit playing flute in the marching band because you were afraid others might catch you taking a wrong step, how you were once so shy that you were tested several times for autism, and they'll say: *No way, not Luljeta,*

Luljeta would never screw up that way.

But Luljeta will.

To them, to the people who know you, this fuckery will come out of nowhere, but you recognize that it's been in your DNA from your very conception. In a recent visit to WebMD, which you consult when seeking explanations for why you often feel so tense and queasy, you learned of a theory that certain autoimmune diseases can lie dormant in the body until triggered by an unrelated illness or injury, meaning a patient can recover from the flu only to be diagnosed with type 1 diabetes. You were exposed to your first antigen moments before the end of last period's study hall, when you received the email you now understand as the universe's final hint that you are not what you have been promised by aspirational posters in the public library you could someday be:

The admissions committee at New York University has carefully considered your application and supporting credentials, and it is with regret that I must inform you that we are unable to offer you admission to one of our NYU campuses this year.

There were a record number of applicants,

43

they explained. Over sixty thousand, they explained, more than half the population of your entire city, though very few Waterburians were actually among those numbers. Not even the students in your honors classes would have considered applying there, since for the most part, honors classes at Crosby High are simply code for "not remedial." To apply to NYU, one should be exceptional. To be exceptional, one must obtain perfect grades in challenging AP classes and a stellar score on the SAT, for which one has been prepared since third grade. One must perform charitable work at Guatemalan orphanages over Christmas break instead of logging in double the hours at the IGA, have a father to insert in the slot about Expected Family Contribution, and have a mother who could navigate you through the world of higher education instead of simply saying, "I don't know, you just better go somewhere if you don't want to end up like the rest of us."

In short, one should be not you.

You're ranked fourth in your class, behind the twin sibling valedictorian-salutatorian duo and their cousin, all children of Crosby High teachers, who can't afford on their public servant salaries to send their children to Sacred Heart or Holy Cross. It has been made clear to these students by their parents that they will attend a Jesuit university and break the cycle of public teaching to which they themselves have been condemned. It's been made clear to you by your mother that you should aim for at least B's and look into the health sciences, since your mother thought once upon a time that she might want to be a dental technician, and there's always work in that kind of field. Your aspirations were always higher than tartar scraper, yet you walked into the SAT testing session with no preparation other than a large extra-light-and-sweet tumbler of Dunkin' Donuts and twelve years of public schooling in a district in which the per capita income is less than half the cost of NYU's annual tuition, idiotically believing that simply paying attention in twelve years of math and English classes was sufficient groundwork for the standardized test that would dictate the course of your future.

And still, you thought not only would you get into NYU but you'd get in with early decision so that you could spend Christmas break feeling less bad about having nothing to do, knowing it would be the last Christmas break in which you would be so bored and lonely that you thought you might actually throw up.

45

This all seems so terribly and obviously naïve to you now that it feels even worse than Christmastime nausea. It feels like a literal punch to the face.

But of course it's not. The literal punch to the face is something altogether separate, bad-news lightning striking twice in one day. The literal punch to the face comes from a girl named after the Señor Pancho's Tuesday night special she was undoubtedly conceived under the influence of.

Margarita never liked you. In third grade she stole the math work sheet you'd been working on, and though you were not a tattle, you were also not a failure, as evidenced by the straight A's in your aforementioned case file. You'd had no choice but to tell on Margarita, because otherwise you would have been the one who ended up with a zero for the day, which, up until a few hours ago, you believed actually mattered. Your case against Margarita wasn't difficult to prove: though hastily erased, your name had clearly been visible on the work sheet under Margarita's, and the handwriting on the rest of the paper was obviously not that of the emerging sociopath who claimed to have done the long division problem that would likely still be impossible for her to this day. Margarita vowed then that vengeance would be hers, and for years she doled it out in little morsels, stealing your regular bra from the locker room while you were in gym clothes for the badminton unit, somehow orchestrating an elaborate musical chairs number that ensured you would never find a lunch seat for the rest of your time in the Waterbury public school system.

But those were children's games. Margarita was now a woman, with a body that had skipped over adolescence and landed straight on forty-four-year-old mother of three. She hadn't actually borne any children, but there were rumors she'd recently undergone her third abortion, the first having been chemically induced and completed in the bathroom off of the food court in the mall, the second brought on by a kick to the gut near that same food court, and the third the old-fashioned surgical kind paid for by her mother's boyfriend, who it turned out had been staying over on nights even when Margarita's mother was working third shift at the twenty-four-hour CVS. Accompanying Margarita's saggy, enormous breasts was the toxic indignation of someone chronically shat upon, whose rage was directed not at her perpetrators but at those who dared to be unburdened with the same traumas as she was. Her targets were those whose mothers weren't on a first-name basis with all the street cops and methadone clinicians in the city, those who remained in school for more than the Head Start breakfasts. Even without the Great Third-Grade Math Work Sheet Caper, even if she could read all the big words in your NYU rejection letter, you would have been the bull's-eye in Margarita's crosshairs.

The punch from Margarita is thus both out of nowhere and as predetermined as the revolution of the planets around the sun. This shittiest of days had been decided galactically, and while, in retrospect, the NYU application seems to have been a practical joke you walked straight into, Margarita was something you had always had the good sense to avoid. Normally it was easy enough, as most of her school days are spent in the modular office trailers where they send troubled students for remedial education. If not for the weekly bomb threats called in by the same barely literate sophomore from the same school pay phone every single Monday, you might have been able to avoid her through graduation day, to which surely she would not be receiving an invitation. However, that day's bomb threat comes during AP History, held in a classroom whose evacuation path empties straight into the lot containing the remedial education outbuildings. This is, you think, somewhat akin to placing the baby zebras just beyond the lion enclosure at the zoo.

Outside, you hear, "Bitch, what you looking at?" and while you shudder at Margarita's voice, the one iota of gratitude you're able to muster at that moment results from your relief that Margarita isn't talking to you. You're not even facing her, in fact, and though you feel pity for her target, you don't dare look for it.

"Bitch, don't ignore me," Margarita says, this time closer. Still, you don't turn. You keep staring straight ahead at the water tower past the football field, wondering if you could slip through the fence separating you from Pierpont Road unnoticed, and if you'll ever have the guts to just walk away, or if there will ever be anything within walking distance worth taking the risk for.

The next *Bitch,* however, is accompanied by a push on your shoulder, hard enough to knock you into the chest of Antony, a six-foot-five freshman who frequently takes on half a dozen guys at a time on the basketball court but who obviously doesn't want to be seen by Margarita as a collaborator with you. He pushes you back upright and walks away, his spot quickly filled in by a group of a dozen rubberneckers eager to take in the carnage that's sure to ensue.

You still can't get yourself to turn around, so Margarita does it for you, spinning your shoulders until you're forced to look at her straight on.

"I saw you looking at me, bitch. You a dyke?" she says.

"I wasn't looking at anything," you say, trying hard to keep your voice from falling apart, knowing your fear will only make you more appetizing prey.

"You calling me a liar?"

"I literally didn't even see you until just now. I literally was looking the totally opposite way."

"I'm a fucking liar, is what you're saying?"

"That's not what I'm saying."

"So I'm fucking stupid, is what you're saying?"

"I never said that," you manage to answer.

"So you call in this bomb threat, you fucking towelhead?" Margarita says.

"No," you say.

"Bullshit, you fucking terrorist. Yeah, Lady Taliban. How they let you in this school? This school is for fucking Americans, you fucking camel jockey," Margarita says, stepping closer.

"My name is Albanian. Albania's in Europe," you say.

"What?" Margarita asks, momentarily more confused than enraged.

"Camels don't live in Europe."

And just to ensure that you're doing what you think you're doing, challenging Margarita instead of fleeing from her, you add, softly but clearly, "Stupid."

You realize, as the word leaves your lips, that you are able to do this because you're feeling something even stronger than fear: rage. Rage is not a new feeling to you, but it's a new word for the feeling, which before you'd always thought of as confusion. But confusion is chaos, and in the second it takes to look Margarita in her hateful, beady eyes, you realize that your rage can have the precision of a freshly sharpened fillet knife. You decide that just as she has done for you all these years, you will make Margarita the surrogate for the world's rejections and injustices and the stain on your favorite Target sweatshirt. You will face her, you will steal her superpower shittiness, and you will destroy her and the random unjust life forces she represents. By simply invoking a two-syllable word, *stupid,* you are attempting to cease being a victim and reclaim your sense of agency, a term that you'd only ever heard in the context of an AP lit class.

Only Margarita's rage is bigger and more experienced than yours, and her practiced fist lands hard on your face.

In movies, the sound of fist on flesh is created in sound labs by men slapping their hands against hanging slabs of beef, and even after Margarita's fist recoils, you expect to hear this same familiar effect. In reality, a well-landed punch makes very little sound. In fact, for half a minute, you hear nothing at all except for the receding waters of Long Island Sound at low tide, which is remarkable, since Waterbury, despite its name, is nearly forty miles from the ocean. And what you see when you look ahead of you doesn't look like an ocean, except for maybe the Red Sea, if that's a name to be taken literally.

The sequence of events after that gets a bit hazy. There are flashes of light, which turn into people, which turn into a single person, namely a physical education teacher who hadn't run a mile in under fifteen minutes since the first Reagan administration. He remains behind in the nurse's office to bring down his blood pressure after you've been ice-packed, ibuprofened, and shuffled along to the assistant principal, where you sit alone for twenty minutes, hallucinating you're sitting behind one-way glass, waiting to point out Margarita to Jerry Orbach, who'll send her along to Sam Waterston, who'll get her to break down on the stand and confess to her theft of your math work sheet and her multiple abortions and her hate crimes against European camel jockeys, yelling that she would've gotten away with it, too, if not for you meddling kids. By the time you realize you're conflating *Law & Order* with *Scooby-Doo,* two syndicated shows you watch in succession every time you stay home sick from school, you're joined not by any members of New York's finest but by the assistant principal and your own mother. It's then that the warm opiate blanket covering your body's pain receptors is snatched off, and the fact of Margarita's practiced fist on your eye socket is fully realized.

"Jesus Christ, what the hell did that animal do?" she cries. *She* is Elsie Kuzavinas, your mother, your own personal creator, and she rushes straight to you and runs a thumb over the swelling as if anointing you, as if her fingers are smeared with holy oil rather than the motor oil left over from the daily engine check that her Ford Contour requires. Instead of healing, though, her hand makes it feel as if every single nerve ending in your body has migrated to your face, which has then been doused in lighter fluid and set on fire.

Despite the pain, which is acute, you feel so entirely defeated that you can't even muster a whimper. Your mother, of course, is the one who rails, because she's the railer, the kind of tough broad represented exclusively by natural brunettes in movies. She could have a second career as the before picture in Botox ads, because even when she smiles, which she manages to do occasionally, the parallel lines etched between her eyes remain, making it clear which of the emotions dominate her life.

She isn't anywhere close to smiling at Mr. DiPietro, the assistant principal. "Why is this girl allowed in school? She's obviously a psychopath. She's been after Luljeta for years," she cries, her voice a half octave higher than even her usual railing voice.

"Margarita has her issues, but she has the right to a public education, too, and until today, her outbursts haven't been quite so violent," Mr. DiPietro tells her. "We're like the police: we can't act, we have to *re*act."

"That's bullshit," your mother says. "You acted when you set up a dress code. You acted when you brought in drug-sniffing dogs last year."

"I understand that you're upset," Mr. DiPietro says, obviously speaking exclusively to your mother, because he looks only at her when he's talking, as if you're not only half blind at the moment but fully deaf. You will most certainly not be mentioning your NYU rejection to her, because you can imagine her on the phone with the admissions office, doing her shrilling with them, as if the key to upward mobility were indignation instead of having enrolled you in a CCD class as an extracurricular ten years ago. She'll try to convince you that the system is bullshit and rigged and that you're better than all of those Long Island princesses anyway, when one look at their eighty-dollar Urban Outfitters maxi dresses and you know that's not true. You're fourth best at Crosby High, you'll tell her, and she'll think you're bragging about it.

You hold a cold compress over your bad eye and fix the other eye on the diploma on Mr. DiPietro's wall, an MEd, cum laude, from some online university you've never heard of. Even with the stark purple bruise already forming over your right eye, you apparently disappear completely in a room. Only your mother and, in a way, Margarita ever bother to drink you in. Even your father ran back to Albania once you stopped causing trouble in the womb, as if you were superboring even to the person whose interest in you was supposed to be innate. Your mother had told you that he got mired in a green card fiasco and decided to stick around once the country formed a tenuous Balkan democracy, but you always suspected the decision was personal, not political. Your mother said he was an asshole anyway, and you were better off without him, but at least she got you out of the deal. That's what she explained, and whenever she said it, you wondered if that last part was supposed to sound as sarcastic as it did to your ears.

Your whole life was supposed to be about proving that you're as unlike your loser transient father as possible.

But you can't beat nature, as NYU has so kindly reminded you. As Margarita's been reminding you for years.

Your mother and Mr. DiPietro continue to argue the nuances of Crosby High's disciplinary policy, and you wonder, not for the first but for the most substantive time, what happened to the man responsible for your hearty gapless thighs, your mane of thick hair, which Supercuts employees admire but which can't be controlled outside of their chairs, the well of rage that you have just begun to lower your bucket into and drink from. You've always known you were unlike your mother, who seems more pestered by rage than driven by it. She wants things easy. She wants you to prep for fields such as nursing and early childhood education, which will lead to the kind of life in which you'll vocate Monday through Friday and vaguely recreate on Fri/Sat/Sun until retirement, which you'll spend in a condo with a trio of small, goopy-eyed terriers. Your mother's plan has been for you to be the first in the family to never have to rely on government assistance, to live a life of such comfort that when early heart disease sets in, you won't even have the will to swallow your daily prescribed beta-blockers. Your plan, meanwhile, is to bloom into something freakish but interesting and impossible to ignore, like a corpse flower. In your room before your mother comes home from work, you've already experimented with the heavy eyeliner and matte lipstick you'll wear, the shade of red on your lips becoming a signature. It's Luljeta Red, your peers will say. Your peers will use your name as an adjective. You'll be wild and mysterious, like the father you're not supposed to want to resemble.

But who knows, maybe your father is actually interesting, like many assholes are. For the first time, you consider this possibly worth a look.

Mr. DiPietro tells your mother that Margarita will likely be expelled.

"I damn well hope she's expelled. I hope she's arrested. I haven't ruled out pressing charges," your mother says.

"Unfortunately," Mr. DiPietro says, "Luljeta will also have to be suspended."

Your mother pauses, throws her right hand to her heart, and shrieks, "What?"

"We have a zero-tolerance policy for fighting," Mr. DiPietro says. "Believe me, I have no doubt that Margarita started this fight, but it takes two to engage."

"Engage? Engage? Standing there while someone rams a fist into your face is engaging?" your mother says.

"Witnesses have told me that words were exchanged," Mr. DiPietro says.

"Do you even know Luljeta? Ask her teachers. Ask anyone. She would never *engage*," your mother says.

"I did engage," you say, interrupting your mother. It stops her midsentence, and she and Mr. DiPietro stare at you, the way patrons in a Wild West saloon might when a stranger steps through the swinging doors.

"What?" your mother says, once she can

move her slack jaw again.

"I did engage," you repeat.

"What do you mean, 'engage'?" your mother says.

"She called me a terrorist and a camel jockey and I told her she was too stupid to live if she thought there were camels in Albania," you say. You're aware that these words are perhaps lightly embellished, but it feels good to release them nonetheless. You're getting the chance for a do-over, and how often does that happen?

"And then what?" Mr. DiPietro asks.

"And then she said she was going to do me like Osama bin Laden," you say, though you are fairly sure that Margarita has no idea what happened to Osama bin Laden, because that would require the literacy to read a newspaper. "So I told her she was late for her post on Cherry Street and I started to walk away, and she hit me from behind."

"She hit you in the eye from behind?" Mr. DiPietro asks.

"No, it spun me around when she hit me from behind, and then she got me in the eye. She had to sucker punch me because she's a dumb sucker bitch, and if I see that dumb sucker bitch again I'm gonna kick her so hard she'll abort her next kid before she even conceives it," you say, and it surprises even you to hear those words from your mouth, just as the immediate endorphin high that follows surprises you. The throbbing in your skull subsides again, and it reminds you that pain, which you've always thought of as an exterior force introduced to the body, is in fact caused by your own nerve endings sending self-preserving Maydays to your brain. If you could just order your brain not to answer, you could win. There are entire self-help aisles in Barnes & Noble devoted to this kind of thing, and look at you, you've read not a single book on it, and yet there you are, feeling pleasantly numb and even slightly awesome.

And then the pain rushes back, because your endorphins, frankly, are not terribly practiced things. You're not used to acting out in ways that satisfy your most primal impulses.

You decide right then and there that you're going to have to work on that. It's in your nature. It's in there somewhere.

For the first few minutes of the drive back home, which is where you're to spend the next three days, per the pink piece of paper signed by Mr. DiPietro, your mother is strangely quiet. It's you, in fact, who breaks the silence, when you ask where you're going, after your mother begins taking roads in the opposite direction of your apartment.

"The hospital," your mother says.

Because of the pain, her words take a little longer to process, but then you remember what a *hospital* is. Hospital is a place people go to detox or die. It handles cases outside of the purview of the walk-in clinic, such as brain tumors, and that's about it, as far as your mother is concerned. You've never had a brain tumor, and thus you've never been anywhere but a walk-in clinic, and even that was reserved for cases of strep bad enough for the white phlegmy spots to travel from your tonsils to your tongue. Everything else is manageable with children's aspirin or NyQuil, and she always buys the unswallowable green liquid kind of the latter, to ensure that you really, *really* need it.

"What do you mean, 'hospital'?" you say.

Instead of looking at you, she glances in the rearview mirror. "Just in case," she answers.

"Just in case what?"

"In case you have a concussion."

"A concussion? But I don't. I'm fine. I'm awake, I'm fine."

"They don't always just knock you completely out. You're obviously acting weird."

"I'm fine," you say again.

"You're not yourself."

"But I am."

"You're absolutely not. That person in Mr. DiPietro's office, that wasn't Luljeta."

"But it was," you say.

"Oh no it was not. Don't try to tell me. I'm her mother. You think I don't know Luljeta?"

"Why are you talking about me in the third person?"

"Because that's the person I know, and it wasn't the person sitting in that office," she says.

"Well," you say. "I guess you don't know all of her. I mean me. You don't know all of me, because that was me, too."

She stops at a green light, and the cars behind you honk like a flock of geese headed south. It appears, for a moment, that she's the confused one, as if she were the one who's had her frontal lobe knocked against her skull.

"Go," you say, and even more strangely, she does what you tell her to.

It takes a few more minutes to convince her that you don't need a brain scan, just a sofa and a cup of tea, that beverage that she thought was reserved for people on the *Ti-*

tanic. Drinking anything besides a cup of burnt Dunkin' Donuts is evidence of putting on airs. It's just one more example of her not knowing all of Luljeta, such as the part of you that thinks Dunkin' Donuts tastes like the carpet of the basement rec room where your grandmother's AA meetings are held.

Your freezer has never held either ice-blue gel packs or bags of peas, since chemical goo and most green vegetables are considered equally inedible by your mother, so back at home, she hands you a frozen box of eggplant Parmesan Lean Cuisine to press against your eye, and she paces around while the water in the kettle heats up. It's not that she yells at you often, but you're certain it's coming, the traditional kind of scolding and punishment that you've largely avoided your whole life, though you aren't sure how much punishment a grounding will be, since you aren't exactly managing a packed social calendar and can watch whatever TV shows you miss on the Internet before she comes home from work. You've already planned your defense, one that, on its surface, seems pretty banal, but that underneath, you think, has a nice little zing to it: *What kind of person would just stand there and take it? Is that the kind of person you want to have raised?*

But she isn't yelling. She isn't talking. She's barely looking at you, until finally, after the kettle whistles and she hands you a cup of fancy Lipton tea, she holds her face in her hands and says, "What did I do?"

Which, of course, is a response you don't understand, and so you go to your planned defense, to try to steer things back on course.

"What kind of person would just stand there and take it? Is that the kind of person you want to have raised?"

And that only makes things worse. She looks at you as if you're speaking some foreign language and raises her arms up in questioning, which makes her look like a portrait of Mary on a dollar store novena candle.

"I mean, what happened? How could this happen?" she says, though you're pretty sure she isn't even directing the question at you, the only other person in the room.

You realize that she's not going to take away your TV privileges or keep you from your nonexistent crew of friends, but you also realize that she's going to look at this as a thing, which, really, it is, only she's going to make it *her* thing, and you feel the same surge in your chest that you felt staring at that message from NYU on the library computer screen, and in facing Margarita earlier that day: rage. Finally you have a name for the thing that's been pressing against your chest when you watch perfectly regular people in the checkout line at the grocery store buying perfectly regular things, like paperback books written by members of the Duck Dynasty, things that make you feel incomprehensibly lonely. It's the thing that you feel more toward Long Island girls who'll be taking your place at NYU next fall than toward the admissions counselors who rejected you, more toward the kids who walked away in the aftermath of the fight, their backpacks sagging down past their butts like colostomy bags in need of emptying, than toward Margarita. It's what your mother triggers in you by insisting you like mushrooms instead of asking if you do — the answer has always been, and will always be, no — and the thing somehow absent when you think about your father, even though he had walked away just like those kids at school. Maybe it was admirable, what he did. Brave. Badass. There are songs written about non-fuck-givers like that.

There are no songs written about your mother.

"God," she says, invoking an entity she uses only as a pinboard for things that make her angry.

"What does God have to do with this?" you say.

"It's just a word, Luljeta. I don't understand why you're being such a bitch to me. I'm not the one who punched you in the face."

"You're not the one who got punched in the face, either, but you're acting like you are. You haven't even asked me how I am."

"What are you talking about? I've done nothing but ask you how you feel."

"No, you've done nothing but tell me how I feel."

"That's not true."

You attempt to look at her wryly with your one good eye.

"Well," she says. "It's pretty obvious how you feel. You feel serious throbbing in your face and you feel freaked out about what being suspended is going to mean for your transcript."

Transcript. Ha.

"And what else?" you ask.

"You're embarrassed that you got hit in front of so many people," she says.

"What else?"

"You think Mr. DiPietro is a damn idiot."

66

"What else?"

"You're mad at me for some reason, even though I'm not the one who did this to you."

You have to stop to think about this last one. You're clearly mad at her, but did she do this to you? It's not like she tried to have no clue. Margarita may have targeted you because of the things you have that she doesn't, such as an intact hymen and at least a single person in the world who gives a shit about you, but is that your mother's fault? It isn't that you want to be altogether unloved and neglected, like Margarita and so many of her remedial peers, it's that often the love your mother gives feels like it's being rejected by your body, as if you're the B-positive recipient of an A-negative blood donation.

"You're crying," your mother says.

"No, I'm not. The Lean Cuisine is melting," you answer. And then you say, "What I felt most was free."

"Free," your mother repeats.

"Yes, free."

"Okay."

"Do you want to ask me why?"

"I don't know," she says. "Probably not."

"See?" you yell. "You just want to hear me repeat what you say. You don't even want to know what I'm really thinking."

"Fine, fine," she says. "Why did you feel free?"

You have to compose yourself to answer, and when you do, it doesn't have quite the eloquence you'd hoped it would.

"Because I did something, and something happened," you finally say. "Something outside of my head. It wasn't just some stupid promise of being good and something one day paying off."

Your mother thinks about this, and you wait for a look of contrition, if not an outright apology. She opens her mouth for a second, then closes it, swallowing whatever she was about to say. The suspense is awful, worse for a moment than the physical pain, or the smell of freezer against your face. You hadn't even realized before then that freezer had a smell, and it was that of delayed decay: a cavern that your mother seemed to believe would revive once-fresh things, and where they instead rested in perpetuity, encapsulated in an ever-thickening shell of frost.

"Luljeta," she says, almost gently.

"Yeah?" you answer.

"But you didn't win the fight."

And with that you do burst into tears and run into your room, not because she reminded you of the obvious, but because she

68

isn't anywhere close to getting the point. It isn't about winning or losing. It isn't even about truth or lies, since your point was premised on an embellished story about standing up to Margarita, when all you really did was call out a factual error in her ethnic slurring. The point was about *doing* and *being,* making the little butterfly ripple that would eventually cause a tornado somewhere on the other side of the ocean, or at least a little chatter on the other side of the baseball field at Crosby High School. It's almost better that it was all based on a lie, because it makes you realize that you can go back and revise your own history, and isn't that almost as good as making your own future, being able to invent your own past as well? You almost want to thank NYU and Margarita for helping you see that, even if you can see it with only one eye for the time being.

At the very least, you're still seeing things more clearly than your mother, who is standing outside the door, saying, "What? What did I do?"

Here's what she did:

When you were a kid and she brought you along to the grocery store, every time you'd ask if you could have whatever gushy,

Lunchables box of fluorescent wonder you passed on the General Mills–sponsored interior aisles, she'd grab the usual Shop-Rite brand pea-gravel granola bars and answer, *Not now.* Not *No,* not *Hell no,* but *Not now.* She must have read somewhere how important it is to instill in children a sense of hope, and for the longest time you held on, but now, at seventeen years old, you finally realize that you're never, never getting that Go-Gurt.

Also: she promised you when you were little that she'd change your name someday, once you were old enough to not want to change it to Hermione. You'd get a normal first name and her last name, which was almost as unpronounceable as Luljeta but was at least shared with another couple of human beings in the world, instead of the last name you had, Hasani, which seemed like a weed growing in the vicinity of the skimpy Kuzavinas family tree. And by the time you had outgrown boy wizards, what you wanted instead of a new name was an explanation for the one you had, and what you got instead was a key chain with your name on it that she ordered special for you at some kiosk in the mall, so you could no longer be sad about the lack of personalized products that were available to Albanian bastard children. You had no keys for the key chain, and no answers to your questions, but you said thank you anyway, because you were sure this was part one in the explanation that was coming someday. Someday, you see, but *Not now.*

And: when you were too young to look after yourself without DCF intervening, she used to leave you with Mamie, your de facto guardian, which was often fine, because Mamie was mostly still able to stand until around 7:00 P.M., when Mr. Carlo Rossi would gently lull her to sleep. But there were also the not-fine times when, upon returning to Mamie's house after an afternoon at Hamilton Park, you found her slumped on the floor in the kitchen, and you would panic and call your mother at work, and your mother would calmly instruct you to check Mamie's breathing, roll her onto her side, and sit quietly in the living room until she was able to get authorization from her supervisor to leave for the day. *See this?* your mother would say when she finally arrived. *This is why you don't drink.* The next day, when you were dropped off with Mamie again, Mamie would point to the door your mother had just exited in an angry huff and say, *See this? This is why I drink.*

And: she told you not to listen to Mamie on those days when Mamie would shake her head and tell you, *God, you look just like your father.*

And: she told you, *God, you take after Greta,* which seemed to you like a good thing, though your mother always seemed slightly concerned when she said it. Maybe she was afraid that once you flew the nest, you wouldn't bother to come home for most holidays like Greta, her too-good-for-everyone sister. You wondered where one drew the line between good and too-good, and if that was something you needed to be concerned about.

And now: she stands outside your door for ten more minutes, ice cube clinking in her own glass of wine, until she's ready for a refill. Then she walks away saying, "Fine, if that's the way you want to be," as if she's ever before acknowledged that *wanting* and *being* have anything to do with one another. You feel like you have some version of that disease which makes people believe that their limbs aren't really theirs, so they travel to Indonesia and pay doctors big American dollars to amputate their not-their arm or not-their leg, only you have a version where you feel like you ended up in a family that isn't really yours, surrounded by bodies that

72

are just a little off. The thought occurs to you now, for the first time, in your bedroom with a now-warm Lean Cuisine compress over your eye, that maybe you were born into the right family but just ended up with the wrong half of it. Maybe it's time to correct that, get proactive, which, you've learned today, can get you bruised and bloody but can also get you moving. Yeah, you think, it's high time to get moving.

CHAPTER THREE:
ELSIE

And then one night Bashkim wasn't waiting outside for me before my shift. It felt like we'd been together for years by then but it was only a couple of months, just long enough for spring to finally stick and the air to stay warm after the sun went down. The first firefly of the season landed on my thigh while I stood by the back door of the Ross and I panicked and smashed it, my uniform now bioluminescent, and I thought: I should teach Bashkim that word, *bioluminescent,* something I remembered from an earth sciences class back in middle school, except I couldn't remember if bioluminescence was a real thing or if it was something like alchemy, nice to think about but debunked by actual science. Then I thought that it had to be real, because my skirt still had a faint yellow light to it, as if I was some raver whose glow stick had sprung a leak while she rolled on E and made out with strangers in enormous jeans and vintage Adidas jackets. I'd read about raves in places like *Sassy* magazine, but the closest I'd ever come to being part of something like that was doing the hokey pokey at the end of the afternoon free-skate session at RollerMagic. I wanted to go to a rave, or to one of those three-story dance clubs in New Haven, and put on heavy eyeliner and pay outrageous cover charges and lean against velveteen so crusted with fluids that I wouldn't dare sit on it, but me and Bashkim had never so much as gone to the movies together. The week before we'd spent date night at the laundromat while he washed his clothes, except I was the one who actually did the work while he stood and leaned against the dryers, crunching on Chiclets from the March of Dimes candy machine. I was thinking that I was going to try to talk him into an actual night out at a place that accepted currency other than quarters, and that's when I realized that it was already ten minutes past my starting time, and Bashkim hadn't even shown up for our standing date, never mind my fantasy one.

I waited two more minutes and then threw a little rock at the employee door, assuming he'd lost track of time and needed to be jarred into checking a clock, but still I found myself standing alone, waiting to be courted in a car before walking into the Ross alone, pretending nobody had figured out what was going on with us. That's when the bad thoughts came: he had an accident and was comatose at St. Mary's, and Gjonni and Yllka never bothered to call me because they were just as aware that I was not Bashkim's wife as they were that I was his lovergirl, to quote the Teena Marie song that was dated even then but on near-constant rotation in the miniature juke-boxes in the booths at the Ross. But the Fiero was parked right where it was always parked, in the farthest-off corner space. I walked over to it and peered inside but Bashkim wasn't waiting in there, either. Then the thoughts got even worse: he wasn't head-injured at all, he had just walked away. Just like that, I was another past he left behind.

I ran back to the employee entrance but walked through it slowly, trying to play it cool. And there he was, Bashkim looking straight into my eyes before he turned his back to me, as if he would turn to salt if he so much as caught another glimpse of my face. So I changed my plan. Screw cool; I was no cool kid, I was no club-hopping New Haven scenester, I was a hard-knocked Brass Valley bitch and I was going to prove it by marching right up to him and turning him around and slapping his face with the spatula I pulled right out of his own greasy hand. But my legs missed their cue and instead marched me all the way out to the dining room, and I sat down in an empty booth and began counting backward from ten over and over again to calm myself and get the nerve to walk back into the kitchen. It was too neon-bright in the dining room, but it was empty enough to hide out in. I had to share it with only a couple of old ladies still mobile enough to walk up the street from the old lady home, and a kid serving his time-out sentence in a booth far away from the one where his mother was sucking down Newport Lights.

"Waiting for someone to take your order?" Cheryl said, once she noticed me there. Cheryl was a skinny pockmarked waitress who I was always stuck working with, obviously a punishment from Yllka, who clearly hated me. "Get up, slowpoke, you're late for your shift as it is."

"I'll be there in a second. I don't feel too good," I said.

"None of us feel good. Look around you. You think you're supposed to feel good?"

"Just a second. I'm coming."

"That's what he said. Get it? No, really,

though, on your feet, girly." She shot me a look that dared me to disobey, and even though she was my elder by about twenty years, she wasn't my superior, so I took my time unfurling, at least until I noticed Yllka at the front counter. She wasn't looking at me, but I bet she could smell trouble even over all the grilled meats.

"Thank you, princess," Cheryl said. "Jesus, what's up with this place tonight? Bashkim's panties are in a bunch, too."

"What's that got to do with me?" I said.

"Oh, nothing, I was just remarking," she said, which she and the other waitress, Janice, found hilarious for no reason I could figure out. Maybe *remarking* was a vocab word on the GED test both of them were studying for, the two of them bosom buddies even though one didn't have bosoms and the other had enough for three or four women. Like a horse, Cheryl lifted her top lip over her buckteeth in something kind of like a smile. Mrs. Ed, I called her under my breath. The name I bet she had for me wasn't quite as nice as *horse,* although it sounded a lot like it.

But who were they to talk, even if they'd figured out what Bashkim and I were up to in the parking lot? Bashkim loved me, he told me so every other night, starting from

78

before he even knew my last name. He got into his quiet moods sometimes, when it was like he'd forgotten all his words, but when he got his voice back he made up for them by telling me about the necklace he was going to buy for my birthday, or what he was going to do to me later in his car. It was Cheryl and Janice who made it through every one of the back of the house staff in exchange for a free meatloaf special or sometimes even actual money, at least a couple of quarters to feed the fortune-teller machine out in the lobby. They tested their fortunes at least three times a night, until finally the fortune-teller fed them the answers they wanted in return for pocket change, which they should've used for ramen noodles to feed their kids.

But never mind them. I wasn't like those ladies. No way would I let their fates happen to me.

I'd gotten some of my nerve back and I steeled myself to walk into the kitchen, but I was intercepted again, this time by Yllka. This whole place was booby-trapped, only as far as I could tell, there were no secret treasures around to protect.

"Where are you going?" Yllka asked me. She held an envelope in one hand, tapped it into the other.

"To work?" I said.

"What do you need in the kitchen? You haven't taken any orders yet."

"A rack of coffee cups?"

"Are you asking or telling?"

"Telling?" I said.

"Cheryl can get the cups. You have a table that was just sat."

I started walking away, grateful for the out, but she stopped me before I took three full steps.

"Actually, here, take this to Bashkim. He forgot it out here," she said and handed me the envelope.

"What is it?"

"A letter," she said. "From Aggie, his wife." She smiled a little, just a tiny little bit, just enough for me to understand that she knew what she was doing.

"Fine," I said, though I was burning so hot that I felt like any piece of paper could turn to tinder in my hands. The white envelope had those red and blue stripes around the edges, the same colors as the American flag but clearly from someplace where Americans couldn't really ever go. France, for example. I'd had a French pen pal in middle school, if you could call someone you exchanged one letter with for a French class assignment a pal. I told *mon ami* I danced jazz and wore *Levis et T-shirts,* and he sent back a photo of what was clearly an actor from a French après école special. I knew how letters could lie. I bet I could pick out all the lies in Aggie's letter without even being able to read the text. I bet it said:

Dear Bashkim,
Everything is fine, really, just fine. The bread I eat for dinner is satisfying, the crumbs make a perfect confetti to celebrate the close of another day. I want for nothing. I feel your love from here.
Love,
Agnes

So finally I had an excuse to talk to Bashkim, but now looking at him was impossible.

"I got something for you," I said, holding the envelope straight out to him like a sword. "It's from your wife."

He blew his nose into a hankie and stuffed the envelope into the pocket of his apron.

"What's it say? Does she miss you so much? She can't wait for that Mercedes you're going to buy her?"

He pulled a Marlboro from behind his ear and lit it on the gas flame before walking outside.

"Asshole," I said, once he was safely out the door. I was going to follow him there, but Yllka had been watching the whole thing.

"I told him not to mess around with that stuff," she said. "I told him, 'Bashkim, there is no shortcut to make money. You work and you save, and that's it.' "

"What stuff?" I said, a little defensively, because I knew she wouldn't be talking to me about anything unless it somehow had the potential to hurt me.

"His investments, as he calls them. You know, the money he probably promised you the world with."

"What about them?" I said. "And he hasn't promised me the world. I don't even want the world. I don't even like the world that much."

"I told him, 'Bashkim, you don't know anything about capitalism. There is nothing wrong with just putting money in a piggy bank.' "

"I don't know what you're talking about."

"I know you don't, Elsie. You two, it's like they call it, the blind leading the blind."

Not too blind to see the reinforced toe of your pantyhose under your sandals, lady, I wanted to say, but because I needed the job, I just repeated, "I don't know what you're talking about. I'm not leading Bashkim or vice versa."

"Okay then, why do you have one foot out the door to follow him? Maybe instead you should get out to your tables," she said, even though she was the one who sent me into the kitchen in the first place.

For the rest of the night I tried to catch Bashkim's eye every time I walked through the kitchen, letting a plate sit in the window when I was right there to run it, asking for a fresh hamburger bun when the drippy coleslaw seeped all over the plate. "It's fine," he said to me, or "What are you waiting for?" Or he'd say nothing at all, wouldn't even glance up, wouldn't even wink an eye with a face so serious that he either meant that wink more than anything on earth or he didn't mean it at all, it was nothing more than a twitch.

Finally I followed him into the walk-in cooler, his arms full of frozen meat. Never had a rump roast looked so much like the skinned dead creature that it was as when it was cradled in his arms.

"Hey," I said. "We need some honey mustard out there."

"You know where it is."

"What's up with you tonight? What did I do?"

"You did nothing. This isn't about you. Not everything is about you," he said.

"Well then what's up with *you*? Your whatever, your investment."

He flinched when I asked it. Those goose pimples on his arm were not just from the cold.

"It's nothing. Don't worry about it."

"I'm not worried about it, I'm worried about you. I don't care about your money."

"Then don't worry about me at all. I will be fine. The money will be fine."

"Jesus, I don't care about the money! I never thought you had any to begin with. Why would I be with a line cook if I was looking for someone with money?"

"Because you like losers."

"No," I said, after a second.

"But I am not a loser."

"I know," I said. "I never said you were."

"It will be fine, it's not a big problem. It's just a little, what you say, burp."

"Hiccup."

"What?"

"You mean *hiccup*, not *burp*."

He looked at me long and hard, and then he said it again. "I am not a loser, Elsie."

"I know," I said.

"So let's get back to work. We're wasting time."

"Wait. Can you just kiss me first?"

"Kissing is not what we're paid for."

"It'll just take a second. Gjonni can dock it from my check."

"Don't be a child. This is for later, this kind of thing."

And he didn't kiss me. He didn't look at me when he opened the door and left me in there alone, surely didn't wonder why I didn't follow him out, why I instead sat on a stack of six dozen frozen beef patties with labels that read grade d but edible. Those boxes were shredded before they were thrown into the dumpster outside, because no customer would accept Grade D, even if the package explicitly said no really, it's fine, what grade do you think you deserve?

I tried to cry but in that cold the tears just froze and iced over my eyes. It was for the best, really, because nobody would then notice my eyes were red and swollen and have to ask me what was wrong, and that worked out perfectly since nobody was going to anyway.

The next night, on yet another one of our parking lot dates, pretending the previous evening never happened, Bashkim moaned *punë muti* into my ear, and I'm telling you, man, I didn't need any translation. I'd figured out a little Albanian by then: the cusses the cooks hurled at the waitresses' wide asses, the cusses Yllka mumbled behind the waitresses' backs for making the cooks look in the first place. I even figured out some regular words, like *hurry,* because Bashkim was always telling my skinny ass to do it.

Shpejtoj, Elsie. Shift started ten minutes ago, lady.

And I understood that *punë muti* meant shit when he pulled out and there was a sticky mess on my thighs, and I swear right then I felt something hitching up, moving like a squatter into my belly. *No trespassing,* I said, but I guess it was like me; where else was it supposed to go?

"Did the condom break?" I asked.

He handed me a wad of balled-up Dunkin' Donuts napkins from the glove compartment. "Let's go," he said. "Inside, lady."

"Jesus Christ, did the condom break? Did it disintegrate? I don't even see it," I said.

"Don't worry," he said.

"Don't worry? What the hell? You didn't even answer me," I said, but that was just a fact, not a prompt. Of course he didn't answer me. I didn't get to ask questions, just wait for him to reveal little bits of himself on his own time. When I asked questions he'd just look at me straight on, long enough for me to catch sight of the tangle of red veins in his eyes, all lit up and glowing like the electric tentacles of the Van de Graaff generator I'd spent two hours staring at on a field trip to the Boston Museum of Science a few years before: millions of currents streaking from a steel orb, a room barely containing what seemed to be the kind of storm that would take out entire third-world villages or midwestern trailer parks if the glass walls were accidentally shattered. Later on I found out that all the Van de Graaff generator could really do was make the hair on your head rise straight up from your scalp, which Mr. Wizard had shown me how to do with just a balloon and a wool sweater.

It was a stupid parlor trick, just like when Bashkim called me pretty girl, like I was a pet parakeet, as he pulled up his brown trousers. Abracadabra, pretty girl, wink wink. I fell for it all, even though his pants had to be called trousers, they were that ugly. Even the leather huarache sandals he wore everywhere — behind the line in the kitchen even, in the passenger seat while we screwed even, his trousers bunched at his feet like elephant skin — not even the sleek leather of a real hustler, not even a slick combed mustache or a necktie as thin as fettuccini to distract me from the ripped seams and grease stains on his shirt, and still, still I fell for it. Who knew if he was a scientist or a magician or just a common con artist, but then again who cared as long as he kept streaming his gibby-gabby into my ear while we rocked the Fiero behind the Muffler Shak before the start of every shift? Who cared? Not me, because I could pretend also that when he said *eja tani! eja tani!* what it meant was my god, my god! instead of: come on, come on! I could pretend when he said *punë muti* that what it meant was: now we have started something that cannot be undone by parents or wives or time clocks instead of: shit.

But no, it meant shit, that I was sure of. I knew it when I pulled my pantyhose back up and they were immediately glued to my legs, and I thought ahead twenty minutes to the chafing I'd get while running trays of coffee and spanakopita.

"I'm going inside," Bashkim said.

" 'K," I said.

"Hey," he said and touched my chin gently, like he must have seen in some movie or another. "Don't worry about it, okay? It will be fine."

"I'm not worried."

"Then why do your eyes look like that?"

"Look like what?"

"Like they won't look at me."

"They will," I said. "They're just doing something else right now." There was a raccoon out there, digging around in a pile of slop that had somehow ended up ten yards from the trash bins. That guy found himself a little Grade D nugget and waddled happily away with it, and I was searching for the lesson in that, coming up empty.

Bashkim opened up my hand and placed something in there, a crumpled-up Dunkin' Donuts napkin from the glove box.

"What's this?" I asked.

"A rose," he said. "See?"

It was a rose, or at least a napkin origamied into a rose shape. I put it to my nose.

"Smells like Tic Tacs," I said.

"The orange kind," he said. "The best kind."

"Thanks."

"I'm sorry I have the bad moods," he said.

"It's okay," I said.

"So much work, you know? I get tired."

I nodded.

"Not tired of you. Tired of French fries. Tired of, you know, other things. Not you, okay?"

"Okay," I said.

"We have to go," he said.

I nodded but didn't budge from the driver's seat when he slammed the passenger door behind him. I just sat there with my hand on the shifter, wondering how much money Bashkim was really down, if it was really that bad, if maybe I could just write Bashkim a check and get him over the bad moods and we could get on with our lives. Then I thought about the seventeen dollars in tips I'd made that night and realized that a check from me wouldn't get us far, maybe just enough for gas to get us to the Poconos, the only place anyone in my family had visited since they crossed the ocean forty years before and figured they'd done enough traveling for one bloodline. There might not even be enough left for a half hour in one of those heart-shaped hot tubs Uncle Eddie said the resorts have down there. Besides, my fifteen-minute break was over, and I had to go back in at least to finish the last hour of my shift, and if I was going to go through all the trouble to go back in there then I might as well just stay a while longer and try to hustle a few more bucks. That's how these places trap you for life. But I was still thinking at that moment, Not me, and on the walk back inside I picked up a penny, heads up, and dropped it into my apron as if anything worth finding would be lying there tossed aside on the street. Good luck, that heads-up penny, as in good luck finding a million more of these in your lifetime so maybe you could pay off, say, your mother's mortgage, or your sister's future tuition bills, or at least treat them to a nice steak dinner at Carmen Anthony's if the other bills were still too high. But at least that heads-up penny proved my mother wrong after all — I wasn't out running around like a ten-dollar whore. I was a whole lot cheaper than that.

Mamie had never gotten the second shift she used to work out of her system, even though that pink slip from Waterbury Buckle had come long ago. She'd been working a daytime gig at the Almond Joy factory a little down Route 8 for a couple of years, but she still lived at nighttime as if she didn't have to rise until afternoon the next day, staying up for news she perked up for only during the weather, and then late-night talk shows with guests she'd never heard of, because the only actors she ever remembered the names of were the ones nobody else on earth did, people like Joel Grey and

Ben Gazzara, guys who were celebrities when life stopped for her right around the time of my birth. After the talk shows were over, the TV went off but the lamp stayed on, with no books or magazines for the light to shine on, except for a *Ladies' Home Journal* with pages dog-eared on recipes none of us had ever tasted. I used to look at the chicken piccata page and wonder who would use wine as an ingredient and not a religion.

The condensed chicken soup I'd eaten for dinner used mostly salt as an ingredient, so the puke I'd just dropped into the toilet tasted pickled and burned my throat on the way up. I licked my lips until they turned in on themselves and somehow still believed, when another typhoon of nausea swirled up in my stomach, that only a sleeve of saltines could save my life. It was my body working against its own best interests, trying to turn itself into dust.

Then David Letterman said something that tore up his live studio audience, and it reminded me of the life that still existed outside of the bathroom. When we were little and Greta and I got sick, Mamie gave us Tupperware bowls to puke in and spoonfuls of brandy to make us sleepy. She'd scratch our heads and do the watusi at the foot of our beds until we cracked a smile, then she'd declare our fevers broken and make us sit up and watch Indiana Jones. That Tupperware puke bowl was long gone by then, ruined when the acids finally ate a hole through the plastic, and the closest things to brandy in our house that night were the caramelized bottoms of the empty Carlo Rossi jugs that lined our kitchen floorboards like buoys keeping our house afloat. I pulled away from the rim of the toilet and dragged myself to the doorway of the living room.

"Mamie, I'm sick," I said.

It came out so soft that I could barely hear it, and right after the words hit the ether I hoped that the television had gobbled them up. At first I thought I'd gotten my wish, because it was half a commercial break before she even acknowledged my presence, and it was less an acknowledgment than a twitch, one of the deeper shakes that I usually made out only when I looked at her for more than a few seconds at a time, which meant not often, because it was confusing to see her start to look old. She was thirty-five. She might've had the beginnings of some palsy, but I wouldn't know, because she hadn't seen a doctor since she delivered Greta, and I'd bet money that she had to be talked into it then. It was in her hair that I noticed the twitch first, the fluffy grown-out bangs of a grown-out Ogilvie home perm swaying just a little as if there were a ceiling fan over her head. One silver ribbon ran through her brown hair like a streaker. She had the kind of soul-deep fatigue that looked sexy in photographs but in real life meant she hadn't thought of sex in a decade.

"What do you mean, *sick*?" she said. Looking at her made it worse. The light from the television was changing color with each scene, so she looked like she were under a strobe light at a disco, like somehow she'd found a bouncer to overlook her elastic-waist jeans.

"Puke-sick," I said.

"What'd you get into?"

"Nothing."

"You been drinking?"

"No."

"Would it help?" She shook her empty glass at me.

"I don't think so," I said. I curled up on the sofa next to her, and she pulled her knees away.

"Well, don't get me sick. I can't afford to be sick, I'm working doubles all week," she said. She pressed her palm against my forehead. "You don't feel hot. You feel cool."

I shrugged.

"Well, what do you want me to do about it?" she asked.

I thought about *Indiana Jones,* how long it'd been since we'd sat down and watched it.

"I don't know," I said. "Nothing, I guess."

"Is it a stomach bug?"

"Maybe," I said.

"I bet it's food poisoning. That crap you eat at the Ross."

"Maybe."

"Are you pregnant?" she asked. "You don't have a boyfriend, do you?"

"What? No. I mean, no I'm not pregnant. I kind of have a boyfriend."

"Then how do you know you're not pregnant?"

"Because having a kind-of boyfriend doesn't mean you're automatically pregnant."

"Shows how much you know," she said.

With that I almost retched again. I wondered if there was a chance she was right, because if Mamie could speak with authority about anything, it was hangover remedies and getting knocked up by accident. But it was impossible; that broken condom incident was weeks ago. I'd stopped freaking out about it after a few days, once I convinced myself that the taupe oval on my underpants was a light period and not an old period stain. I hadn't even introduced Bashkim to Mamie or Greta, I hadn't even gotten that birthday necklace he promised me yet.

"No, I'm not pregnant," I said again.

"Who is this guy, anyway?"

I thought for a second and realized I didn't really know how to answer that question. Mamie wasn't going to like that he was a foreigner, unless he was Lithuanian like Bobu and Grandpa, because once her parents made it into the U.S. the whole family assumed every other immigrant was just there to mooch off the system. But Bashkim was a hard worker, which she'd be okay with, especially since the thing he worked hard at was manual, thankless, low-paying labor, and Mamie didn't trust any other kind. He was married: that was a bad thing. He dreamed of a better life: also a bad thing. Anyway, once I made it through high school without getting knocked up she stopped being interested in who I was dating, so none of that seemed worth mentioning.

"Just some guy I work with," I said.

"Well," she said. "Sounds like a winner."

"I mean, he's more than just that."

96

"What is he, then?"

I pulled the afghan from the back of the sofa and wrapped it around my shoulders. The afghan wasn't finished, one of Mamie's monthlong hobbies, so you had to choose the part of you that felt the coldest, then move it to the other parts later. It didn't help much, but it helped more than nothing at all.

"He has a really broad chest. It looks like he's been breaking horses," I said, finally, during the commercial break. "And nice eyes."

"Oh Christ," Mamie said. "You're done for."

She was seventeen when she'd had me. I'd seen a picture of her eight months along, in a bikini, cannonballing off a dock at Scovill's Dam. Dad used a cooler as a bench, his denim shorts soaked because he'd already taken his turn, maybe shown her how to land just so in the water to make the biggest splash. He held a can of Schaefer in his hand, but he hadn't yet drunk enough of it for his belly to be swollen with a half keg, the way it looked in pictures taken a few years later. His arms were swollen instead, biceps that were ready to be used, one of them tattooed with a cobra, its head puffed out at the widest part of his arm.

"Anyway," I said.

"We don't even have a flight of stairs to throw yourself down," Mamie said.

"I'd probably just break a leg anyway, with my luck," I said. Then I'd have to ask Bashkim for help, and it was not the right time for that, with his mind on his money in another part of the world. Sometimes I understood what a burden I could be, and why I seemed to line Bashkim's blue eyes red, which really just made them prettier, those two primary colors dueling with each other.

Mamie had blue eyes, too. According to the Punnett squares in biology class, if I had an offspring with a blue-eyed man, it'd have a 25 percent chance of having blue eyes, too.

But I wasn't pregnant, I reminded myself, so never mind about that.

"I don't know what happened to you two. I really don't," Mamie said. She was looking at Greta's latest progress report from the school social worker, and apparently *progress* wasn't really the right word to use to describe how she was doing.

"No idea?" I said.

"I don't know who's worse. Your sister tests like a genius, and look at her, pulling her hair out in chunks like a crazy person. I mean, I broke the vacuum following her around. The thing literally choked on hair."

"It's a sickness. She can't help it."

"She can't help being sick, you can't help being sick. I don't know how I'm supposed to help it. There comes a point, you know?"

"When?" I said. "When does the point come?"

Mamie looked at me. The television had gone dim for a moment, so she was half-shadowed, her right eye just a dark socket, the jawline of her square face an abyss. She looked beautiful and harsh like that, in a way fashion photographers try to stage.

"What are you talking about?" Mamie said. "You really must have a fever."

I nodded, draped the afghan over the back of the couch, and headed off to bed.

By morning, I was seized with sickness, though there was no fever to break, and it hurt me to think she might be right. I might have gone and gotten myself pregnant.

CHAPTER FOUR:
LULJETA

Once upon a time, before school administrators were gently persuaded to reconsider their annual superlative categories, you'd swept the A.M. Kindergarten Award Day, taking home construction-paper blue ribbons in the prime categories of Prettiest, Nicest, Smartest, and something else — you can't remember the last one, but you're sure it was a good one, and that your prizes totaled four, one for each of the still-gangly skinny girl limbs you kept until approximately age nine. At recess on at least two occasions, different boys grabbed on to your arms and declared *Mine!, No, mine!,* and because this was years before third-wave feminism blogs and because their testes were still years from dropping, it was flattering and exhilarating. You sat daily in a pod with Miguel, Latoya, and Samantha, imagining the world was made of the Cool Ranch Doritos on which you wished to subsist entirely, and you never bothered to disrupt the fantasy to voice your fear that this world would literally crumble and become overrun with cockroaches, the creatures that had chased you and your mother out of two previous apartments before you landed in the one it seemed like you'd never get to leave. And anyway, you didn't even need a fantasy Dorito world. Your real world was amazing. It was perfect. You were warm and stuffed with blocks of melted, delicious government-surplus cheese, your mother let you watch all the television you wanted, you were admired and respected but not feared by your classmates, and your teachers were sure they'd read about you in the paper years later, in one of the good Civic sections, surely, not the police blotter, where they were equally sure they'd read about some of your peers.

You don't remember one moment where it all ended, though by the time you'd had your first menstrual period, at age eleven, your glory days were long over. It wasn't like an explosion had rocked the school and sent you all flying up into the air and landed you down in a place where you surely were not meant to be, estranged from your friends and ignored by teachers who felt they didn't need to worry about you and thus didn't. There wasn't one specific day where Miguel up and left to run exclusively with a crew of Puerto Rican boys, and Latoya with black girls, and Samantha, who was a white girl like you, with one black boy at a time.

In the end, you managed to keep one friend, Teena, who isn't a friend so much as a carpool partner. She's willing to drive you around to places on nights when she isn't being driven around herself by twenty-something-year-old mall security guards in their creepy white vans or douchey Mitsubishis. You two are stuck together because she, like you, has been rejected by all the other girls you know. Unlike you, she's been rejected because she's been branded a superslut — really, she's only a standard slut, not nearly as bad as the jealous girls who tend to call her that — and also unlike you, she truly does not give a shit what people have to say about it. It hasn't yet occurred to you how awesome and advanced a thing like that is, something that aging actresses say in interviews came to them in their forties. For the time being, you're still seventeen and kind of embarrassed to be seen with Teena at school. Since your plan is to go to Pandora's Box, a.k.a. the Betsy Ross Diner, however, you're happy to be with a friend who attracts the kind of attention you secretly want but from which you typically flee.

"Ew, the Ross? Why don't we go to Chili's?" she'd asked when you suggested a trip there.

"I keep hearing about how good their gravy fries are," you'd answered.

"Ew, gravy fries?"

"And there's this guy I'm kind of into who hangs out there," you'd said.

The guy to whom you're referring is the one you've suddenly decided you can't live without, the one who will make you make sense, the one whose failures of both nature and nurture constitute the sloppy human pieces you've attempted to assemble into a functional unit. Before, your father was something whose existence you were told of only so that you'd know to avoid it, like poison ivy or crystal meth. But, as with recreational drugs, you have become aware that you have not been told the whole truth about things. There's got to be something good about something people will ruin everything for just to get ahold of, the way your mother once apparently did with your father. Finding him has, in the three days of your out-of-school suspension, become an obsession, the way Beyblades were when you were little, and making unwearable hemp jewelry was two years ago, and Fleetwood Mac secretly is to you now, after hearing "Landslide" on some classic rock station and weeping like you'd lost something instead of discovered it. It's clear to you now that those things have all been surrogates for what you've actually been looking for, red herrings meant to trick you into not seeking out the one true thing. Your father, you are certain, will make everything else fall into place. You are two broken parts that must be reassembled in order to serve any purpose at all.

At the very least, maybe he can cough up seventeen years of child support to cover a security deposit on an apartment near Washington Square, where you'll work out a feasible Plan B and feel not even a pang of envy for the kids on the street power-walking to their classes at NYU.

In any case, it's nothing you can explain, and it's not the kind of thing Teena, with her French Canadian auto mechanic father who fixed her up an Acura coupe the second she turned sixteen, would understand. So you talk instead about a random guy, and she indeed agrees to go with you one Friday evening, on the early side, before the latest of her security guards gets off for the night, in multiple senses of the phrase.

The Ross was the only place to begin this search, not because of the gravy fries but because the place is known in Waterbury as Little Albania, staffed and frequented by guys with eagle tattoos and dark jeans with elaborate embroidery on the ass pockets, and of course their women, 100 percent of whom could serve as Pirelli calendar models but instead study chemical hair-relaxing techniques at the local cosmetology school. These are the Kosovar Albanians, the ones who began to migrate in the late nineties, when the Serbs began their ethnic cleansing in the Balkans, learned English fluently in two weeks, and briefly broke their parents' hearts by dating Italians and Puerto Ricans before marrying, of course, fellow Kosovars. You know this type of Albanian from your school, and thus you know that they are not your people. You were descended from the ones who sponsored the Kosovars' visas, the older crew of Albanian Albanians who run the Betsy Ross Diner, old-world people who'd come over beginning in the seventies under the false impression that there was still work in Waterbury's brass foundries. The Albanian Albanians found the Kosovars slightly stuck up, raised as they were with a relatively benign Yugoslavian form of Communism, and put them to work cleaning bathrooms and running cheap Greek food to cheap American tippers. You knew that your mother had done the same kind of work once, before the Albanian Albanians had begun serving strictly as an employment agency for displaced Kosovars and were willing to take a second-generation Lithuanian girl on, if only to get her knocked up with one of their very own. While it had occurred to you in the past that your father's people might perhaps still run the joint, it was a recent revelation to realize, as obvious as it should have been, that your father's people are also your people. You have people! You do, you do, you do, and they aren't Miguel or Latoya or Samantha, which maybe explains why things hadn't worked out with them. You *do* have people, regardless of what your mother has to say about it.

Your mother never has much to say about it, is the thing. It's as if she believes that the blanker your slate, the more room you'll have to fill it in with better things. It seems so naïve to you now that you once believed that, too.

As you enter the Ross, you see people with deep pockmarks, people who likely have no Social Security numbers, people who you would guarantee have lived lives you cannot and do not want to imagine, each of them most decidedly not attractive. Funny how a tattoo goes from a cool thing to a terrifying thing once it's applied to a face. For a moment you wonder if it might not be better to choose ignorance over these prospects.

"Chili's has those really good seasoned fries," Teena says, scanning the room.

But that email from NYU flashes before your bruised and bleary eye, and it gives you courage to ignore Teena and ask for a seat. The young male host manages to convey both utter disinterest in moving from behind the counter and simultaneous rapt attention to your boobs. At least they distract from your black eye, or from the quarter inch of Maybelline cover-up you'd Pan-Caked on top of it.

"You want to sit? Why don't you keep me company up here?" the host says, his smile not really imbuing his tone with any charm.

"No thanks," you say. "Booth, please." And you smile, because you're still young enough to think you're supposed to be polite to everyone, even lecherous diner hosts who must have been made aware of the statutory rape laws in this country, no matter their citizenship.

You scan the room and notice a couple of

waitresses floating around whose feathered hair and cankles give them away as Waterbury lifers rather than Albanians, and some busboys who would probably rather retain their virginity than give it away to the likes of those old broads, but nobody who fits your profile.

"Is he here?" Teena asks.

"I don't think so," you answer, and you don't have to act to convey your disappointment. What a dumb idea this was in the first place. Your people probably sold the Ross and fled years ago, also carriers of the Hasani cut-and-run family inheritance you are well aware of despite never having met a single damn one of them. Your family's coat of arms likely consists of a giant middle finger and the tailgate of a chariot.

One of the ragged waitresses takes your orders — coffee and a side salad for Teena, coffee and gravy fries that you have no actual intention of eating for you — and before you can ask for a straw so you don't have to put your lips to the plastic tumbler of water, you're approached by two young men, who, from the neck up, are actually not un-hot, though their Fast and the Furious fashion sense, all tight T-shirts and leather jackets reinforced with yet more leather at the elbows, is not quite up your alley. You imagine yourself with an intentionally messy-hair type, with jeans that came off the rack but are clearly built to his specs at the denim factory, someone with whom you can discuss the Nabokov that you're obviously going to read someday, once the Stephen King stuff stops being so damn good. Basically, you're waiting for someone who doesn't hang out in alleys, never mind yours.

"What are you girls up to tonight?" one of them asks, both of them dropping into the seats next to you uninvited, their motorcycle helmets like giant reptile eggs they've been charged with protecting.

Teena sizes them up, analyzing whatever slutty data her eyeballs feed into her brain. She's so pro about it that she actually, without ever directly looking at you, manages to convey: *Nah, but we can let them pay for your fries.* You instantly begin sweating under your sweatshirt — so that's where it gets its name — because you have absolutely no idea how to talk to guys, be their hair pleasantly messy or, like that of the ones at your table, shellacked. Once again, you realize what a stupid plan this has been all along, because even if you had spotted someone who looked promising, someone who perhaps shared some obvious physical feature with you, what did you think you'd say to them? *Hey, my nose looks like yours; what should I bring over for the end of Ramadan?*

You're assigned the shorter and darker of the two, who introduces himself as Matt, though if this guy's real given name is Matthew, yours is Rapunzel. You don't let on much of anything, including that you're a native English speaker yourself, because you volunteer no response to the chatter he offers.

"What's the matter, cat has your lips?" he asks, and you, like an idiot, nod, as if that were actually a question that warrants a response even if it had been asked correctly.

"It's tongue," Teena says, interrupting the inane conversation happening on her side of the booth.

"What's tongue?" her guy asks.

"It's 'cat got your tongue,' " Teena says.

"Maybe I get your tongue later," her guy says.

"Ew, get the fuck out of here," she answers, and her guy smirks because he thinks she's flirting, whereas you know that she won't actually put out — that's the part of her reputation that people get wrong, that she just gives it away to whomever. You don't quite understand what her standards

110

are, but you understand that she has them, and these guys aren't meeting them, which makes it even harder for you to come up with something to say. What you don't understand is that your silence makes you into something even better than a bad girl; it makes you into a *good* girl, and turns Matt's interest in you from passing and situational to one ripe with potential. This makes him nervous, and makes everything on your half of the table even more awful than it already was.

"You need some more coffee?" Matt asks and immediately knocks over your tumbler of ice water, which somehow manages to miss the table and pour directly into your crotch. You try to stand, but Matt has you trapped in the booth, and doesn't seem to comprehend, though you aren't even speaking in a strange American tongue, that you need to get away from the waterfall that's somehow still streaming into your lap. Finally you just point, while Matt repeats, *"Mut mut mut,"* and Teena tries not to laugh.

"What? Oh," Matt says, and goddammit, maybe you are a stupid good girl, because as you squeeze past him to run to the bathroom, you're the one who offers an apology, and when you get to the bathroom, you're the one who begins to die from

111

embarrassment in the stall instead of trying to dry yourself off under the hot-air blower, which doesn't even have enough power to get hands past damp. You were an idiot for coming here in the first place, for pretending you have any kind of heritage to salvage. Did you think you were going to fill in the holes with anything other than gravy fries and ice water? This trip has already turned into the kind of failure you'd always avoided by not attempting anything too risky. You want to cry, but if you do the tears will make the Maybelline run and your eyes will become bloodshot, and your face will be layered in pink and purple and red, a colorscape that's mesmerizing during a sunset but would be hideous on your face, so you manage to hold back the tears. Instead you punch yourself in the thighs to replace your disappointment with quiet rage. When the quiet rage rises to a respectable level you release it by kicking the stall door. So this is what *agency* is really about: going out and making yourself look like an idiot instead of waiting for someone else to do it for you.

The bathroom door swings open just as you're ready to emerge from your stall, so you stay in there, hoping to avoid as much humiliation as possible on the walk back from the bathroom to the table. The person who enters stands by the sinks, her feet pointed toward yours. The shoes don't belong to Teena (not sensible enough; that's another unexpected thing about Teena, she wears the most sensible shoes, sneakers and ugly slip-ons with too much sole, shoes meant to be worn by home health workers and grocery baggers instead of part-time skanks), and after a minute or so, the person literally begins tapping one of her pumps up and down, as if in a bad movie where the director told her to telegraph impatience.

"There's another stall," you say.

"I know how many stalls there are here. Are you going to stay in there all night?" the voice says. The accent sounds like a gypsy's, almost exaggerated compared to the vague Eastern European lilt of the guys at your table. Your stomach drops, and you try to get a look at her in the crack between the door and the framework, but all you can make out is the impatient folded arms to match her impatient, poorly directed tapping toe. Who really does that, other than someone mimicking an adopted language? Someone who'd been in this country long enough to learn idiomatic English expressions but will never call this place home?

"I can't leave yet," you say. "I'm not ready."

"It's just water, sweetheart. Ahmet knows it's his fault. He's more embarrassed than you."

Ahmet. Ha. You knew it wasn't Matt, just like you know that this woman out there could be the key to your entire shrouded family history, the person who could double your DNA's helix, which heretofore has just been a limp noodle with some random kinks and coils. It really had been as easy as you secretly believe nothing ever is; just think, you could've done this years ago, since at least age twelve, when your breasts had grown enough to attract the sloppy attention of the young men of the Ross. And yet the bravery you'd walked in with seems to have been extinguished with that douse of water, because there you are, inches away from — what, your grandmother? Your third cousin twice removed? — and you're paralyzed, wondering what episode of *Grey's Anatomy* your mother is on by now, questioning just what the hell you hope to accomplish by opening this can of worms. It's not that ignorance has been bliss for you, really, but it's been okay. It's been a low-fat pound cake, not entirely satisfying but better than bread and water.

"I need another minute," you say. Yes, another minute. Seventeen years hasn't been quite long enough: seventeen years and one minute, that's just the right amount of time.

The lady sighs, another cue from the bad-acting handbook. "Fine, take your time, stay for hours. What difference does it make, we'll be open. We're always open," she says, before she clicks away on what may actually be tap shoes.

After she walks out, you bend over the commode but don't quite retch. You try to retch; your stomach seems swirly enough, and the drama heightened enough, but nothing happens, and it occurs to you that you're simply pantomiming what you think someone might do in a situation like this, which is freak out, cry, hit your head on the porcelain, wake up in the hospital with a new perspective and an inexplicably British accent, like you saw on an episode of *Mystery ER* a while before. What you feel instead, after a minute kneeling before the bowl with your sweaty head in your hands, is the same old slightly pissed and mildly panicked feeling you feel pretty much every day at one point or another. What is wrong with you? Besides looking a wreck, with your poorly concealed black eye and a bot-

115

tom half that looks as if you've pissed yourself, what the hell is wrong with you? You're right here. You traveled the entire three miles to get the first sentence in your origin story, and you're going to walk out of here with nothing to show for it but some clammy denim and the phone number of a surrogate Albanian dude who might just let you call him daddy?

No. No, that is not going to happen. You rise to your feet and fling open the stall door without even stopping to look for the screw that drops from the handle. You check the mirror and smooth out the makeup that's settled into creases you don't even have, and you cup some water from the tap into your mouth. You give yourself the kind of pep talk that you imagine varsity wrestlers give themselves before meeting their middleweight nemeses: You can do this. You are stronger than them. You do not give a mighty fuck about how dumb you look for the next ten minutes.

You glance over at your table, where Teena is waving you back with a pleading look that means she's ready to get out of there. Matt/Ahmet & Co., meanwhile, are avoiding all eye contact with both you and Teena, which is just as well. You wave back at Teena, though she doesn't know it's a wave goodbye. You have work to do now, lives to disrupt, starting with your own and radiating outward. You march straight over to the counter, where the lady from the bathroom is staring through drugstore readers at a scroll of receipts, and you tell her, "I'm ready for the check."

The lady barely glances up, then throws her eyes over to your table. She says, "You don't need to pay for this. Ahmet will pay for this."

"No, I don't want him to pay for it," you say.

"He is going to pay. He's an idiot, but he's not a jerk."

You're glad that Matt/Ahmet is a gentleman idiot, but that's not the point, so you pull your debit card from your wallet and place it on the counter. "No, really. Please. I need to pay."

The woman sighs, pulls off her reading glasses, and finally looks at you, first with mild annoyance, and then — you think, though it's possible that you're imagining this part — with vague confusion, as if she'd met you before but can't place exactly where. She takes your card from you, finally, but she runs it through the card reader without even a glance at it. The whole point was for her to glance at it, to see your name and then, maybe, to see you for what you are: one of them, part of an indefinable something you've always been chasing, whether or not you knew it.

But she doesn't.

"At least let him apologize," she says and waves Ahmet over.

"No, seriously, I don't want —" you start, but it's too late. Ahmet weaves his way to you with more finesse than you imagine he'd ever have steering his motorcycle through a parking lot of orange cones. He touches your elbow with the gentle consideration of a Boy Scout guiding an elderly woman through a busy intersection.

"Hey, are you okay? I'm so sorry, Lulu. Lulu, right? Your friend said."

"It's fine. It's just water," you answer.

"Lulu?" the woman at the counter asks.

"Yeah," you say. And then, because she's already handed your card back without seeing your name and all the things you suspect it might stand for, and because this is your last chance to ever make her see it, since you know you'll never have the nerve to come back in here ever again, you add, "Well, no. Luljeta, actually. It's actually Luljeta."

Ahmet's face instantly flushes with excitement, even more than when he'd first taken notice of your boobs. "You're Albanian?" he asks. What a prize you are, suddenly, all things in one, an American girl that could make his parents happy, a halfsie who can pull off whorish American necklines but is probably still a nice Albanian virgin. The woman at the counter's face, meanwhile, turns approximately the same color as the split pea soup on special that evening. She looks down at the receipt you've just signed. She pulls on her glasses and then flings them off again to get a good look at your face.

"Oh my god," the woman says.

"So, like, do you have a boyfriend?" Ahmet asks.

Teena taps your shoulder. "Are you ready to go?" she asks.

You take it all in, this circus around you. Your heart is racing, your mouth is dry, and you instinctively unwrap the peppermint candy you'd been handed with your receipt and pop it into your mouth.

"I'm ready," you say to all of them at once.

CHAPTER FIVE:
ELSIE

Greta wasn't looking so hot. All the things in the world I should've been thinking about at that moment, like the tiny cluster of cells threatening to become human in my womb, and I kept coming back to that: someone's got to do something for that girl. Greta was a trick, which was idiot-speak for trichotillomania, meaning when she was stressed out or sad or bored, when normal people bit their nails or puffed on cigarettes, she pulled out her hair one thin oily strand at a time. Who could blame her for wanting to dismantle herself: take a sixteen-year-old girl with a hairline like Willard Scott's, no daddy, Carlo Rossi for a mother, a report card that had never seen anything less than an A, and a library card that got worn out every six months, and plop her in the halls of a high school in a place like Waterbury, where studying to be a nail art technician counted as postsecondary education. The girl was like chum in a tank of sharks. I wasn't exactly vying for the homecoming court in high school, but at least I was unremarkable, just your standard minor slut who consistently failed to live up to her potential, a phrase so often used in my report cards that the teachers should've had a rubber stamp of it made to save themselves some work. Greta didn't even get bullied anymore; she'd been picked clean, her predators had to move on to an obese girl with psoriasis just so they wouldn't starve to death. She hadn't come home crying in months, her face was now perfectly aloof, except for her eyes, which still always jumped around, looking for a place to run. But I'd lured her into the bathroom with me and there was nowhere for her to escape to, except for maybe the bathtub, which reeked of Jean Naté so strongly that it would have made her gag. I hadn't had an actual friend since high school ended and my bestie-and-only ran off to marry and divorce the Marine recruiter who used to hang out in our cafeteria scouting for fresh blood, so my sister was the only person I could think of to wrangle into my mess. And now I'd managed to do what even her tormentors had given up on doing: I'd gotten her to cry.

"I want to hit you so bad," she said. "I want to kill you."

"You're going to push a turd out if you keep rocking on the toilet seat like that," I said.

"This isn't funny. This is serious, Elsie. You're going to wish it was a turd going down the toilet instead of your life."

"It's going to be fine," I said, even with the pregnancy test in my hand telling me otherwise. The pregnancy test, in fact, was telling me to fuck off, one slim pink middle finger stuck straight up the center of that stick. I flipped it right back off but Greta didn't see it, or she didn't react if she did see it. She blew her nose on the neck of her T-shirt and groped for strands of hair that she'd already mostly gotten to.

"Hands off your head, Greta," I said.

"What's wrong with you?" she said. "Why don't you even care what's happening?"

It was a fair question. The E.P.T box was ripped apart on the counter, both of the tests undeniably positive, at least in one sense of the word. All the evidence was laid out in front of me: the two pink fingers, their tsk-tsks; the bile stain on the linoleum in front of the toilet after the latest round of sickness; a witness. When I blinked my eyes the facts went away for a second, but they kept coming back. Like cockroaches, they always came back.

"I do care," I said. "It's just, like, there's no point in freaking out about it."

"I've seen you freak out when your good pair of socks got a hole in them. This is your life, Elsie. And not just your life, another person's life."

"Bashkim will be fine."

"I meant the baby, the baby's the other person. Of course this guy will be fine, whoever he is. All he has to do is take off to Myrtle Beach and never think about it again."

"He's not going to do that. He's not like our father."

"Then why was I the one you asked to be with you while you peed on a stick?"

"Because," I said, and that was all I could come up with. Even if I wasn't ready to face Bashkim with this yet, why would I turn to Greta? Why not just do it alone, like I always claimed I could? The two of us had slept within five feet of each other our whole lives without ever saying good night. We didn't even look alike — she was pale and I had the acne-red complexion of a rug burn, she pulled out her dirty blond hair while I spent hours trying to fluff up my dirt-brown — but it was obvious we came from the same peasant stock, because neither one of us had any cavities in our teeth and both of us shared a kind of loneliness that was so innate it had to be built into our DNA. Still, most of the time we each looked at the other like a foster kid Mamie had taken in for extra money. We could outline all the things we had in common, write them out on index cards and not even have enough to fill up an hour of conversation after lights-out. She'd take a flashlight and a book under her blanket, and I'd take a Walkman loaded with *Led Zeppelin I.* In the morning, we'd stand behind the closet door to undress and re-dress.

"Because you're the smart one," I said, finally. "I thought you might have something to say other than boo-hoo."

"You don't have to be smart to see how this is going to turn out. Look at Mamie. Jesus Christ, look in the mirror."

"It doesn't have to be that way. It could end up like you."

"Fuck you."

"I meant that as a good thing. You're going to be fine. You're going to get a scholarship somewhere and leave us all behind and you won't even come back for Thanksgiving. You said so yourself."

She shook her head, and I pushed her

hand away from it before she could pinch a hair out.

"Anyway, who says I'm even going to have this baby?" I pressed down on my stomach, and nothing pushed back, so it didn't seem possible that there was any kind of life in there. "I'll take care of it. In two weeks none of this will make a difference in the world."

Greta stood up from the toilet. She hadn't used it, but she flushed it instinctively, so I was never really sure if I heard what she said correctly. What I heard was "We need a fucking difference."

But she probably just said something about fun indifference.

I closed the door behind Greta and lifted my shirt in front of the mirror. How was something supposed to fit in there, anyway? I imagined a bicycle pump with its nozzle in my belly button, Bashkim at the other end, pumping away. Then he'd come back with a sewing needle and pop it. He'd pop it, right? He wouldn't want this kid, and his wife certainly wouldn't want this kid, and I of course didn't want this kid. It would be insane to go ahead with it, because children killed dreams, and because car seats don't fit in Fieros. Look at Mamie, not a dream left in her soul, not even a nightmare to wake her up sweating on the couch. Just nothing, the worst thing in the world, worse than war and famine, worse than the labor camps in Albania that Bashkim talked about. Nothing. But I mean, of course I wouldn't do it like Mamie did it, and just quit right out of the gate. I'd at least put headphones over my belly and make my kid listen to Beethoven like the yuppie moms on TV, I'd have my kid in state-run daycare only until I got my dental technician certification, then I'd get a real job and work days and switch off babysitting with Bashkim, who still worked nights, but at the pizza shop he always talked about opening someday. I'd carried a sack of flour around in high school, I knew it'd be hard at first, and then eventually it'd get better. Eventually we'd buy a raised ranch the next town over in Wolcott and only ever go back to Waterbury for grocery shopping and to visit the graves of poor dead relatives, great-uncles and -aunts who lived at the Lithuanian Social Club and were laid to rest at the Lithuanian cemetery, not having left the city limits in decades, never mind gone home to their motherland. Our kid would spend summers with his cousins in Albania, learn how to ride a horse and brine things, come back and be bored by our strip malls and discount second-run movie theaters, talk about one day busting out like a Springsteen song.

I pulled my shirt back down and turned away from the mirror. There was no use thinking of the ways things would be different when in a couple of weeks they would be nothing. Stupid, endless, soul-numbing nothing, the kind of nothing it'd be merciful not to pass on to some poor doomed offspring.

Greta was on her bed, staring at the ceiling, when I finally left the bathroom.

"Don't say anything to Mamie, okay?" I said.

"I haven't said anything to Mamie in about ten days. She hasn't even noticed," she said.

She was so thin she was almost flush with the bed.

"You're almost out of here," I said. "Don't fuck it up."

She looked over at me. "You're giving advice about fucking up?" She didn't even sound mean about it, just confused.

I shrugged and sat down on my bed to put on my pantyhose. "I guess that's stupid. Never mind. Do your thing."

She went back to staring at the ceiling, and I got ready to go back to the Ross.

When our father died seven years before, Mamie threw out the *Waterbury Republican* so me and Greta wouldn't come across his name in the obituaries. Greta only ever opened the paper for the Garfield comics, me for the Bob's Stores ads, hoping for a mythical one-day sale where the genuine Levi's and Reeboks dropped in price to match the generics. I was twelve, Greta was ten. We weren't yet checking every day for the names of schoolmates who might've died in 2:00 A.M. car wrecks on the way home from the Brass Pony, we didn't wonder if our former elementary school teachers finally let their two-pack-a-day Pall Mall habits take them down before retirement did, we didn't care enough about distant relatives to figure out who was still alive and who wasn't. Mamie was the one who subscribed to the paper for the death notices and circulars only, sometimes the classifieds when Waterbury Buckle announced another round of layoffs, or when the LTD rusted off a part that looked like it might've been too important to ignore. Greta and I probably didn't notice that the paper wasn't on the table as usual. We probably read the previous day's as if it were new, because it always looked the same anyway. That Bob's sale was never in there.

Then, on my next birthday, my father's parents, Grandma and Grandpa Kuzavinas, sent a card with a fifty-dollar check enclosed. I'd never held that much money in my hands. They said they were sad that Greta and I didn't come around for Christmas anymore, even though they were just down the road in Naugatuck, that we left them when Dad left us, as if that were something me and Greta had, as kids, made a conscious decision to do. They were disappointed we weren't at the funeral because Dad's son was there and he looked a little like us, and we should get to know him because blood is blood, signed the Kuzavinases. The card had irises on it and said THANK YOU.

"What funeral?" I asked Mamie. "What kid?"

She read the card. "Fifty dollars? They expect us to believe that's all they got out of that?" Her hand shook while she held the check, maybe on purpose, maybe trying to get it to vibrate so fast that it'd look like there were hundreds of fifties flying about.

"Got out of what?"

"The insurance settlement, the whatever.

Even people who aren't worth nothing alive are worth something dead."

"Who are you talking about?"

"Your father, Elsie. I thought you knew that." She handed the check back to me, but it missed my fingers and fluttered slowly to the floor. "At least it didn't bounce, right?" she said when it landed.

I'd always believed Dad would try to come back someday. I'd planned the whole thing out. I would be wearing those genuine Levi's when he knocked on our door. Or sometimes I'd be wearing a corduroy skirt instead, short and black though, not preppy and stupid. Mamie was at work; it was just Greta and me, sitting at the kitchen table we never sat at in real life, me doing the homework I didn't do in real life. We wouldn't let him in. We wouldn't cry or anything, we wouldn't yell, we'd just tell him from behind the screen door that it was too late. *It's too late,* we'd say, *we're all grown up. The work is all done, and you don't get to come in now and reap the harvest.*

"I didn't know he died. How was I supposed to know?" I asked, and at first I didn't hear her because her back was turned and the water was on full stream, and she was always saying that she didn't know why we bothered to talk to her when she was washing dishes, she couldn't ever hear anything over the faucet.

But then she shrugged. "What's the difference anyway? That's what I thought. I thought what's the difference if he's alive or dead?"

I didn't know. I think that's why I was crying, because there was a correct answer but I just couldn't tap into it, like when I tried to learn the past perfect tense in French class.

There had been only a couple of cereal bowls and coffee mugs in the sink to begin with, but the water kept running, Mamie kept her hands underneath the stream, and I wondered if she was like me, if her hands got cold when she was upset about something. "The bastard couldn't handle it here. He did jack shit, and he still couldn't handle it. Don't miss him, okay? Don't mourn him just because you think you're supposed to. He was already gone, Elsie. Nothing has changed."

"Yes it has," I said. "Now I'll never be able to tell him to fuck off."

Mamie finally shut the water off. She turned back to me and pressed her wet palms against my cheeks, but hers were wet, too, and not from dishwater. "Oh, but there will be so many other men that you can tell to fuck off, baby, I promise you."

I didn't want Bashkim to fuck off. I wanted the opposite of that, for him to fuck on, or whatever you'd call it. It was impossible to predict from night to night which version of him I'd be getting: the one who was going to take me away from the tedious, sweaty, forevermore kind of life lived in ugly sensible work sneakers, or the one who was condemning me to live it forever. Some nights he was a month away from cashing in, because fortunately he had *diversed,* because he wasn't an idiot — *I am not an idiot,* he'd say, to me or to Gjonni or whoever he thought was secretly accusing him of being one — so the money he lost in one account was being made up for in another. On those nights, he was already in contact with a divorce lawyer back in Tirana, and on those nights he would drive me to his place on his break so we could lie side by side on his air mattress, not even screwing, just lying there until his stopwatch beeped ten minutes later and we had to head back to the Ross. On those nights, I would go home with a plan to tell Mamie that I was done paying her rent to keep living under her roof, that I had a new home with a guy named Bashkim, and that she'd better just deal with the fact that he wasn't Lithuanian, and that we had made a baby together and the baby would be a mutt, which everyone knows are stronger, smarter, healthier breeds. I never really said those things to her, though, because she was always passed out on the sofa by the time I got home, and because eventually I'd remember that I wasn't going to have this baby, especially since I didn't even have the guts to tell him about it.

On the other nights, Bashkim was so far away from me that he might as well have been back in Tirana. Those were the nights when I realized I was never going to tell him, because I didn't want him to have to pay for me to get rid of the thing. I was afraid he'd get so bent out of shape about it that we'd never have one of the good nights again.

And then there was Greta, who kept asking, "Do you have an appointment yet?"

"In two weeks or so," I'd say.

"You said that two weeks ago. You're going to be ready to pop in two weeks."

"I'm telling him tomorrow, okay? Lay off already."

But once again, last night's tomorrow was already the past. Once again, I'd shown up too late for Bashkim to sneak out to the Fiero before my shift, and once again, he didn't get mad, or corner me in dry storage because he couldn't live without me, or at least without *it,* for one more night.

"Slowpoke," he finally said one night while I waited for him to scrape the blackened cinder off a burnt grilled cheese. "I rang that bell two minutes ago."

"Who do you think I am, Pavlov's dog?" I said.

"You're getting fat," he said.

"You're getting bald," I said. "We're even."

"You look better. You look better with boobies," he said.

I almost smiled before I remembered there was nothing to smile about.

"I want to talk to you," he said. "When you're finished tonight. You're running away on me all the time now."

"I'm not running away," I said, right before I ran out of the kitchen and into the bathroom to purge the latest round of sick.

After my shift I went outside, hoping for a few minutes alone to air out my pits and figure out what the hell I was supposed to tell him. What new could I come up with about the oldest story in the book? Whatever, I got knocked up, I'd say, it was bound to happen at some point when you buy your rubbers from the clearance aisle at Joey'z Shopping Spree. But Bashkim was already outside waiting for me, leaning with one arm against the wall of the Ross. Dust and asbestos stuck to his skin when he pulled his weight away, like confectioners' sugar over the pink dough of his forearm. I wanted to gum it, even if it would infect me with something worse than the bug he'd already made me come down with.

"So," he said.

"So," I answered.

"You, ah. How are you feeling?"

"Fine," I said. I pressed my palm hard against my stomach to shut it up.

"You are acting funny lately. Tired. Sick." He pulled me toward him and kissed me on the mouth, but I must've forgotten how to do it, because I couldn't breathe while his lips were on mine, and I had to come up for air.

"See? Like that. Pulling away from me," he said.

"I'm not," I said. "You're the one who's been pulling away."

"Look at me. Is this called pulling away?"

"I mean, not tonight you're not."

"I'm right here," he said.

"Well, I'm here, too," I said. "I've just been busy."

"Busy doing what?" he asked.

I shrugged. "Not busy, really. Distracted.

Thinking about other stuff."

He shook his head. "You are sick. You have been a long time sick."

"Maybe it's cancer," I said.

He didn't laugh. "It's not cancer. Don't be dumb, Elsie."

"It was a joke," I said.

"For you everything is a joke."

"Take my wife. Please."

I knew Bashkim didn't get the punch line but he didn't bother asking me to explain. Nobody wants to admit they're not in on the joke, right? We just stared at each other for a minute, waiting to see who would draw first.

"Yllka says you have to tell me something," he said finally.

I felt my skin catch fire. "Yllka doesn't know anything about me. And she definitely doesn't speak for me."

"You should thank her when she does the dirty work. You don't speak for yourself. You say things against other people, not things for yourself."

"That's not true," I said.

"You're having a baby," he said.

"I'm not," I said.

"You can't pretend that."

"How does Yllka know anyway?"

"Everybody knows. Nobody here is blind."

136

"I'm not having a baby," I said. "I'm pregnant. It's not the same thing."

He looked sucker-punched for a second, his lips pursed out as if they'd swelled instantly from a perfectly landed uppercut, but then he recovered, like he always did, and said, "It is the same thing. What did they teach you in high school?"

"They didn't teach me anything at school. This is the kind of thing you learn on the bus on the way there."

He stared at my feet, and I shifted my weight to disguise my pigeon toes. I was embarrassed about them, suddenly, among all the deformities I had.

"I think it is not the right thing to do," he said.

"It's a little late for that," I said.

He looked up at me finally with those salesman's eyes, those big blue things that could sell words as big and combustible as the *Hindenburg*. "It's not too late," he said. "Right? You haven't."

"Doing it, I mean. Having sex. Getting pregnant. I meant it's a little late for that."

"Oh," Bashkim said. "It is, yes."

I kicked more sand over the wad of spit he laid into the ground after he'd said those last words. If I was crossing the desert, if I was dying of thirst, I bet I could've found it

137

again and drunk from it. It looked like an ocean to me.

"I wasn't going to ask you for anything," I said.

"Ask me," he said.

"I can't. You need your money. Or should I say Aggie needs your money."

"I would say yes," he said.

"Yes to what?" I asked, but I didn't want him to answer that. It was like uncovering the last number on a scratch-off ticket: it was the last part that would kill the dream.

"Yes to —"

"To what, now?"

"Yes, I will be your father."

"You'll be my father?"

"The father to your baby. Our baby. I will have this baby with you. I want to have this baby with you."

Oh, I meant to say, but I just breathed out a spit bubble instead. It coated my lips like cheap gloss and it didn't taste like Bonne Bell, like cherry or root beer or peppermint, just recycled dirty spit. I could taste my own breath on it, oily and flat like shortening.

I will have this baby with you, he'd said.

I want to have this baby with you, he'd said.

He wanted anything from me at all.

I tried speaking again. "Oh," I said. The veins in Bashkim's forearms filled thick with fluid and bulged from his skin like garter snakes. My father used to kill them when he caught them sunbathing on the front porch even though Mamie said they weren't poisonous, they were good for the yard, even, feeding on the stuff nobody wanted around. Then Bashkim pulled his arms tight to his chest and tangled the snakes together, the way they look on a medical bracelet, when they're warning you about something.

"Are you saying what I think you're saying?" I asked.

He nodded.

"But that's crazy, this is a problem we can solve. I wasn't going to ask you for anything like that," I said.

"Why crazy? Why a problem? I want this. I didn't know that I wanted it but now I have it and I don't want to give it back."

"You don't?" I said.

He pulled in close to me and took my hands. "No. You don't, either. I know you don't. If you did you would not have let it come this far."

"I don't know anything," I said. "I don't know what I want. I don't know who you are. The person I thought you were wouldn't be saying these things to me right now."

"You will have to get to learn, then. You will have to let me take care of you. Isn't that what you want?"

I couldn't remember wanting that exactly, but then again, wanting for me was mostly a feeling that didn't have anything specific attached to it, other than stupid things like a used car or that bag of Bugles by the checkout line at the Pathmark. Bashkim seemed so sure of himself that I thought maybe I should trust him with my wants, too. I just had to train myself to ignore my instincts, which, I reminded myself, had not ever been terribly reliable things.

"I guess so," I said.

"See?" he said. I would've thought seeing him smile like that would settle my stomach, but for some reason it kept churning, a tornado brewing in there. It's hormones, I thought, a body all out of whack. The heart palpitations, the sweat, the terror: all biology.

He pulled me close, and I said into his chest, "Where will we live? How am I going to keep working like this?"

"Shh," he said.

"Your wife —"

"It's not for you to worry about my wife," he said.

"And what about school? I was going to apply for that dental tech program at Mattatuck. I'll never make it through the year."

"You don't care about school," he said.

I nodded as if that were an order, and I thought that it was probably a good thing, not having to make up my own mind about anything. I was getting nowhere doing that.

"My mother is not going to like this," I said finally. "This will kill her dead."

"You have me now. You don't need anyone," Bashkim said. "This is what I want. This is what I came here for. To make a son, an American son so he can do whatever he wants to do from the day he is born."

"A son?"

"Yes. Isn't that what you want?"

I couldn't make my head move up and down in agreement, so I just rested it against his chest, listening to his heart in case it was giving anything away. It sounded like it was beating *uh-oh, uh-oh, uh-oh,* the droning pulse of a dirge, and that made me feel a little better. That dread was the same kind I felt the first time I saw Bashkim, the same kind I felt when I listened to the best minor-key ballads, and that inspired the kind of love that was easier to nurture than kudzu. It didn't even need light to grow.

CHAPTER SIX:
LULJETA

Yllka gave you her address and told you to come see her anytime, the sooner the better, the next day if you could. The next day is Saturday and so you can, at least feasibly, though you have no way to get there other than walking or biking, neither of which is considered, in Waterbury at least, a valid method of transportation for people who aren't hookers or have fewer than three DUIs. You brainstorm reasons you can tell your mother you need to borrow the car: school project (but you would have already told her about that); a date with a boy (but you would never have told her about that); a trip to the mall just to get out of the house (but you'd explicitly sworn off the mall because it held essentially the same human contents as Crosby High, only walking around in a fog of kush and vanilla-scented Yankee Candle napalm). By the time you emerge from your bedroom with some

142

excuse about needing to drop off a book or a sweater that you'd told Teena you'd let her borrow, it's too late: your mother has already taken the car, a note on the table in her surprisingly meticulous penmanship explaining that she had to catch up on some paperwork at the office and that you'd have pizza for dinner that night.

You don't need a note to tell you about dinner. You've had pizza for dinner every Saturday night for the past six years, a tradition that began at the intersection of your Student of the Month honors and your mother's first hire to the front office rather than the manufacturing side of a factory, a move that was more titular than remunerative, just enough extra in her paycheck to spring for a weekly to-go order from Dominec's. It's like she'd never stopped celebrating, and last year, when she started adding two cannolis to the pizza order to celebrate her finally getting her associate's degree from Mattatuck Community College after five years of talking about it and five more years of actually going for it, you weren't sure whether to find her triumph in such small victories adorable or depressing. Not like getting a degree isn't a big deal, but what next? She still works at some barely-hanging-on car parts manufacturer, the latest in a long line of jobs at factories a year or two from relocating to Georgia or Mexico. It's still just the two of you in your little second-floor apartment, which she always mentions is near a bus line that neither one of you ever uses. The most substantively positive development was when she began dating one of her former Mattatuck professors after he tried and failed to get her to switch from accounting to poli-sci, even though she did meet him halfway and switched to sociology, which was how she got stuck forever as a clerk in accounts payable, the department where no-bullshit women with a head for numbers and a preference for husbands in motorcycle gangs go to die. Those were her exact words, the same ones that made Professor Robbie fall for her, even though the two of them are still, after a year, just casual, because your mother doesn't want to take anything with him too far, too fast. Robbie's got a thick Brooklyn accent and a denim jacket full of crusty-punk pins and you think for somebody who'd willingly moved to Waterbury from the 718 area code of your dreams, he's pretty all right. And what does your mother say about him?

Robbie's great, Lu, I love him, but I don't need all that in my life.

She doesn't need all what in her life, love? Then what does she need instead, cannolis?

She needs you. She's said as much herself — she didn't necessarily ask for you, and she doesn't always know what to do with you, but you're what kept her waking up in the morning to go to dead-end jobs and sign up for the classes from which she'd previously withdrawn two or three times. It's sweet enough to give you pause now momentarily, and feel bad about stalking the other unknown half of your family line, because you know it would break her heart to learn that, despite all of the pizzas and Italian pastries and crappy jobs and associate's degrees, you do need *that* in your life, whatever *that* is. You can't define it, but you can feel it; there's a hole somewhere in you that nothing has thus far even begun to fill, even that whole box of cinnamon Life you ate one time for dinner when your mother and Robbie went on a date to Bosco's and you insisted you didn't want to go. You don't know what dating entails, but you're certain it isn't a teenage daughter gnawing on bread sticks off to the side like some pathetic street urchin in a Dickens novel.

And then it's infuriating, your mother's need for you, because it feels manipulative at worst and a little creepy at best. It's not fair that you should serve as her primary motivation for getting out of bed in the morning, especially considering that you have no idea what the hell you want from your own life, other than to get out of this crap town and figure it out elsewhere. And you'll be doing that soon, really soon, even without stupid NYU. You're determined you'll still find your way to New York, the only city that matters, where Aunt Greta will tell you where to find the good Chinese joints, if not the answers to all of life's questions. And it isn't fair to deny other people a shot at knowing you, because what if it turns out you're the hole in someone else's life, the way Yllka, ever so briefly, made you feel last night? Maybe your father is suffering from the same condition as you. Maybe you're the two jagged edges of a best friends locket, designed from the start to fit perfectly together, each side kind of meaningless and tacky without the other.

Three miles to Yllka's. For seventeen years you've been three miles from an alternate version of your life, and now you have the Google Maps route pulled up on your phone and no way to get to it.

There are barely enough contacts saved on your phone for you to be able to scroll through, and none are people you can call for a ride without having to explain where you're going, including Teena, who'd caught on at some point that you weren't hanging out at the Ross because of some mystery messy-haired boy, which meant she lost interest in driving you around. There's your mother, Mamie, Greta, and a dozen or so schoolmates with whom your friendships either have fizzled or were only circumstantial to begin with, group-work partners who paired up with you knowing that you'd do 90 percent of the assignment yourself. It's depressing to even look at your phone as anything other than a handheld gaming device, a silent Scrabble partner. You have to play against the computer, even. You don't even bother with Words with Friends.

God, you can't wait to get out of this shithole.

Except there is Matt/Ahmet, that guy with the Kawasaki motorcycle, someone whose number you'd forgotten to delete and who would be more than happy to shuttle you back to your Albanian roots on a Japanese machine weaving through the Italian part of town. Huh. How about that.

You call. He can't believe you called, but he plays off his shock by coughing for a few seconds. Radiator heat, so dry, you know?

He says he'll be there in an hour, which seems, after already having waited approximately 149,000 hours, like an ungodly amount of time.

He arrives in a Civic hatchback with ridiculous rims but no ridiculous spoilers or the faux-carbon vinyl wraps wannabe dragster drivers apply to their four-cylinder Japanese automobiles. He must've run out of money before he got around to installing a noise-maker exhaust pipe and a decal of Calvin pissing on a Toyota. But still, he has both a motorcycle and a car, whereas you don't even have a bicycle without a bent wheel, so either he or his parents are doing something right. On the drive he explains to you he's a sophomore at UConn, no doubt referring to the auxiliary Waterbury campus, where students wear UCLA sweatshirts because California feels just about as far away to them as UConn's main campus in Storrs, and you nod and say *cool* without asking what his major is or what he wants to be. You don't want to give him the wrong idea, or at least more of the wrong idea than you'd already given him by calling him out of nowhere the day after he poured ice water onto your crotch. He's been a gentleman, opening the door for you and offering to buy you Dunkin' Donuts or a breakfast McWrap, both of which you decline, but he's also just a ride. He is not the Albanian man you are looking for, not even an acceptable surrogate.

"So Yllka is what, your aunt or something?" he asks in a small-talky kind of way, as if he were remarking about the rain that's expected later in the day.

"Something like that. It's hard to explain," you answer, and, gentleman that he is, he doesn't press you to explain hard things.

The ride to Yllka's is mercifully and maddeningly short: mercifully because what are you supposed to say to Ahmet other than *thank you* or *no thank you* a dozen times, and maddeningly because really? That's it? Yllka — and the rest of the Hasanis, as far as you know — has seriously been ten minutes with traffic from you all this time?

"So, should I come up, then, or just wait?" Ahmet asks.

"Um, could you just, like, wait outside? Or, like, I could text you when I'm done?" you say, knowing that all he'll hear is that you'll be in contact again and thus of course will agree. For someone with no experience with boys, you're surprised at how easily you're able to navigate this whole Ahmet situation. Who even needs to read all those

Cosmo advice columns instructing women on how to keep a man under your thumb, in between all the other *Cosmo* advice columns instructing women on how to keep the man from seeking out other younger, hotter thumbs? You aren't even wearing a push-up bra or terrifying fuck-me pumps and yet there's Ahmet, glancing back at you on the walk to his car, pretending the sun is in his eyes and he can't see you.

But it isn't only eager young men on whom you can cast a spell, you see when Yllka flings open the door before you can even tap the knocker a second time.

"Oh, it's you!" she declares, full exclamation-mark declares, as if she's waited for you all night and yet was convinced you wouldn't really come. And suddenly you wonder, once again, if you should have, if this whole thing is going to prove to be a horrible mistake. There's a good chance this woman is a nutjob who wants to sell you out to some underground network of skeezy Albanians, according to the rumors you've heard. You've heard these people marry off their daughters at age fourteen, or if the daughters refuse, human-traffic them to fat sweaty businessmen in industrial parks off the highway. In an hour you might find yourself in a Chevy Suburban with some pork-fingered Budweiser executive with a secret penchant for girls not much older than his own chubby, spoiled children.

Yllka doesn't look like a pimp, though. Pimps probably wouldn't cry tears of joy at the sight of you the way that Yllka does. She grabs you and pulls you to her bosom — it can only be called a bosom when it's so in-your-face like that — and tells you to come in, but you can't move, and in fact can hardly breathe, with her holding on to you so tightly. Eventually she releases her arms and steers you by the shoulders into the apartment, the first floor of a triple-decker a lot like the one you live in with your mother, if only because half the people in Waterbury live in triple-deckers that are essentially identical to the one you live in with your mother. Yllka's is spotless, though, not a speck of dust anywhere, which is particularly notable since nothing in there appears to be any less than sixty years old, from the china to the doilies to a Frigidaire that's possibly one model year past icebox. There are so many crystal and porcelain knick-knacks lined up on the shelves that if you squint your eyes it all melts together into some ornate wallpaper, and behind all of that stuff is actual ornate wallpaper, the kind you'd seen at elementary school birth-

151

day parties thrown by kids being raised by their off-the-boat grandparents. Even the functional stuff on the dining table is some kind of knick-knack-paddy-whackery: the salt and pepper shakers are doves, the napkin holders are brass trumpets, the pot holders are the same angel's wings that Mamie has in her kitchen, which is surprising to you since you assume that Yllka, like most of the Albanian kids at school, is a Muslim, while Mamie is a Catholic who'd been reborn somewhere between her fourth and fifth steps in AA.

Yllka sits you down and places a serving platter in front of you, the thin pieces of fried dough it holds stacked six inches high and drizzled with honey. You normally don't like to eat in front of strangers, because you think they're glancing down at your farm-girl haunches and silently questioning whether you really need the calories, but you also realize that you can't be expected to talk with a mouth full of food, and now that you're in front of her, you realize you have no idea at all what to say. So you take a bite, and it gives you something to say.

"Oh my god, that's really good," you choke out — choke because your mouth is still too full of sweet mush to really attempt speaking, but the words come out involuntarily. There has to be something in those fried dough squares besides flour and water and sugar. Nothing can taste that good without the use of black magic and/or generous amounts of bacon fat, neither of which you think a Muslim with angels on the wall would be allowed to use.

Yllka looks relieved, like she's just advanced to the next round in *Iron Chef.* Then she pours you coffee and brings out cheese and bread and you spend the next two minutes convincing her that you really, really don't want or need anything else to eat, and that you really, really aren't too skinny like your mother always was.

"I'm good, I'm fine, I'm full, I promise," you say, and eventually she sighs and sits down across from you at the table, petting your hair as if you were a runaway dog she'd retrieved from the shelter.

"Gjonni couldn't be here, unfortunately," she says finally, but she doesn't really look sorry about it. She's so grabby, and the way she stares, it's like she's greedy for you. You've never been looked at like that before, not even by Ahmet back in the car — and he was much more circumspect about his desire. It's strange, and not entirely comfortable, and yet not entirely awful, either. Yllka had told you last night that she's your great-

153

aunt, which is family, a word that doesn't quite seem to fit but absolutely does. What other word is there, other than an Albanian one that you don't know?

"Who's Gjonni?" you ask, and immediately Yllka looks ready to cry.

"My god, do you know nothing?" she asks. You don't shake your head, but of course you know nothing, and of course you're embarrassed about that, as if you'd been caught neglecting your duties. How are you supposed to know about these things? Is there some Wiki you don't know about that could have unraveled all the mysteries of your own life? "Gjonni is my husband, your uncle," she says, and you mouth the word *uncle,* something you'd had few occasions to say, other than crying it when Margarita pinned your arm against your back once in third grade. Your mother has never mentioned the names Yllka and Gjonni to you. She's never mentioned that these people whose blood you share live in an adjacent zip code to you and not on a different continent. You could practically forget your own father's name, your mother has said it aloud so few times to you. When it comes up at all, it's to assign blame for something, and his name then becomes Your Father, pronounced with a detached, clinical tone that makes it sound like a medical condition. As in: *I don't know where your frizzy hair/eczema/cat allergy comes from, must be from Your Father.*

"So you're a Hasani?" you ask, excited by the prospect of your name having a history. For the first time, your name doesn't seem to you like some random collection of letters put together by a spambot. You're glad your mother has never followed through on her lifelong promise to legally change your name to Kuzavinas, something even more unpronounceable and somehow equally unsuitable.

"I was, before I was married a hundred years ago. Now I am Shehu, Yllka Shehu," she says, and once again you are alone on an island of Hasani. "But you can call me Teto. It means 'auntie.' " She pauses. "You don't know that, do you? You don't even know the words for your own family?"

"No," you say.

She shakes her head and strokes yours. "You poor thing, i dashur. So lost from what you are."

It takes a minute for that to sink in, and then you're fully convinced that this woman is not a human trafficker or a run-of-the-mill weirdo after all. She's a genius. She'd had you pinned as the hungry, stray animal you'd always felt like from the moment you walked in the door.

Yllka brings out a photograph, a black-and-white shot of a man with eyes as wrinkled as his shirt staring into the camera from under a white knit cap. He looks like he's deciding what kind of punishment to dish out to whatever asshole is trying to steal his soul with that little plastic box in their hands, his face veiled with smoke from a cigarette that didn't make it into the frame. He is ghostly, and you have no doubt he was the kind of man whose spirit would have hung around long after he died from consumption or a mule kick, the kind of man who isn't about to let a thing like death keep him from getting his work done, whatever his work is. From the looks of him, it's farming or arms dealing.

"That's my brother. Your babagjysh," Yllka says. "I know, the picture looks terrible. We just had cheap Chinese cameras in those days. Toys, really."

"Babagjysh," you repeat.

"It means 'grandfather,'" Yllka says.

"I know," you say. "I figured that out. I just never knew I had one."

"Of course you had one. He's gone now, rest his soul, but you had one. Everybody has one, silly." She takes a wisp of your hair and pushes it aside and looks at you like you're much younger than you are, a toddler that the whole world has to be explained to. "Let me show you more people from back home," she says and scatters the photo albums across the table.

Home, she says, like it's yours, too.

"There are no Hasanis left in the village," she says, after you make it through the first album, more black-and-white shots of more people who looked like they were allergic to good times, which you hope isn't genetic. "Except for the dead ones, I mean. Lots and lots of dead ones. We were there forever, hundreds and hundreds of years. And now, poof, all gone."

"How come? What happened?" you ask.

"Oh, Luljeta, it became a terrible place. You must have heard about how terrible Albania was under Hoxha."

You can't get yourself to admit that you haven't. You don't even know what a Hoxha is.

"We weren't allowed to even feed ourselves. Hoxha would rather us starve than to grow food that wasn't for the State. His own people he did this to. We were the cattle, why would we need to raise our own? And so many people put in the prisons and the camps, and so many people put to death, and so many lies that we believed, that Albania was the most powerful country in the world, and every nation was an enemy, everybody wanted to get us. Do you know what it's like to feel so alone like that, like the whole world, even your own people, wish you not to live?"

You try to come up with a good answer to that before you realize it's a rhetorical question.

"Of course you don't," she says. "Thank God you never knew that life."

Yes, thank god, except that there is a secret part of you that is thrilled to be only a degree or two away from that kind of suffering, the same ugly part of you that, when you were little, sometimes secretly wished for type 1 diabetes like your classmate Aisha, who got to wear a cool medical bracelet and received endless attention from her parents and teachers. Sure, she almost died twice a year and would probably eventually go blind and might not make it to fifty; what was fifty to you other than some diffuse, faraway threat, like purgatory? Aisha, at eight, understood suffering and mortality. It made her serious and above reproach. You'd had a couple of stomach bugs and a respiratory illness once, and that was about as close as you came to Aisha's innate stoicism. You'd never even gotten the chicken pox, even after your daycare closed for two weeks when it swept through and infected just about every other child in a half-mile radius. You are hearty, almost ridiculously so, but maybe that's because you've inherited the gene for overcoming adversity, which means that you are tuned in to adversity in a way that your schoolmates are not. After all, look at what your uncle and aunt had lived through. Your father. Your babagjysh.

"But I want to know that life," you say. "Or at least know *about* it."

Yllka takes your hand and kisses it. "I know, darling, and you will learn. I am so happy you're here."

"I am, too," you say, and god, it's embarrassing to talk like that, all gushy and goo-goo-eyed, to be called darling, which you thought was a word used only by old ladies to describe white waffle-knit capris from Talbots. Mamie would never call you darling. Mamie possibly doesn't even know the word.

"Of course, then we leave Albania and we find out we're no enemy to the world," she says, opening the next album. "We're not number one, we're nothing, just some strange backward Communist country. Nobody cares about us at all. It's almost worse, right, to just be nothing?"

"I don't think anything's worse than nothing," you agree, which seems to confuse Yllka.

"Well, who knows what's worse. I shouldn't say that. Anyway, it all turned out okay for us Hasanis in the end. Better than we dreamed back then, anyway. Mostly. Of course there have been some stumbles. It's never going to be perfect, not even in America."

"But it's better? Like, it gets better?"

"Usually. It depends, you know, if you want it to be better. It was hard for some of the people who came over, because they thought you land here, boom, life is wonderful. They didn't know you still had to work for it." She shrugs. "Mostly everybody figured it out, but it's hard at first. It's hard to be a stranger anywhere, I guess."

"So the Hasanis are all here now?"

"Oh, no, the Hasanis are everywhere. We're here, obviously, Gjonni and I. Your aunts are in Switzerland with their husbands, you have one uncle in Turkey, one in Greece. Cousins everywhere, my god, *everywhere* — New Jersey, someone's on a fishing boat in Alaska. A couple of them not much older than you are in Tirana running a bar that caters to tourists. Tourists! Can you imagine, tourists in Tirana?" She laughs and shakes her head, and you laugh, too, not wanting to let on that you have no idea what's funny about that.

"And, um," you say, and she keeps shaking her head but stops laughing.

"I was waiting for this," she says and pulls out the last album. "I'm not sure why I was waiting. It wasn't fair of me, to make you wait longer. I wasn't trying to be mean, I swear to you. I just . . ." She looks at you, and then takes a deep breath, as if she's about to drop underwater and has to rely on that single lungful for a while. "I'm just still not sure what to tell you."

The album opens to the kind of boy you see in documentaries on PBS, in shorts, unsmiling, the kind of boy who looks like he's already broken horses and sold brothers and sisters into indentured servitude. The picture, in both quality and content, should have been taken a hundred years ago instead of in the seventies. It looks like it's from a time before cameras were invented, before anyone was supposed to have had a happy childhood.

"Your father, when he was little," Yllka says.

She lets you be in charge of turning the pages, and you do it slowly, so your father grows up just a little bit at a time, a flip-book in slow motion. There's a big chunk of him missing, though. He goes from boy to man in the flip of a page, from wrinkled soiled cotton standing in a field of rocky dirt to a wrinkled soiled apron in a sea of stainless steel, obviously the kitchen of the Betsy Ross.

"We didn't see him for a long time," Yllka says. "Between when we left home and when he came here."

On the last page is the only picture of him smiling, the only one where he isn't posing like the star of a low-budget action flick about a play-by-his-own-rules ex-cop with nothing left to lose. He's leaning back dangerously in a folding chair, surrounded by guys who all kind of resemble him. Playing cards and beer bottles and loose cigarettes are scattered over the table, the detritus densest in the semicircle he's claimed for himself.

"It was a party for you, to celebrate when your mother was pregnant."

You'd have thought Yllka was lying if you weren't seeing it for yourself. All of the other pictures in the photo album matched perfectly the idea of your father you'd had since you were capable of abstract thought: stony-faced, too hard to give a shit even about the things everyone's supposed to give a shit about, one's own offspring, for example, something that even most wild animals manage to be capable of. And yet there's your father in two dimensions, smiling in a way that's impossible to fake for the camera.

"He was drunk," you say.

"What? No, he was happy, that's all."

"Happy about what?"

"Happy about you," she says.

"That makes no sense. People aren't happy about things they don't want. People don't celebrate, like, having cockroaches in their house."

"Oh, Luljeta," she says.

"What? It's the truth."

"No, no, that's not the truth. That wasn't it at all."

"So then what is the truth?"

She looks at you, then looks away, as if she suddenly doesn't speak your language anymore, or maybe the words to explain it don't exist in English. She exhales long and slow, and then starts to say something, but she stops before the first syllable is out. She tries again, and fails again, and then she says, finally, "I still don't understand it all myself, and I can't apologize for your father or your mother."

"You don't have to apologize for my mother. She's the one who stuck around."

"Yes, but she also . . ."

"Also what?"

Yllka closes her eyes a second, hits reset, and lets out a deep whistling exhale from her nostrils. "Never mind, never mind. It's not for me to say. But I understand that you are angry with him, and you have a right to be angry, but you also should know the story, and that he wasn't a terrible person. He was a very hurt and confused and scared person, and, you know, he left Albania but everything he tried to leave came with him anyway, do you understand?"

"No," you say.

She nods. "I know. I hope you can understand one day, though. I don't want to make excuses for him. He was stupid, there is no denying that. But I think he thought he was doing the right thing at the time. Both of them did, your mother and father. You know what they say, the road to hell and good intentions and all."

"So that's where he ended up? Hell?"

She shakes her head. "No. Texas. Eventually, anyway, after Albania. Houston. His wife's brother lives there."

You regret the fried dough now. It's so close to coming back up, and you have to work so hard to keep it down that you can barely talk. "He came back?"

"Yes," she says.

"And he never even tried to see me?"

Yllka looks embarrassed. "I guess he thought you wouldn't want that," she says.

"I was a kid. What would it matter what I wanted?"

"Well, your mother wouldn't want it."

"So it's her fault?"

"It's nobody's fault, Luljeta. It's not a fault. It's just mistakes. Or, I don't know, not mistakes, just decisions that led to other decisions, and on and on, and in the end the first decision seemed too far buried to get back to and change."

You think for a moment about the first Christmas you were old enough to remember. It was back in the Toys for Tots days, the Play-Doh-workshop-courtesy-of-the-U.S.-Marines days, the days when charitable strangers had to do the work that those charged with caring for you could not. Even then, the magic of new Play-Doh could not entirely compensate for the desertion you felt not by your family but by Santa Claus, that bastard, who you believed had forsaken you, because that was easier to explain to a child than the true source of neglect. "We don't have a chimney, Lulu, what can we do?" your mother had said when you asked why Santa skipped over your apartment, her eyes welled with tears as if she was the one who'd failed, and man, you hated that fat man in red for making her feel like that. But it's occurring to you just now: what if there had been an answer to that question all along? *Lulu, what can we do?* What if the answer was: Let your father do the job he apparently was open to doing, instead of waiting for another mythical white man to do the providing?

Up until now, you've been mostly annoyed with your mother, thinking she believed you too fragile to handle the truth about your father. You've believed she's been trying to protect you from him, this creature who, like a male grizzly emerging from hibernation, might tear you apart to sustain himself. Now, though, it's becoming clear: *she* is the one who's sustained herself on you. He'd never even gotten a taste before she scuttled away with you, claiming you as hers alone. Her what, though? Her cub? Her trophy? Her prey?

"Texas," you say, trying to get the word to sound natural in your mouth.

166

"Yes, Houston," Yllka says.

"Texas," you repeat. It seems as far away to you as the Balkans, and slightly more oppressive. Texas is to you a land of giant pickup trucks, tiny trailer homes, and evil oil tycoons, just like the television would have you believe. Their toast is good, though, that frozen Pepperidge Farm stuff you'd add to every meal if you could.

"Is he a cowboy?" you ask.

"Cowboy? No, no," Yllka says, confused. She pauses a moment, then says, "He opened a little pizza shop. Amici's."

"Pizza?"

"Yes, pizza."

"Pizza? Like Italian pizza?"

"Albanians are very good at pizza," Yllka answers, almost defensively. "Half of us lived in Italy before we came here."

"Who's Amici?"

"It's just a name," Yllka says. "You can't put Hasani on a sign for pizza. It's not good for business."

Business. Not only had your father actually been excited about you at one time, but he actually has the means to care for you now the way he didn't then. You never imagined that someone with your own blood would be able to run anything, let alone an entire business. That would make him a businessman, right, and — don't think it, don't even dare think it — but there it is anyway: aren't businessmen rich? Sure, Yllka owns the Ross and still lives in a triple-decker in Waterbury just like you, but that's because immigrants do that, save every penny under their mattresses and then make their kids millionaires when they die. It's so, so inappropriate to think it and so, so impossible not to, but maybe your father is doing the same for you. Maybe there's some savings account in your name that you'll find out about at precisely the right moment, say, when it's time to cut the cord to your mother, when it's time to pay your own rent in a dope loft far from these triple-deckers, and generally live a life that others will envy.

Then you remember that you were not the offspring that was chosen to thrive.

"He has kids, my father?" you ask. You want to know who's the beneficiary of that savings account. "I mean real ones?"

"Three. Two boys and a girl. Adnan is the oldest, just a couple of years younger than you."

"Adnan? Is that a boy or girl?"

"Boy. Golden boy, the oldest child, a son."

You don't point out that Adnan isn't really the oldest child.

"Do they know about me?" you ask.

Yllka shakes her head. "I don't know. I really don't. I get into trouble, talking so much, but I have not brought it up with them. They're just kids, and anyway it's not my place. Maybe it's your place," she says, suddenly hopeful. "Maybe someday you could tell them."

"I have no idea what my place is," you say.

"You have to make your own place, i dashur."

"Is that true?" you ask. "Is that really true?"

Yllka starts to nod, but her neck freezes when she lowers her head, and it stays there, seemingly unmoving, until you detect a tiny little quake. She reaches over and clutches your hand and squeezes it until it almost hurts, and she dabs her eyes with a napkin she'd crushed in her other hand, as if she was trying to make a diamond out of it.

"This is hard. This is very hard. There is so much to tell you and now I can't come up with any more words," she says.

Yllka mistakes your dead-eyed automaton stare for stoicism, like the kind your envied classmate Aisha showed throughout her bouts of diabetic ketoacidosis.

"Look at me falling apart and you being

the brave one," she says. "You must be strong like your mother."

At that moment, being compared to your mother doesn't seem terribly complimentary. Strong — that's one way to put it. Margarita is strong. Margarita could beat any member of the football team in arm wrestling, and she doesn't deserve admiration for it.

"Maybe," Yllka says, then pauses. "I would like to see her, too. I miss her. I hope she's not angry with me. I hope that's not why she's stayed away."

"Why would she be mad at you?"

"Oh, who knows how these things work. I hope she's not. And will you . . . Will you make sure she understands that I'm not angry with her? That I understand why it might have been too hard to stay in touch with me?"

You understand that you're supposed to nod, but you just look straight ahead with your dull Aisha stare. A few minutes ago you'd felt like you were getting somewhere, but suddenly you're right back to where you started, understanding nothing.

"Never mind," Yllka says. "That's too much to ask of you. I'll tell her myself, if you can just get her to visit next time. Do you think, maybe, she would?"

"I don't know," you say. "I doubt it."

"Oh," she says. She finds your eyes again, and cups her arms around your shoulders. "Well, in any case, you will come back? I can't tell you how I've missed you."

"But," you say.

"But what, love?"

For the first time, you're beginning to feel annoyed with this woman for making you say everything out loud. "But what about my father?"

Silence. Yllka doesn't seem like a big fan of it, but it's what she offers in response to your question.

"So he doesn't want to see me," you say.

"It's not that," she says.

"That's what it sounds like," you say.

"But it's not right," she says, dropping her head into her hands. "I just don't know what to say. Maybe this is what we talk about next time? You'll come back next weekend, maybe?"

"Maybe," you answer. It's a response that seems to both encourage and devastate her, but it's at least gentler than what you're really thinking, which is that she's perfectly nice, this Teto Yllka, and you could maybe make room for her someday, but you didn't come here looking for another maternal figure, a great-aunt to supplement your mother and Greta and Mamie, even if Yllka can at least offer magical pastries and photos of people you sort of resemble. The little morsels she fed you, those pieces of sweet fried dough, don't have the kind of sustenance you're hungry for. There's a whole feast for you somewhere in Texas, and like a hunter, you have to track it.

CHAPTER SEVEN:
ELSIE

The year before, a girl in an uppity town just down the highway from Waterbury had kept her pregnancy a secret for nine months, delivered the kid in her bathroom, left it bundled in a Starter sweatshirt outside the volunteer fire department, and went to a varsity football game that same night. That kind of denial was nuts. Me, I wasn't nuts. I was just waiting for a good time to make my condition known. It was just that good times were so hard to come by.

In the meantime I told Mamie that I'd be moving out. I thought she'd finally be happy to be rid of one of her two beasts of burden, but instead she looked worried, even a little sad.

"What?" she said. "How are you going to do that? You have the money for that kind of thing?"

"It's not going to be much more than you charge me," I said. "And anyway, it's time I grow up."

"Well, I don't have to charge you," she said.

"Then why do you?"

"To give you an idea of what it's like out there."

"You did a good job. Now I know what it's like out there, and I'm ready to take it on."

"Your rent here is only a hundred fifty bucks a month. That's not going to cut it anywhere out in the real world."

"I'm going to be sharing the rent."

"With who?"

"My boyfriend."

"What boyfriend?"

"The one I told you about."

"You never told me about any boyfriend."

"I did, too."

"When?"

"One night. That night I was sick."

"Oh, that? The 'some guy' guy? Since when has it been that serious?"

"Since recently," I said. "It got serious recently." I hoped she might know what *serious* implied, and then I wouldn't have to come out with it myself. Why was I afraid to tell her I got knocked up, just like she had when she was even younger than I was? Did I think she'd pummel me until I miscar-

174

ried? That she'd beg me to abort it or give my one potentially valuable thing away, when I was reserving it as a gift for Bashkim?

I was afraid she'd shrug and say something like *Of course,* like I was exactly what everyone expected me to be.

But she didn't even shrug. She just got quiet for a minute, poured another glass of wine over a fresh ice cube, and swallowed half of that sweet nectar like it was an antidote to the poison I was always feeding her.

"What's his name?" she asked.

"Bashkim," I said.

"What?"

"Bashkim. Bosh. Keem."

"What the hell is that?"

"It's a name."

"What kind of name is that? Is he black?"

"No," I said, annoyed at her obvious relief. "But what if he were?"

"I mean, I don't care about that kind of thing, but you'd run into some trouble in the world, I bet."

"You wouldn't be okay with it," I said.

"Of course I would," she said.

"No you wouldn't. You totally wouldn't."

"Stop trying to turn this around so that I'm the bad person here. You're the one telling me you're moving out with a guy whose name you barely know."

"I know his name perfectly well. I just never told you because I knew you'd say 'What kind of a name is that?'"

"What I'd say is exactly what I'm about to say, which is that it's a really stupid idea to move in with someone who's not even important enough to you to tell your mother about. Whatever happened to going on a few dates first?"

"What, am I supposed to come home with his letter jacket? I'm an adult. We're adults. We know what we're doing."

"Oh, every eighteen-year-old girl in the world knows exactly what she's doing. Yup, nobody smarter in the world than an eighteen-year-old girl."

"Well, smart or not, I'm an adult. You can't stop me."

Mamie swirled the ice cube around in what was left of the wine in her glass. The burgundy was watered down by then but still unmistakable, like a bloodstain on bedsheets.

"I'm not going to try to stop you," she said, that sad look back in her face. "It's too late for that. I'd have to go back in time to the day you decided I don't know a thing in the world and never wanted what was best for you."

"That's not fair," I said. "I never said anything like that."

She shrugged, grabbed her jug, and walked away, and for the first time in weeks, I felt a sickness that had nothing to do with hormones.

Gjonni and Yllka were the only people not flying the red, white, and green outside the triple-decker they owned in a Sicilian compound on Harpers Ferry Road, so when the neighbors came out on their porches to clap the dust out of their welcome mats, Gjonni and Yllka got only the smallest of nods, just enough to let them know that those welcome mats wouldn't ever be dusty from their feet. It didn't seem to bother Gjonni and Yllka, because in Waterbury moving on up meant trading in whatever ghetto you started off in for an Italian one, where the front porches were swept three times a day and decorated for Christmas six months of the year. Those poor Italian grandmas, looking over at Gjonni and Yllka, thinking: Marone a mi, first these Turkish-coffee-drinking bastard sons of Europe wash up on the shores of Sicily, now they follow us here? But Yllka fit in just fine, greeting me from the same Welcome Wagon that her neighbors greeted her with, her arms crossed like she was fighting off a chill on that eighty-seven-degree day.

"We can get more money for that apartment. We're losing money on it now," she said, in English, so that I could understand clearly how little she wanted me there.

"Beh, family is not for making money," Gjonni said, while Bashkim walked by us all with the last of the four boxes I'd packed. All of my worldly possessions had fit in the trunk of the Fiero, and Bashkim didn't even break a sweat carrying them up three flights of stairs. It would've depressed me if I thought about it, but I was drinking from the half-full cup that day, and thought instead how easy it would be to unpack and settle in.

Bashkim and I were moving into the third floor of Gjonni and Yllka's triple-decker. It was a glorified attic, twelve degrees hotter than the ground floor, and most of the square footage was cut off by sloping walls at every corner. But it was ours, even if it was really Gjonni and Yllka's, even if Yllka probably wanted us to be late with the rent so she'd have a reason to evict us. I very nearly wept when Gjonni handed over the keys to us. "You will be happy here. The water is good, the electricity is strong. You could run an air conditioner in here no problem," he said.

I nodded. We didn't have an air conditioner to prove it, or even a box fan. We didn't have a toaster, a fry pan, a can opener, a television, a spare blanket, or a single piece of silverware. We had one bath towel between us and a glove box full of sporks from Lee's Famous Recipe. We had each other and the makings of a country song.

We also had an almost-set of old dishware and a scratch-off ticket from Mamie, which she left along with a note on the table that morning: *You can come back here if it doesn't work out. Love, Mamie.* It was nice of her; *Love* was a word Mamie didn't use much. She signed our Christmas cards *Sincerely.* She still hadn't met Bashkim and she didn't know yet she'd soon be signing cards *Sincerely, Grandma,* but I took it as a good omen that the scratch-off was a winner, sixty dollars, so I could invite her over for a spaghetti dinner and afford the saucepan and the box of pasta both. I figured we could borrow silverware from the Ross until we could get ourselves a cheap cutlery set sometime before the baby was born, although the baby wouldn't come out using a fork and a knife, so maybe we could buy some time on that, too.

How much time, I didn't know. I had no idea when a baby learned how to eat with something other than its hands, if it was before or after the first words, and if the first words were before or after the first step. This was assuming, too, that we made a baby that would be able to speak and walk. There was a whole lot that could go wrong. I hadn't been to a doctor yet, but I'd been to health class in high school and paid attention every once in a while. Plus I'd seen the canisters collecting money for the Ronald McDonald Houses or worse, Jerry's Kids, the ones that never even had a chance to be Regular Kids first. They were the kids that didn't even get to run and play and be tormented for their overbites before being stricken by lymphoma at age four.

I told myself to stop. Our baby would be fine. It would call me Mama and run to hold me when it scraped its knee, or else it would scrape its knee and just point because it hadn't learned how to say Mama yet. God, when did that happen again? It didn't matter. I knew what tears meant, and when the baby came I would know what to do about them, just like I would know how to wrap a present with perfectly crisp corners like all moms, even Mamie, seem to be able to do. I figured they taught those things in the maternity ward after you gave birth.

"Elsie, Gjonni asked you a question." Bashkim snapped his fingers in front of my face, like the customers that annoyed me the most at the Ross.

"Huh?" I said.

"Which is your room and which is the baby's room?" Gjonni asked. "I will bring you the dresser we're not using."

"We were using it," Yllka said. "I don't know where we'll put the towels and the washcloths now."

"There is room in the closet for those. Elsie, which room?"

"Oh. Uh, the big one I guess, the one with the two windows."

Bashkim and Gjonni walked off and left me standing outside with Yllka alone.

"Thanks for letting us have this place," I said.

"It has a nice bathroom. You should use it to wash up or you will stink for work," she answered.

I smiled and nodded, trying to remember that she was doing me a favor.

We showered, we screwed, we showered again. The water was freezing but it was sweltering that day, so standing in the shower felt like being in fresh air and being in air felt like wading. Bashkim loved my new swollen breasts, which weren't boobs anymore, not tits, because now there was a point to them. They'd gotten a promotion. He teased them, pinched and bit them, and I bit my lip to keep from crying out. He came inside of me and it didn't matter. Or it mattered, but it didn't have any consequences. Then we slept. Not a nap, hard sleep. Our limbs twitched and jerked and even though we were aware of them, they didn't wake us. It was the downstairs neighbors that did that, the bass shuffle intro of "Hot for Teacher" butting into our dreams. The one I'd been having was of a tiny, stampeding elephant that I held in the palm of my hand, its wildness adorable because it was small and didn't pose any real threat, unlike the air mattress we slept on, which was doing actual nerve damage.

"God, this bed. I don't think I can move my legs," I said.

"Too bad you can always move your mouth."

"When do you think we might get a real mattress?"

"There is nothing wrong with this."

"It's an air mattress that doesn't hold air. It doesn't do its job. That's the definition of wrong."

"There is air in there."

"Not enough air. It looks like a taco when we're in it. We're like taco meat."

"This is better than what I slept on most of my life."

"Most of your life you lived in a zoo."

His eyes turned animal. He was the elephant, suddenly, only not as adorable.

"I was just joking," I said. "You were the one who said you lived like animals over there."

"That was not a joke," he said. He stood to pull his briefs back up. He'd slept with them around his feet, like stained white cotton shackles. Without his weight on the mattress, I sank farther down, almost to the floor.

"Sorry," I said again. "But this isn't going to work forever."

He pulled on his socks.

"I mean, it's okay for now. I'm not, like, huge yet. But."

"But what?"

"But we should start to put some money aside."

"Don't worry about money. It's not a problem."

"Well, we don't have any. Cash money, I mean. Like, the green stuff in our hands. And we're going to have to get a lot of stuff for the baby."

"I have money. I told you that."

"But the kind of money we can use. Now. Or soon, anyway. Paper bills that stores will take as payment."

"Elsie," he said. He blew a puff of air through his nose, the warning before the stampede. "I told you."

"I mean *real* money."

"Real money? There is no such thing as fake money. Money is money."

"I don't know," I said.

"Yes, you don't know. Look at you. What would you know?"

I knew that was meant to hurt, and it did, but I didn't understand why.

"Get ready for work," Bashkim said. "If you're so worried about money."

"Five minutes," I said.

"I am leaving in five minutes."

"Three minutes," I said.

He got up and stared down at me before walking off to take a piss that it sounded like he'd been holding on to for a while. He splashed around in the sink, and I hoped he'd save a dry spot on the towel for me. There was no point in us duking it out together in the bathroom at the same time, so I lay on my side and dragged my finger along the floor beside the air mattress.

"This floor is filthy. It looks like I dipped my finger in cake batter," I said.

The toilet flushed.

He walked back in and looked at me, tucked his wife-beater into his pants, and grabbed his keys from the pocket of the pair he left lying on the floor like a police body-tape outline.

I stood up finally. "I'm coming, I'm coming."

"I'm leaving," he answered.

"What? I'll be ready in one minute. I just have to get dressed and brush my teeth."

"I told you I was leaving in five minutes. That was five minutes ago."

He started to walk away, and I sprang out of bed to follow.

"Are you serious?" I said. "I didn't even get a chance to use the bathroom."

The door was opening. He was walking through, going down the stairs, loping across the parking lot.

"Wait," I said, but he kept going. I yanked my pantyhose up so fast that tiny holes appeared where my fingers had grabbed on to them. He thought he was teaching me a lesson, and he was, I thought: I learned that he had the patience of a gnat and that he needed to hydrate more, because I could smell the sharp tang of his piss all the way out in the kitchen. "Son of a bitch," I said. I grabbed my purse and ran down the steps to catch up with him, but by the time I got there his parking space was empty except for a black rose of fresh oil on the ground.

I walked to the front of the building but he wasn't waiting for me there, either, so I returned to the parking spot and stood there and waited for him to come back. I waited, and when the sun beat down too heavy and started burning my scalp I moved underneath the eave of Gjonni and Yllka's porch. When I thought that Yllka might open the door and ask what I was doing standing there for twenty minutes when I should've been at work, I walked quietly up the stairs and cried into Bashkim's side of the air mattress. It would dry long before he got home, and he wouldn't ever have to know it happened. When that was over, I counted the change in my purse and took the rest of what I needed for bus fare from the pockets of the pants Bashkim had worn the day before. On the ride over to the Ross, I practiced mouthing *I'm sorry,* but my mouth didn't seem to want to make the words, so when I walked through the back entrance into the kitchen and saw Bashkim, I just turned away and set a new carafe of decaf on to brew.

It seemed like a good sign that Mamie didn't complain about the food we served her when we had her and Greta over for dinner. It was spaghetti with ground meat and a can of Manwich, which we called Bolognese, which I'd guessed was a favorite of hers because she'd served it at least once a week since I was old enough to eat solid food. That was just a guess, though, since I don't think I'd ever heard her mention food in my life, other than asking how in the hell Greta and I managed to go through it so fast. It was just another thing essential for survival and yet always standing in the way of it. Since there was nothing standing in the way of her bottle of Blue Nun at my and Bashkim's table that night, she kept mostly quiet through dinner, but when the food was gone, Mamie was suddenly ready to talk. I recognized that light in her eye, set off by the flint that sister hid underneath her blue habit.

"So where are you from again?" Mamie asked Bashkim. He looked like a kid eating for the first time at the grown-ups' table, sitting on his hands because he ran out of napkins to shred. "What did Elsie say,

Armenia or something?"

"I live here," he said and slid an empty fork into his mouth.

"No, you know what I mean. Where are you *from.*"

"I came from Italy," he said.

Greta looked up at the plate of spaghetti-art she'd been working on for the past twenty minutes. "You said he was from Albania."

I looked at Bashkim. "He is. Italy?"

He shrugged. "I was there for a year before coming here."

"That wasn't the question," I said.

"But you're Albanian really?" Greta asked.

"I lived in Greece for a while, too," he said.

"But yes, he's Albanian," I said, since Bashkim didn't seem to want to. He looked embarrassed, like I'd given something away, as if he thought Mamie wouldn't notice his accent, or his skin, or his pinkie ring with tiny flecks of diamonds encrusted in it. Guys from around here didn't even wear wedding rings, just thick gold ropes and brass knuckles if they were from the east side. If they were from the north side, they tattooed the names of their children's mothers around their ring fingers. Gold rings, meanwhile, seemed to wash up on the shore of the Adriatic instead of seaweed, since every Albanian guy I've ever seen, including the ones who could barely afford Ring Pops from Joe's Corner Grocery, had them wrapped around at least one of their fingers.

"Most people don't know of Albania. I tell them what they know," he said.

"Don't tell me what you think I want to hear. I know about Albania," Mamie said. "I mean, at least I know that they're coming over here in droves. I've worked with some, too. Remember, Elsie, when my hubcaps were stolen and I bought a new set from one of the guys in the shop? He was Albanian, that guy."

"I thought that guy was Puerto Rican," Greta said.

"Well, I don't know. I just remember an accent."

"Bashkim doesn't steal hubcaps," I said.

"I'm not saying he does. Don't put words in my mouth."

"It's the Blue Nun did that," Greta said.

"Why would I have anything against Albanians? My parents were immigrants, too."

"Not Albanian immigrants," Greta said.

"No, they were just the regular kind," said Mamie.

"At least he's not black, right, Mamie?" Greta said.

"He's kind of tan," Mamie said. "But I don't care about that. I'm not racist, is the point."

What Bashkim was at that moment was red, and somehow half the size he was at the beginning of dinner. I wondered if his feet could even touch the ground from his chair.

"We have dessert," I said. "An Entenmann's, if anybody wants."

"So are you Catholic, then, or Orthodox, like the Greeks?" Mamie asked.

"What difference does it make?" Greta said, dropping her head down to the table. "This is embarrassing."

"What's embarrassing? I'm just making conversation. I'm interested. I think Bashkim is very interesting."

"I am nothing, really," Bashkim said.

"Oh, that's not true. Everybody's something. We're Catholic. It was very unpopular in this country to be Catholic."

"Everybody in Waterbury is Catholic," Greta said.

"Not everybody. There used to be a lot of Jews here, too. And there's that Jehovah's Witness temple or whatever they call it up on North Main."

"Mamie, nobody here is religious. I don't want to talk about this," I said.

190

"Don't speak for me. I'm religious," Mamie said.

"I've literally never been in a Catholic church with you except for funerals," Greta said.

"That doesn't mean I'm not religious. It's a faith thing."

"Anybody want coffee?" I asked. "I got Chock full o'Nuts."

"The Albanian kids at school are Muslim," Greta said.

I kicked her underneath the table. I think I grazed Mamie's shin on the way but she didn't notice. She held herself perfectly still, and even shut up for a second.

"Muslim, wow," she said. "Wow. That is really interesting."

"I am not really anything," he said.

"But I mean, is that what your family is?"

"In Albania, you were nothing. There was no religion, except for the Party."

"The Party?"

"Communist," I said. "Like Lithuania."

Mamie shook her head. "No, not like Lithuania. We didn't want to be Communist. The Russians made us. Why do you think we all ended up over here?"

"The same reason Bashkim did," I said.

"And we didn't come looking for hand-outs. We wanted to work."

191

"Like Bashkim. Bashkim works really hard," I said.

"The Russians had nothing to do with us," Bashkim said.

"I'm just saying, you came here because you wanted a better life, just like everybody who comes to America does," I said.

"And he ended up in Waterbury. God," Greta said.

"Yeah, with Elsie!" Mamie said. "What a gyp."

"Thanks. That's great," I said.

We all stared down at our hands on the table like dogs playing poker. Bashkim had taken the whole night off from work for this, and instead of melting behind the grill he was melting right there before us, beads of sweat forming at the roots of his ridiculously thick hair. The strands were thick like pipe cleaners, and on other nights, nights when Mamie wasn't there, I would shape them into whatever I wanted while we sat together on the love seat we picked up from the Salvation Army, watching the thirteen-inch Panasonic Janice at work had given us when she'd saved enough for a new twenty-seven-inch for herself. We were getting by, just like everybody else, that's what I wanted Mamie to see, that we were no worse off than she was. We were better, even, because I had someone else's hair to run my fingers through, at least until he got sick of it and pulled my hand away.

He wouldn't even look at me now.

"I like the built-in china cabinet in the kitchen," Mamie said, finally. "Not like there's china in there."

"Thank you," Bashkim said softly.

"But I mean, who has china these days? I don't have china. You don't need fine china to heat up a can of Progresso, do you?"

"No," I said.

Mamie bounced her pack of Basics on the table but didn't pull one out to smoke. "It's not like this is the olden days. People don't get china for their weddings, they get, I don't know, bread machines. You ever see how many bread machines there are at Goodwill? They've got their own aisle. Every one of them a dead marriage."

"Who needs bread machines? There's a Hostess outlet right down the road. Bag of Wonder bread for ninety-nine cents," I said.

"Who needs bread machines is right. Who needs china. Christ, who even needs marriage. Don't need a husband for a family, right? Look at us. Me and my girls. We did all right, eh? You guys never wanted for nothing, right?"

Greta looked at me from across the table,

193

and shook her head just enough for me to see it.

"Not really," I said.

"Bullshit," Mamie said. "You wanted for everything. You still want for everything."

"Mamie," Greta said.

"No. I know I fucked this all up. I can admit that. I know I wasn't sitting at home with you, helping out with your homework and dragging you to Girl Scouts and what-not, but I really thought you'd learn something from that. You both wanted so bad to get away from me. And for what? For this?"

My hands were asleep from sitting on them. My neck was strained from looking down. "There's nothing wrong with this place. You said you liked the china cabinet," I said.

Mamie pressed her palms into her eyes. "I do. I love the china cabinet. I love the big empty china cabinet."

"We keep our plates in there," I said.

She slapped her palms down on the table. "Just, god. When are you going to come out with it?"

I shrugged. There was no point in denying anything, it was why we had her over in the first place, to come out with it all. But I didn't come out with anything. It oozed out of me somehow, but I couldn't come out and say it.

"I mean, I guess at this point you're having it, right?" Mamie said.

"Yes," Bashkim said. His voice was confident again, his again. "We are having it."

"What?" Greta said. "You mean keeping it? You told me you took care of this weeks ago."

"We did take care of it. We decided to have it," I said.

Greta stood up from the table and stomped toward the door. "You're a liar, Elsie," she said and slammed the screen door behind her. "A stupid liar. Have fun, is all I have to say. I'm not going to be helping you out in nine months, if that's what you think."

"Nine months?" Mamie said. She finally lit up that Basic. "Six months, if you're lucky. Isn't that about right?"

"I don't know," I said. My face stung as if she'd slapped it, but she was sitting there perfectly calm, her crossed leg bouncing over the other the only sign of what was bubbling inside. "I haven't gone to the doctor yet."

She laughed as she exhaled. "Perfect."

"Well, nothing's been wrong yet. I haven't had to breathe any secondhand smoke yet," I said, swatting her Basic stream away from my nose. Finally I looked up, and Bashkim was smoking, too, blowing perfect rings of Marlboro wisps that floated like tilted halos over our heads. "He usually goes outside for that," I said.

"I do, yes. Tonight, no. Tonight I will smoke here, because this is my home, and I decided that I would like to do it in here," he said.

"It's only your home so long as you don't run off and leave her alone in it," Mamie said.

"Mamie, it's not going to be like that. Not every guy is like that."

"Even then, it would still be my home," Bashkim said.

Mamie smiled a little and stubbed out her cigarette only halfway through it. "I'll tell you what, I'll take some cake now, Elsie. And some coffee if you got it."

I looked at her but didn't move, thinking I'd be walking into a booby trap.

"Go ahead. Better get used to serving people," she said.

"I will have some, too," Bashkim said, looking at Mamie.

It was definitely a booby trap, then, but I stood up anyway and walked to the counter, where it at least felt safer. I waited for it to start, *it* being Mamie crashing the empty bottle of wine over Bashkim's head, *it* being Bashkim pushing Mamie to the door, still in her chair, as if she were a patient and he the orderly, *it* being the ultimatum: it's him/her or me. But they only watched each other, Mamie's hands folded under her chin, her head cradled in there like a hammock; Bashkim's arms folded over his chest, his biceps round like ripe fruit. I dropped saucers of cake off in front of both of them and drew back, scooped spoonfuls of coffee onto the counter because I couldn't stop watching them. They took delicate bites, as if at a tea party.

"Will you not be getting married then?" Mamie asked. "Elsie, coffee?"

"It's coming," I said. I swept the grinds into a filter, my shaking hands not even steadied by the counter. I shook my head at Bashkim, begging him not to tell her, but he hadn't really looked at me all night.

"No," he said. "Getting married would not make things any different."

"Of course it would make things different. It would make it harder for Elsie to get out when she has to. *If* she has to, I mean."

"Getting married does not make someone stay. You should know that," he said.

"If that was supposed to hurt," Mamie said.

Bashkim shook his head. "If I wanted to hurt you, there would be no confusion about it. We did not have you here to hurt you. Elsie is not having a baby to hurt people. This is right, Elsie?"

I nodded, for no reason since neither looked over at me.

"Then why is she having a baby?"

"Because she loves me. This is right, Elsie?"

I didn't bother nodding this time, and instead walked to the door. It was still hot out there, but not like inside, which was just a few degrees away from ignition. I breathed in deep and leaned against the railing, which gave a couple of inches under my weight. We were twenty feet or so up, not enough for certain death if the railing gave way, but there would be plenty of broken bones, and almost certainly a blank image on a sonogram. The doctors would say they were sorry for my loss, the way they were trained to, but they probably wouldn't be, just like plenty of people wouldn't be. Mamie wouldn't be, Greta wouldn't be, Yllka, Aggie, wherever she was, whatever she knew. I would be. Of course I would be. I'd be drugged up and broken and sorry, somewhere deep underneath all that gauze. I'd get all the plastic cups of apple juice I asked for. Magazines, balloons, *The Price Is Right* on Channel 3, whatever it took to make me unsorry.

"What do you want?" Greta said. She was crouched in the corner of the porch, invisible under shadow.

"Jesus Christ, you scared me," I said. I pulled my weight away from the railing and felt woozy when I looked back at the twenty-foot drop. Suddenly it was cold out there. I shivered.

"You've got bigger things to be scared about, if you ask me," she said.

"I'm not asking you," I said.

"I know."

"I'm not asking anybody, in fact."

"They're telling you anyway."

I stopped to listen to Mamie and Bashkim, but all I heard was fork scraping against plate, like they thought more cake was buried underneath the surface. It was going better than I'd thought it would. No screaming, nothing shattered. It made me nervous, though, knowing all that fuel was inside just waiting for a spark.

The screen door popped open, nearly whacked me in the face, and slapped back against the frame. Mamie stepped out, a little unsteady on her feet, and held her purse in tight against her as if she thought we might rob her.

"You should get a spring for that door. Greta, you're driving. Elsie, coffee's ready. I decided I didn't want it after all." She looked me up and down, nodded toward the stairs. "You want I can toss you down those. It's not too late."

"I'm good," I said.

"Score one for the kid, I guess." She leaned on the rail, didn't even notice it was loose. "Just so you know, not killing a baby isn't even close to giving it any kind of life."

"It's not an *it*, it's a someone," I said.

"Even worse," she said and began walking down the stairs, taking one step at a time. "Good night and good luck, sweetheart."

She called people sweetheart sometimes instead of asshole, so I didn't bother echoing her goodbye. I looked instead at Greta, who ignored me and squeezed past.

"I'll call you," I said to her.

"Save your dime. You'll need them," she said, and then she was gone, too.

Inside, Bashkim still sat at the table, the haze of smoke around him making him look like a dream sequence, or a low-budget version of heaven. That's what I'd call his biography, I thought: *A Low-Budget Version of Heaven,* and then realized it said more about me than about him. What kind of heaven did I want? It took him an hour's work to pay for that bottle of Blue Nun. One whole hour of his life sitting in the bottom of Mamie's belly, and he didn't complain once. And he had all kinds of money on the way, he said. And was a good-looking guy, underneath the ugly clothes that were either Communist issue or Salvation Army castoffs. He'd taken off his short-sleeve button-up, and look at how nice he filled out that undershirt. Strong, not just the muscles. I stepped back inside and walked over to him and kissed the top of his head.

"Thank you for dealing with my mother," I said.

"Go clean that mess up," he said, pulling a cigarette to his lips. "The flies are going for it."

I thought about arguing for a second, but decided that it was a fair trade, him taking care of me in exchange for me taking care of everything else.

CHAPTER EIGHT:
LULJETA

The addition of your mother's boyfriend, the postanarchist Professor Robbie, brings the total number of guests gathered for Christmas dinner to five, one more than the quartet of you, your mother, Mamie, and Greta, which had gathered for Thanksgiving and all other previous holidays you've sat through your entire life. Even with the addition of a Y chromosome, your Noel looks mostly like a nativity scene staged by a militant women's separatist group.

"Ooh, where'd you get these?" Mamie asks, pointing to the holly berry–printed napkins that, you've been warned, are for display purposes only.

"T.J.Maxx," your mother answers, though she doesn't add the comment about caving in to the commercial holiday bullshit like some consumerist blue blood, as she had when she suffered through the twenty-minute line to purchase them two weeks before.

Blue blood was one of the terms your mother picked up in Robbie's class at Mattatuck Community College, and from what you can tell, it's used to describe the class of New Englanders whose families had settled here long, long ago. These are the people who had come to control things like local government and who had things like "money" and attended events called functions. But because neither you nor your mother has ever ventured farther outside of Waterbury than Six Flags New England in Agawam, Massachusetts, Misquamicut State Beach in Misquamicut, Rhode Island, and annual trips to visit Aunt Greta in Queens, New York, you believe the Italian-Americans who dominate Waterbury constitute blue bloods, since they make up nearly all the elected officials in City Hall and run the classy eating joints like Carmen Anthony's and the Pontelandolfo Club. This perhaps explains why your Christmas meal begins with a breakfast lasagna, served up with coffee at 11:00 A.M. while the Shop-Rite turkey roasts to 170 degrees, a full thirty higher, and thus, to your mother, better, than the minimum internal temp recommended by the USDA.

Hosting a holiday that encourages the cooking of nonboxed food products means that your mother has been too consumed with prep and chores to notice the silent treatment you've given her since your trip to Yllka's a few days prior. Robbie is there to dice celery and onions and shake up the Good Seasonings while your mother twirls the Pillsbury dough from triangles to crescents, because she wants full credit for what is invariably everyone's secret favorite part of the meal. You've been tasked with making the salad, which essentially consists of opening a plastic bag of iceberg and shredded carrots and dumping in a few cucumber chunks and black olives to solidify its place as the least desirable foodstuff at the table.

"Take it easy on the olives, Lu," your mother says to you. "It's a salad, not a pizza."

You briefly think about telling your mother where she can put the Good Seasonings cruet, but Mamie will be arriving from the train station with Aunt Greta momentarily, and you don't want the sole Kuzavinas who has a clue to think of you as an asshole.

What you want, in fact, is for Greta to think of you as amazing, because she's the only one you could think of who might have any idea of what *amazing* means. Greta's going to be the first and possibly only person you tell about your meeting with Yllka, because if anyone knows what it means to feel homeless in your own bed, to be an explorer without a vessel, it's Greta Kuzavinas. Greta is the Kuzavinas family's pilgrim: first ever to go to college, first of the American-born to leave Waterbury, and not even for one of the boring little suburbs where some of your second cousins had settled after they'd been promoted to fore-man or head purchasing agent at Highland Manufacturing, maker of little stamped metal parts for a variety of industries in which you're not interested. Greta lives in New York — not the upstate part, which is no different than Waterbury, but the New York City part, which is different from all other places in the world — where you still hang on to the hope that you belong, just not in the cheater NYU way you'd previously planned, lounging in dorm rooms among the sons and daughters of packaged Greek food scions. No, this whole NYU rejection was for the best, because now you can prove that you're still smart enough to do New York right, like Greta does it: count-ing Bloody Marys as meals, having friends who work in things like media, having friends at all. You'll be living, per your plan, your mother's worst nightmare. All the streets and buildings, and worse, all the people — it's just too much, your mother frequently says, reminding her, like a Neil deGrasse Tyson special on PBS, of just how inconsequential each one of us is in the grand scheme of things. In contrast to your mother, that kind of thing is comforting to you, who would rather be inconsequential in a context so great your smallness isn't even registered.

When Mamie and Greta walk through the door, though, you're reminded of just how unlike Greta you are, at least in any obvious physical way. Even in the black military-style puffy coat that's pretty much standard issue for people of a certain demographic in the city, Greta is someone people look at. Her hair is buzzed, because despite having fled Waterbury and her family, the two main triggers for her trich, the only real treatment has been removing the target, which is somewhat akin to quitting a nail-biting habit by removing your hands. She'd explained this to you during one of your annual visits, while you two squeezed into a counter space for one at brunch in Greenpoint, the neighborhood she'd told you Williamsburg hipsters go to to retire. For you, it was like watching *Sex and the City* in a foreign language: you had no idea what she was talking about, but you were sure that it was glamorous.

"Lulu!" Greta says, and when you lean in for a hug you wonder for a moment if Greta has eaten anything since that long-ago brunch, because you can feel her sharp ribs beneath her puffy military jacket. In Waterbury, her kind of skinny is mostly seen on late-stage drug abusers, but in New York it's just how you look awesome in clothes that are bizarre outside of the boroughs. This is perhaps why, with your thigh juncture instead of gap, your clothes never seem to hang quite right on you.

"Lasagna!" Greta cries when she notices the pan, and you wonder if maybe she's been starving herself to fit into those teeny jeans, because, to your disappointment, Greta appears as excited to see a casserole as she does to see you.

"Look at this girl, right?" Mamie says. "She looks like a cancer patient."

"Jesus, Mamie, that's not nice," your mother says.

"What did I tell you about saying His name like that?" Mamie says.

"That only you get to do it?" Greta says.

"Hi, baby," Mamie says to you. "You look healthy, baby." This is Mamie's way of saying you look chubby, though not saying it explicitly is Mamie's way of being nice, so you force yourself to say thank you and quickly run for a celery stick before Mamie reminds you again that your ample bosom and butt don't come from the Kuzavinas line.

"Turkey will be ready in an hour or so," your mother says. "Help yourself to some lasagna."

But Greta is already helping herself to some lasagna, and Mamie to some of the coffee that she makes very clear is to be kept ready at all times during her visits, lest she be forced to wet her whistle with the Carlo Rossi your mother keeps hidden from Mamie to avert any relapses, which your mother still braces for even three years into her sobriety. Your mother sits with them at the kitchen table, picking out the stray hairs or particles of dust that have fallen into the raw crescent rolls, which she has shaped into something more like the twisted claws of a neglected junkyard Rottweiler. Robbie is in the fourth chair, compulsively shaking the Good Seasons dressing every twenty seconds, the panic on his face apparent whenever the oil and vinegar even hints at separation. They all look right together, you think, even Greta, back in her regressed, anxious state, and the too-tall, too-skinny interloper who is the first-ever male at your family's annual Christmas Day showdown. Each of the four chairs at the table is already filled, and from where you stand it looks like they are on the bow of a ship, a little *Mayflower* setting off for some land where a bunch of freaks would be able to piece a collective life together.

"Ah, crap," your mother says, looking up at you. "We're gonna need another chair."

"I'll stand," you answer.

You don't stand. You end up on a twenty-five-dollar Office Max office chair that rolls away from the table every time the anchors of your feet lift off the floor as you reach for another crescent roll.

"I just don't understand where you put all that food," Mamie says to Greta. "You haven't stopped eating since you walked in the door."

"It's Christmas," your mother says. "Let her enjoy herself."

"You're like that hot dog–eating lady who weighs about ninety pounds. Do you just hollow yourself out so you can eat once a year?" Mamie says.

"First you tell me I'm too skinny and then you won't lay off me for eating. What is it that's going to make you happy?" Greta says.

"I am happy. What makes you think I'm not happy, just because I'm concerned? Would you be happy if I wasn't concerned?"

"Yes," Greta answers.

"So how's work?" Robbie asks Greta. He'd assured you and your mother that his own family's holiday dinners had primed him for whatever the Kuzavinas family would dish out in addition to food, but he's been sitting at the table silently throughout dinner, responding to every line of conversation with the same weird, tight smile that makes him look a little Botoxed, as if he's an out-of-work talk-show host instead of a gainfully employed community college instructor.

"It's great. Last week a patron stabbed himself in the stomach in the bathroom and then came to the reference desk asking for help putting his intestines back in," Greta answers through a mouthful of candied yams.

"Oh, that's disgusting," Mamie says.

"You have to say that at the dinner table?" your mother says.

"I'm the only one still eating," Greta answers, looking truly a little pleased with herself. "And Robbie asked."

"Vet?" Robbie asks. "Homeless?"

"Both, probably. You know how it is, it's a public library. Part daycare center, part VA hospital, part sex shop for middle-aged moms who don't want to pay the fifteen bucks for their own copy of *Fifty Shades.*"

You sometimes almost forget that Greta is a librarian, because you think of her so exclusively as Greta, as if that is itself an occupation: buzz-cutted, lesbian bar–hopping, get-the-fuck-out-of-Dodger. Her apartment is the kind of place where there's only room to sit on the floor, which is dingy enough to be the last place you want to sit, but she goes to parties in breathtaking lofts owned by rich people who dress like poor people and raise organic chickens on their rooftops. When rent and student loan payments eat her paychecks three hours after she receives them, she makes do on slices of Ray's and appetizers made by chef friends who've been on TV and don't even make a thing of it, as if being on TV is something as natural as having a thigh gap. You admire her so much it hurts.

But you're just her kid niece, she reminds you, when she asks, "So, Lu, have you sent in your college applications yet?"

Instantly you regret stuffing down that last crescent roll.

"Yeah, a couple weeks ago," you lie.

"Exciting," she says. "Where did you apply?"

"Western Connecticut State University and, you know, NYU," you say.

"And where else are you going to apply?"

"What do you mean, *where else*?"

"That's it? Two schools?"

"A reach and a safety. That's what the guidance counselor said to do."

"Yeah, a reach and a safety. What's wrong with that?" your mother asks, not rhetorically.

"You're going to listen to a guidance counselor?"

"That's their job. Yeah, we listened to them," your mother says.

"Please, the guidance counselors here basically just feed people into the military. Why do you think they offer the ASVAB instead of SAT prep at school? And the kids who can't pass the military fitness test get pushed into Mattatuck. No offense."

"None taken," Robbie says.

"Some taken," your mother says. "I went to Mattatuck. What's wrong with Mattatuck?"

"She owes a whole lot less on her student loans than you," Mamie chimes in.

"I'm sorry, I know that sounded douchey.

I'm just saying that it's not what you want for Lulu, right? And Lulu, it's not what you want, right?"

"No," you say.

"No," your mother echoes, though she seems to be waiting to be told whether or not she answered correctly.

"Well, why not? Why do you think everybody has to go to some name-brand college?" Mamie says.

"Because the people who run the places we all work for send their kids there, and they never think to call them name-brand colleges."

"Those people. Who even wants to be one of those people?" Mamie says.

"We should want Lulu to be one of those people," Greta says.

"I do," your mother answers. "I think she can be one of those people no matter where she goes to school."

"Anyway, they shove college down all these kids' throats nowadays, and yet half of 'em don't know how to work worth a damn. They don't know how to do anything without Mommy and Daddy holding their hand," Mamie says.

"I never have to worry about that," you say, but nobody seems to hear it.

"We're just doing what we were told to

do," your mother says. "I mean, how many applications is she supposed to send out?"

"That's up to Lulu. Five or six, maybe? Did you look into any other places?" she asks you.

You don't respond. It's what happens instead of saying *no,* which is the real answer, which you figured out recently was the wrong one, and you feel a bit like Greta has ganged up with NYU and Margarita to remind you of what an idiot you've been. In truth, your criteria in selecting NYU had been, in this order: location; having heard of it; and it not being Columbia, an ivy where in a million years you wouldn't have dreamed of applying. You hadn't let yourself consider what would happen if you weren't admitted to NYU, since you never really considered the other option an alternative. Western Connecticut isn't really a safety, it's a freebie, a school that practically guarantees admission to anyone with a high school diploma and the willingness to drive I-84 west at least a few days a week.

"I wish you would've told us this a little bit sooner," your mother says, looking first at Greta, and then turning to Robbie. "You, too. Aren't you supposed to know about this stuff?"

Robbie looks deeply embarrassed, and is

clearly regretting turning down Christmas in Bay Ridge, where the meal would be served cacciatore style and suffused with the kind of Italian-mother guilt to which he had long ago become inured. "I mean, I'm happy to answer any questions, but I didn't want to overstep my bounds. She's not my," he begins, but doesn't finish what obviously doesn't need finishing.

"Daughter. I'm not his daughter. It's not his job," you say. "And it's not Greta's job, either, and it's not a stupid guidance counselor's job."

"No, actually, it *is* a guidance counselor's job," your mother interrupts.

"No, actually, not really," you say.

"Are you telling me I'm supposed to have done everything? I am one person, if you haven't noticed," your mother says.

"No, you weren't supposed to have done everything. You just decided to," you say.

"Really," she says, though there is emphatically no question mark at the end of it. "I decided to make both of our lives as difficult as possible."

You shrug, your shoulders rolling high in the pantomime of a shrug, a shrug that the people at the back of the theater would tell you to tone down.

"Guys, come on, it's Christmas. I wasn't

trying to start anything. I was just trying to make conversation," Greta says.

"That's what happens when you make conversation about the rest of us being idiots," Mamie says.

"I never said you were idiots, I just said don't rely on people around here for academic guidance."

"Well, who is she supposed to rely on, you? You who checks in once or twice a year when there's free food on the table?"

"Yeah, I wonder why I would possibly want to not come back here," Greta says, finally pushing her plate away.

"I know, it's *so* awful here, and it's *so* great where you are. You're doing *so* much better than the rest of us with your name-brand college degrees."

Greta appears shocked that her well-being is not apparent to Mamie.

"I'm happy," Greta says. "I'm so happy."

"In any case, it's not like it's too late. She can still send out more applications if she needs to," your mother says.

"No, I can't. It's like seventy-five dollars for each one," you remind her.

"They'll waive the application fee for some people," Robbie says, deciding to be helpful now that you've decided there's no point in bothering with any of it.

"Really?" your mother says.

"*Some people.* That means poor people," Mamie says.

For a moment the silence that everyone was hoping for comes to be, and it brings none of the relief that, seconds ago, it had seemed to promise.

"What?" Mamie says. "That's not us. We're not poor. All of us work. All any of us have ever done is work. We don't need hand-outs."

"It's not a handout. It's like a scholarship to apply," Greta says.

A need-based scholarship, which you earn by being a docile, poor, free-to-reduced-lunch–getting bastard child. You think that, but you don't say it aloud. You've stopped saying anything aloud, in fact, and once again, it doesn't even matter. Everyone else is doing the talking for you, deciding what's right or wrong for the Luljeta Hasani they decided is sitting with them at the table, whether or not she should be proud or ashamed of being an aspirational charity case. You don't even have the same name as these people. You resent being their obliga-tion as much as you suspect they secretly resent you for the same. You don't even want the parents of some packaged food product heir to cover your application fee to

Wesleyan or Bucknell via their contributions to the school's never-ending capital campaign, so happy were they that the school found no hard evidence of the trumped-up allegations lodged against their son the second semester of his freshman year. Their boy was a good boy, their boy was a gift bestowed upon them late in life, after eight rounds of fertility treatments and, ultimately, the egg of a well-compensated nonsmoking Bucknell coed with no family history of heart disease, addiction, mental illness, or brunettes. It's dumb, maybe, but you wonder what it would be like to be a gift to your family instead of a burden. You wonder what it would feel like to be a happy surprise, the kind a father celebrates in a smoky room among friends who'd never seen him smile quite like that, instead of the kind a mother doesn't really know what to do with when she wants to go bowling with some co-workers on a Tuesday night.

Your phone buzzes in your pocket. There's a message from Yllka: *This year my present was you,* it reads. And another from Teena informing you that she's told her parents she was with you, in case they call looking for her. And another from Ahmet, not really a message but a series of seemingly unrelated emoticons that you'd have to be an

Egyptologist to decipher. Three texts from three different people in a day; it's possibly a record for you. Meanwhile, the people whom you sit among continue shrilling at each other, supposedly over your future but obviously really about their own histories, begrudging each other for past betrayals and ingratitude and dinner conversations turned ugly.

"Well, don't worry about me ruining everything, I have to catch the six-twenty train back anyway," Greta says.

"What?" you say. "I thought you were staying overnight." Six-twenty is three hours away, not enough time to clean up, eat dessert, clean up again, watch two hours of *NCIS* reruns on TV, and confide in Greta that you were on the verge of something big, that you'd received an invitation to explore your past and, you assume, form a future that is tenable on account of a stronger, reinforced foundation.

"I'm sorry, Lulu, I've got a thing I have to go to that I really can't get out of," Greta says.

"But you can get out of being with your family? Lulu's been counting down the days till you got here," your mother says.

Greta looks at you with the same smile she always gives you, which previously felt tender and affirming and seemed to say: *Save yourself. We are not your sole progenitors and we are not your sole fate.* Only now it feels condescending and obligatory, as if, in addition to learning how to be cool from her stupid rich friends, she also learned how to smile in the gracious, empty way of well-bred rich people, mimicking the smiles her friends give their doormen when they hand over a Christmas card with a pathetic twenty-dollar tip at Christmas. You realize that you've had Greta wrong this whole time: the lesson hasn't been look what you can do when you apply yourself, it's look what happens when you don't stop running: you turn around to find that the life you thought you abandoned has been only one crescent roll behind you this whole time.

"It's fine. I don't feel good, anyway," you say.

"Don't be like that, Lu. I wish I didn't have to go," she says. "You should come see me next weekend, okay? And we'll see each other all the time once you're at NYU, right?"

"Yup," you answer. "All the time."

"Well, silly me, I thought I'd get to spend a whole holiday with my family," Mamie says.

"If we don't get to spend the whole day

together, then let's just not be assholes for the time we do have, okay?" your mother says. "Now who wants cake?"

"I do," Robbie chimes in.

You think, Yeah, who wants cake indeed.

CHAPTER NINE:
ELSIE

It looked like I was the only person on the
East End who didn't get an invitation to the
party happening in our apartment when I
walked in after my double shift at the Ross.
Bashkim and Gjonni were sitting at the
heads of the kitchen table, the other chairs
filled with guys I'd never met, all of them
leather-brown, all of them with scars across
their brows or cheeks or necks, like factory
seconds from a set of dishware. A few others improvised seats, like an Igloo cooler
that wasn't ours, a stack of telephone books
stolen off of every front step in the neighborhood, a case of industrial-size stewed tomatoes stood upright, obviously borrowed
from dry storage at the Ross and almost
certainly going back there afterward.

"Beautiful, beautiful!" the men called out,
so I turned behind me to see what they were
looking at before I realized they meant me.
When I turned back to face the room, I was

surrounded by wet lips searching for my cheeks. They grabbed my hands and shoved wrinkled dollars into my palms, which I wasn't ready for, so the bills floated to the floor.

"Look at her, just like a woman, throwing away money," Gjonni said. He gathered the bills in his hand and pressed the pile into my arms, and I cradled it tight like a child against my chest. "But see, a good woman, a natural mother," he said, pressing his hand into my belly, which was as puffy from Pepsi bloat as it was from the future human living in there. The men laughed, and then somebody said something I couldn't understand, which made them laugh harder, and made me want to run.

I looked at Bashkim and did my best to smile.

"I didn't know people were coming over," I said.

"It's friends," he said. His smile was distorted behind a bottle of Heineken, so many empties scattered on the table that the light in the room was tinted green, the way it looks when a storm is coming. "I wanted them to meet the mother of my child."

One of the men held a bottle to the ceiling. Cameras were pulled from nowhere.

Pictures were snapped.

"Të lindtënjëdjalë," he said, and the others followed. *Të lindtënjëdjalë,* they said, not really in unison, so it circled the room like some weird school chorus round.

"It means, 'May a son be born,' " Yllka said. She was standing beside me, and I noticed then for the first time the women seated in the living room, presumably the wives of the men in the kitchen, a bowl of potato chips towering untouched in the center of the coffee table. They stared at me with eyes that were bored and vicious at once.

"Go introduce yourself to the girls. Yllka, go introduce Elsie," Gjonni said.

It was a den of lions in there. Except for an old lady in a babushka, they had thick manes hairsprayed around their hungry faces, and their noses twitched as I got closer. I stared at Bashkim, but he wouldn't even look over. He was concentrating on the playing cards splayed in his hand, wearing a poker face that could run Atlantic City.

"I was actually just on my way out," I said.

"Go on, go on," Gjonni said.

Yllka sighed. She pulled the money from my arms, ironed it smooth with her hands, and folded the wad neatly into my pocket. "Come," she said and pulled me into the

224

living room. It looked like the women had gotten palms full of money before, too, and had spent it all at Kay Jewelers. There were gold bands wrapped around their index fingers and thin gold hoops hanging from their lobes. The old lady wore a gold plate over her right front tooth, which I could see because her lip was curled back into something that was not a smile.

"This is Elsie," Yllka said. They nodded and stared at my stomach. I recognized the youngest one in the room, a girl maybe my age, from the Ross. She sometimes stood in the lobby for an hour at a time trying to pluck a stuffed toy with a metal claw for twenty-five cents a shot, even though she had to have known that those things were wedged so tight that she'd have been lucky to grab some fuzzy dice with a pair of pliers. A New Kids on the Block pin was fastened to her denim jacket, not ironically as far as I could tell.

Yllka nudged me and started pointing at the women. "This is Klarita, Lindita, Dardata," she said, and I remembered that I heard the young one, Dardata, called Dottie by her friends in the parking lot. After that the names fell apart into clumsy syllables that I'd never remember, and I figured it wouldn't be worth trying, since chances were slim they'd be inviting me over for Tupperware dems anytime soon. When the introductions were over, the golden-toothed woman rose from her seat and took hold of my belly with both hands, keeping her eyes on me but cocking her head to aim whatever she was saying at the rest of them.

"Vajzë," the lady said.

"She thinks she knows what kind of baby everybody is going to have, even though she's wrong half the time," Dardata said.

"She doesn't think she knows, she tries to make the baby whatever she wants it to be. If she likes you she says boy, if she doesn't she says girl," Yllka said.

"What does she want me to have?" I asked.

"A girl," said Yllka.

I tried my best to smile and waved the smoke snaking in from the kitchen away from my eyes so I could pretend that was why they were glazed over.

"I wish Bashkim would've told me that you were coming over," I said. "I could've been prepared."

"What's there to prepare? We got chips." Dardata waved her hand over the coffee table like a model on *The Price Is Right*. "It's like a king's spread."

"Just prepare," I said.

"You'd think he'd tell his wife those

things, right? Oh, wait, but you're not his wife . . ."

"She's joking," Yllka said and said something to Dardata that sounded more like a warning than a joke.

Our eyes moved in circles around the room. Yllka said something to the woman in the recliner, and the woman reluctantly stood up and shuffled over to the arm of the couch, where she sat on one cheek and resumed a blank stare. "Sit," Yllka told me, and I didn't argue about it.

"Thanks," I said. "My dogs are barking."

"What?" Dardata said. "What dogs? I don't hear any dogs."

"It's just an expression. When your feet are tired, your dogs are barking."

"That doesn't make any sense. Feet don't make sound."

"It's just a saying," I said.

"It still doesn't make sense. No wonder half of us never learn English. It's full of nonsense."

"Every language has expressions that don't make sense," Yllka said. "Mos më shit pordhë."

Dardata rolled her eyes, and a couple other women covered their mouths as if holding back a cough.

"What does that mean?" I asked.

" 'Don't sell me farts,' " Yllka said. "In other words, 'Don't mess with me.' "

I pitied the soul who ever dared to sell Yllka farts.

Dardata began looping her hair around a finger. "So, are you having a boy or a girl?" she asked.

"I don't know," I said.

"Can't they tell yet? Aren't you going to find out?"

"I'm not sure yet," I said.

"Don't find out," Yllka said. "It's bad luck to know."

"How is it bad luck? It just gives you time to get ready. So you know what color things to buy," Dardata said.

"Fine, not bad luck, just bad. Some people might stop caring if they found out the baby wasn't what they wanted," Yllka said. She looked into the kitchen, straight at Bashkim, but we didn't exist anymore to the men out there. They pulled on bottles of Heineken as if they contained mothers' milk and kept backup cigarettes behind their ears, the rest of the loosies scattered across the table to use as poker chips. Bashkim was ahead by at least a pack.

"They won't stop caring altogether," Dardata said. "Even men know not everybody can have a boy."

"We don't really care about that kind of thing," I said.

Yllka cocked her head at me. " 'We' don't, or you don't?"

"We," I said. "It's not something we talk about."

Yllka folded her arms and leaned against the wall. "Of course it doesn't matter one way or another. Mothers know that."

A woman on the sofa reached for a potato chip. The rest just sat there and looked at us, like they were watching a foreign movie without subtitles. Yllka said something to them in Albanian, and they leaned back and nodded and kept watching.

"Well, how much longer before we all find out?" Dardata asked.

"Huh?" I said.

"How far along are you? How long before we know if it's a boy or girl?"

"Oh," I said. "I think about four or five months."

"You think?" Dardata said. "What does the doctor say?"

It was too hot in that room. No air. The windows had been painted shut, and the ceiling fan just recycled our own breath back down into our lungs.

"I haven't been to the doctor yet," I said.

Everyone seemed to understand that one.

The women got more quiet, their heads shaking like they'd caught some tic from whatever was in the drinking water.

"What? Why not?" Dardata said.

"Nothing's gone wrong," I said.

"You're not supposed to wait for something to go wrong. You go to the doctor to make sure that nothing goes wrong. I haven't even had a kid and I know that."

"I've been busy. Working, moving," I said, and I realized that those things made up my entire to-do list. "And anyway, doctors are expensive."

"Bashkim's got money. He's becoming a millionaire, I hear," Dardata said.

I shrugged. "My mother didn't go until the very end and everything turned out fine," I said.

"Did it?" Dardata said.

"You should see a doctor," Yllka said. "This is not the old country, you don't have to do it like these ladies did it."

"And I thought we were the ones living in a time warp," Dardata said.

"Hesht," Yllka said. "When you have a baby you will mess things up, too."

"I have to get some air," I said.

Bashkim's eyes tracked me as I rushed through the kitchen, but he didn't lay down his hand and follow me outside. It didn't matter, though, because for once I didn't want his attention, or anybody else's. For just that minute I wanted to be left alone, and then my stomach cramped up and reminded me that there was a little person in there, and that I wouldn't be alone again for a long, long time. Already it was a needy little thing: it needed me to eat so it could eat, it needed me to empty my bladder so there was more space for it inside of me. No doctor was going to be able to tell me what I really wanted to know, which wasn't boy or girl, healthy or monster. I wanted to know just what kind of person this thing was going to be. Like, *be.* Muscly and quiet and serious like Bashkim, or skinny and smart and broken like Greta, or bitter and tipsy and mean like Mamie? Or would it be like me? I thought for a minute and realized that I didn't even know what that meant, what few things I could be boiled down to. Acne-prone waitress who deferred acceptance to a community college? Was that really it? And then there was Bashkim's whole history, a black hole that I wouldn't even know existed except that Bashkim had to come from somewhere, he hadn't just rolled in from nowhere like a thunderstorm, although those blue eyes did resemble storm clouds. And even if genetics didn't determine it all, if this thing relied mostly on nurture, did that mean it had a better or worse shot of turning out okay?

"She is right, you should go to a doctor," Yllka said. She'd slipped outside with me silently, like a ninja. "Dardata is wrong about most things in life, but she is right about that. Babies are hard enough without something going wrong."

"I'm going to go," I said, though I hadn't really thought much about it until that night. My people weren't doctor people; we went from healthy to dead in one fell swoop. Mamie had had to be talked into going to the hospital when she lost a finger at the knuckle, afraid that she'd get in trouble with her boss for missing work or bloodying up the machine she'd been assigned to, back when there were still a few jobs at the mills. We'd never been to the dentist, we treated strep throat with mint chocolate chip ice cream, we collected scar tissue from infected wounds like tribal body art. Mamie agreed to send Greta to the shrink only when the guidance counselor threatened to call DCF on her like she was some worthless junkie.

"Those are all the wives inside, you know. The wives of the men in there," Yllka said.

"I figured," I said.

"So what do you think they think of you?"

"Not much, obviously."

"You are here with the wives. Not the girlfriends. That happens other nights, with other girls. They don't understand why you're here."

"I'm here because I live here," I said.

"That's what I mean. Why are you *here,* in this house, instead of the places where they keep girls like you? Those women know Bashkim is married, and it makes them wonder what kind of company their husbands kept before they made enough money to bring their wives over."

"That's their problem. I'm not some dumb mistress. Agnes didn't even want to come over. It's done, it's over with her, she lost her chance, and now it's my turn. And it was his idea to move in together, anyway. I don't see why I have to be the bad guy for the rest of my life."

"I think you are young and dumb. I don't think you're bad."

"I'd rather be bad than dumb."

"Well, you're off to a good start. A woman who doesn't know enough to go to the doctor when she's pregnant is dumb. One who knows better but still doesn't go is bad."

"I am going to go to the doctor," I said. "So after that, what will I be?"

She shrugged. "I guess just regular."

233

"That's a start," I said.

"Yes, just a start. Listen, Bashkim is family, and you are not, but that child inside of you is my family, too. And while it is inside of your belly, it eats the food you eat, but that's not all. It feels what you feel. You feel sad, it is sad. You are hurt, it is hurt, too. I want what is good for that child, and so I don't want you being hurt. That's all."

"I'm not trying to get hurt, either. I'm not looking for pain," I said.

"You should be," she said. "You should look all the time for it, so you know where it is, and you can stay far, far away."

She walked inside, her shadow a moment or two behind her, a ghost of rosewater perfume always the last part of her to leave. Once that faded I sat alone in the dull light that the kitchen window let out, looking at all the other dull lights in the houses to my left and right. There were lights on in most of them, and swarms of moths panicking at each. What a shitty, sad life moths led, I thought. They'd do anything to get at the warmth of the light, and as soon as they reached it they burned up and died.

Those kinds of flaws were everywhere in nature. I wasn't saying I had everything figured out, that I wasn't making mistakes all over the place, I just didn't see why I had to be singled out for it.

The next morning Bashkim collected the money his friends had shoved at me, which I'd crammed into the pockets of my jeans and looked forward to counting.

"Where are you going with that?" I asked.

He shrugged.

"Wait," I said, sitting up on my elbows, or trying to anyway. The air mattress had deflated enough that it couldn't support things like right angles. "I was going to use that to go to the doctor."

"You don't need this to go to the doctor."

"Yes I do. I don't have any other money."

"Why do you need money to see a doctor?"

"Because they cost money," I said. I watched Bashkim take in that information, process it for a second, and then reject it.

"This is America," I said. "Everything costs money."

He thought about it some more. "You don't need to go to a fancy doctor. Nothing is wrong with you," he said.

"I'm not talking about a fancy doctor. Just a regular doctor, to make sure everything's going okay with the baby."

He looked down at the money in his hands and sighed. "How much?"

"I have no idea. I just know that it costs money to go to the doctor."

He handed me forty dollars.

"I don't think that's enough," I said. "It's probably a couple hundred at least. Doctors are rich. They don't get rich charging forty bucks at a time."

Bashkim was getting frustrated, which was probably compounded by the hangover he had to have. "Why don't you find out how much it is going to be first?"

"Bashkim, this is your *child*," I said.

He hesitated.

"Your *son*, remember?"

He looked at the knot in his hand again, then looked me up and down, wondering if my rounded belly were some kind of elaborate hoax, before he put the money back on the dresser.

"Yes, we should make sure everything is okay," he said, as if the whole thing were his idea.

He stood there for a second, waiting for me to thank him, but I couldn't get any words of gratitude to form. He eventually walked out, and I collapsed back onto the mattress, wondering how much longer it was going to be like that, me having to convince Bashkim that there was going to be a return on his investment in me.

The cheapest doctors, the clinics that advertised on billboards on the sides of buildings that were one lead brick away from being condemned, were mostly downtown, in walking distance from the most busted-up, hope-defying neighborhoods in the city. The gas tank in the car I'd borrowed from Mamie was riding E, so I shifted into neutral and coasted down the hills into the valley, rolling down East Main, past what used to be Scovill Brass Works, except it hadn't worked in years, and was being demolished to make way for a mall that I was guessing wouldn't work any better. I rolled past the half dozen Puerto Rican shops hawking shrink-wrapped white pleather couches on the sidewalk, rolled past open windows that piped spirituals and salsa out of speakers that'd been bought off the backs of white box vans tagged with graffiti from the Bronx.

By the time I had to shift back into gear, I'd managed to roll almost all the way to the town green and into a spot that could make you believe, for two or three minutes anyway, that Waterbury was still somewhere you might actually want to be. For three or four square blocks municipal buildings and bank headquarters made this place look like an actual city, the kind that casts heavy shadows over one-way streets. It could have been a set from *Hill Street Blues,* the kind of cop show set in some generic northeastern city where crimes are committed and solved in time for happy hour. All that marble, all those men in suits as gray as the steps of the courthouse, lawyers stuffing thick wedges of salami on Portuguese rolls into their mouths, not even pausing from their conversations to do it. A block away, inscribed into the marble above the entrance to City Hall, it said *Quid Aere Perennius?* What is more lasting than brass?

That's what my sixth-grade teacher had told us it meant, but she hadn't told us the answer. Nobody had. It was a trick question, see, because once your eyes stopped being dazzled by all the slate and those Revolutionary War memorials, it turned out almost everything in the city was more lasting than brass. The toxic mud the mall was being built on was more lasting than brass. The hunger of the wailing baby in the stroller outside the social services office was more lasting than brass. The rubber on my sneakers, secondhand New Balances with still a good inch left to the soles, I bet even they would be more lasting than brass. Everybody here was more lasting than brass, and that made us stronger, didn't it, wasn't that what we learned in biology? All of us who came from ancestors who survived the bubonic plague, famines, those constantly finding new means of survival, moving from farms to villages, villages to cities, cities to different cities in new countries half a world away. We were a hearty brand of people and we had reached the end of the line, right? What was even left for the next generations?

In the waiting room at the clinic I was surrounded by women who didn't look like they wanted to think a day ahead into the future, never mind a generation. There were girls younger than me in there, with scabs on their knees as if they'd come straight from the jungle gym, and some women who, if not for the bulges beneath their muumuus, could've been young grandmas. There was a lady in a baggy puff-painted sweatshirt and thick eyeglasses who looked like she'd been planning her baby since meeting her husband at a Christian mixer a year or two before, and another woman with an electronic monitoring bracelet around her ankle sitting next to a stern lady who was either her mother or her parole officer. We all picked up parenting magazines, traded them in for *Highlights for Children* magazines, traded those in for pamphlets about smoking and fetal alcohol syndrome and low birth weights. Nobody touched the adoption pamphlets, because none of us were prepared to give anything of potential value away.

I was trying to fill out the paperwork, on the question that asked whether I was using or had ever used intravenous drugs, when a little boy wobbled over and took the pen from my hand. He brought it to the woman who I guessed was his mother, who huffed and banged the pen down on the coffee table and closed her eyes again. He picked the pen back up and handed it to another woman, who slipped it into her purse. I stood up and asked the lady at the desk for another.

"I don't know if we *have* any more," she answered. I saw at least two other Bics within grabbing distance of her hand. "What happened to the *other* one?"

"I don't know," I answered, and as she slid over another pen she sighed like she regretted every moment of her life, up to and including that day.

Do you have other children? the form asked. I checked off no, and for good measure filled in a zero when the next question asked how many. The little boy reached for my pen again, but I held on tighter and looked at his mother. Her eyes were closed and her mouth open. Her purse was balanced on a stomach so enormous it must have housed more than just a fetus.

The boy was cute, in a feral kind of way. His hair made him at least three inches taller than the two and a half feet he actually was, and it was orange — not red like a redhead but orange like rust, like he'd been left out in the rain. When he walked he kicked his legs straight out instead of bending them at the knee. He sang something with words that meant nothing but followed pretty closely the tune of "Eye of the Tiger."

I smiled at him a little when he looked at me, but he turned back to the stack of magazines he was streaming to the floor.

"Dwayne, sit down and quiet up," the woman said. She didn't open her eyes.

I went back to the questionnaire. *Has your partner ever hit you, kicked you, or threatened to harm you?*

No, I responded.

It asked all about my health history. I had never had diabetes, cancer, gallstones, hepatitis, anemia. I didn't know if it was panic attacks or indigestion keeping me up at night, so I left the questions about those blank. Depression? What a stupid question to ask in a place like this, I thought, so again I left it blank.

"Dwayne, you hear me?" the woman said. Dwayne kept singing, picking up the magazines he'd pushed to the floor so he could do it again.

The questionnaire asked if my partner had had any of those conditions, or my parents. I left those blank, too.

Dwayne's mother opened her eyes and lunged forward so fast that it seemed like she was waking from a nightmare, and she grabbed on to the boy's arms as if bracing herself.

"You shut that mouth up or I will punch it. I will punch you in the fucking mouth," she said. Her purse had fallen off of her belly when she leaned forward but she didn't make a move to pick it up, and a Vicks inhaler and a quarter pack of powdered Hostess Donettes rolled out. The boy dropped to his butt and wasn't singing anymore, but his lips still moved, opening and closing and making spit bubbles that popped just before they could float away.

Nobody else in the room looked up during the outburst or after it, and that made me want to run.

"Elsie?" a nurse called, and I was surprised

to find that I was already on my feet, halfway to the door. I stopped in my tracks, caught in the middle of my jailbreak, and I had to remind myself that this wasn't a jail, it was just a gyno's office, one that didn't seem to care whether you were insured or not. What was I so afraid of? Wasn't this the easy part?

I was an amateur. I giggled when the nurse moved the little bud of her stethoscope over my back.

"Sorry, it tickles," I said.

"One more deep breath," she answered.

I stared when she poked a needle into my arm, watching the cylinder turn crimson as it sucked up blood.

"You have good veins," she said, and I felt proud, like all these years, when people said I was busy doing nothing worth talking about, what I was really doing was working on my veins, making them nice and plump for overworked phlebotomists.

"What's it say?" I asked.

"What's what say?"

"My blood."

"I don't know yet. We have to send it out for testing."

"Oh," I said.

"But it's red like it should be," she said,

trying to help me feel not stupid. "I bet it's got all of what it's supposed to have and not too much of what it shouldn't."

Unlike the ladies in reception, the nurses were cheerful, kindergarten teacherish. They must have been used to dum-dums like me, baby incubators too young or too stupid or in need of twelve steps to be mothers. I didn't trust their soothing voices, their Snoopy and Woodstock scrubs. They'd play peekaboo with us, and then, by the time we uncovered our hands from our eyes, DCF would be waiting with a net to scoop up our litters.

"The doctor will be right with you," the nurse said.

The doctor wasn't right with me. It took another twenty minutes for that, and in between another white-smocked woman came in, short and smiling, and I thought I recognized her from back at Crosby High School, someone who graduated a few years before me. I looked at her name tag and it was no help, because it just said Marisa or Maria or something, one of the names that was assigned to every third baby girl that went through the maternity ward at St. Mary's Hospital between the years of 1974 and 1983. Marisa or Maria was doing all right for herself. She had the money for a spiral perm and acrylic nails and something put a smile on her face that wasn't fake. It must've been a good field to get into, ultrasound tech, and I put it down on my mental to-do list as a career to look into once things were settled down.

Marisa/Maria smeared some cold jelly over my stomach.

"Cold, right?" she asked.

But I wasn't shivering from the cold. This was the moment, just like that, when everyone would really get to see whether I had done this whole thing wrong. The Albanian ladies — the *gruas,* Bashkim called them — they would probably be happy to see tentacles on that screen instead of arms and legs. They'd remind me of those Marlboro Reds I'd taken drags from before I realized I was knocked up, those swigs of Mamie's Carlo Rossi. *This* is what can happen, *this* is what you go to the doctor for, they'd say, the behind-the-scenes, the coming attraction, the sneak peek at the mess you'll be cleaning for the rest of your life.

"Wait," I said.

"What's wrong?" Marisa/Maria asked, and my face must have answered for me. "Oh, don't worry, this doesn't hurt. The wand just goes on top of your belly," she said and illustrated on her own stomach, which probably hosted nothing more than an Italian grinder from Nardelli's, nothing that could turn monstrous.

"It's just," I said.

Marisa/Maria smiled her infinitely patient smile, and I had no good response to it.

"Never mind, I'm ready," I said. I closed my eyes like I did for the last two clicks up the hill on the Cyclone roller coaster, the last moments of peace before the velocity of the fall would force my eyes open again.

She was right, it didn't hurt. It almost felt good to have someone press into my belly like that, a little massage, a little feeling that the weight there wasn't all mine alone.

"Do you want to open your eyes?" she asked.

"Oh," I said. I'd forgotten that they were closed. Marisa/Maria pointed at a monitor, which was swirly and gray and came in like a premium cable channel the clinic hadn't paid for.

"Do you see it?" she asked.

I shook my head, and she began pointing. "Arm, leg, head. See?"

It was as if we were looking at a cloud, and she was describing a shape that wasn't really there until it was, and then it was so obviously there that I couldn't not see it.

"Oh my god," I said.

"See?"

"Oh my god," I said again.

She kept moving the wand and let us sit in silence for a minute. There it was, the star of this show, up on a screen with an audience and everything. It wasn't much of an audience, just me and an ultrasound tech, and I felt bad for the little thing, starring in a show that nobody had come out to see. And then I felt bad for me, that I was sitting alone out there, trying to muster enough applause with my two little dinky hands to reach the stage. And then I didn't feel so bad anymore, because it was mesmerizing, that little graceful modern dance going on in front of me. There were tiny little movements you really had to focus on to see, but I did see them. My eyes trained to them pretty quick, and I felt like I suddenly understood why dancers dance, not to get a whole theater full of people to pay attention but to get just one person to really, truly see.

"It's two arms, right?" I asked.

Marisa/Maria nodded.

"And two legs?"

"Yup, two and two and nothing extra."

I was relieved but not that relieved. It surprised me, because I realized that if she'd said *No, something's missing* or *Oh god it's*

247

got horns, I'd still have been fixed to the seat, mesmerized.

"Do you want to know the sex?" Marisa/Maria asked.

"I don't . . . I mean, should I?"

"It's up to you. Some people want to plan for it, some people want a surprise. No harm either way."

That didn't seem entirely true. It felt like Bashkim already had something to lose.

But Bashkim wasn't there, so I guessed he didn't get to say.

"Yeah, I want to know," I said.

"Congratulations, you've got a baby girl!" said Marisa/Maria.

I choked up and I wasn't sure why. I didn't feel sad, and I didn't feel disappointed. Maybe I was disappointed that I wasn't disappointed, knowing I was letting Bashkim down and not giving a shit about it. Maybe I was happy that I wasn't carrying a Dwayne-to-be, which meant I was one step further away from ever being Dwayne's mother, that terrifying Donette-fueled entity out in the waiting room. Everybody said girls were harder, but maybe that just meant I was going to have to try more and, for once in my goddamned life, really mean it.

"I'll get the doctor," Marisa/Maria said, and I nodded. She pulled the wand away and the show on the screen was over, but really, it wasn't. When I thought about it I realized what I saw wasn't even the show, it was a dress rehearsal at best. Really the curtain hadn't even gone up yet.

I was even further along than I thought, twenty-six weeks, which in real-life time meant six months, right on the cusp of the third trimester. I wasn't ready to hear that number, and I got a little pukey when she said it, but other than that, the whole trip was fine. It was better than fine, even, it was beautiful. That's what the doctor said: beautiful. It was a word I didn't know could be used to describe a condition like mine. I thought the only words were *pregnant* or *not, healthy* or *not.* But she said *beautiful,* which up until then I thought was just a word someone called you when he wanted a blow job.

"You could stand to take in a little more iron, but otherwise everything looks beautiful," she said. She was corn-fed and tall, had to be from somewhere like Indiana sent to do mission work in a place like this, with a helmeted blond hairdo that looked like it belonged on someone twenty years older than she was. But still I wanted to tell her: *No, Doctor, you're beautiful, you're the one who makes everything you touch okay.* I felt like a moron for having been afraid of this all this time. On the way out we passed a corkboard covered with thank-you notes and pictures of newborns, and I told myself that I'd have to send a card to the clinic. It would say: *Thank you, ladies, for doing what nobody else in my whole world had even attempted, for making all of this okay. Thank you, Doctor and Marisa/Maria, for showing me how to do the part that comes next, and thank you, Donette Lady, for showing me what not to do.*

The doctor sent me off with vitamins and the name of a book, *What to Expect When You're Expecting,* which she said would answer most of my questions and teach me how to eat actual food and do actual yoga like a California hippie and continue to enjoy sex with my partner without harming the baby. I guess it was the book she recommended to all of her literate patients, because all three copies were checked out of the Silas Bronson Library by the time I got there. But no worries, because there were shelves of instruction manuals to get me through this. *Pregnancy for Dummies,* even, a book written just for me. I guess I was feeling smarter by then, after the doctor's visit, so I chose a serious hardcover published right around the year of my birth, something with footnotes and illustrations instead of photos, tables and charts instead of stupid jokes and cartoon lightbulbs with bright ideas for pregnant dummy readers. I checked out a VHS copy of *The Miracle of Life* and popped it in as soon as I got home, and I fell asleep for most of it but woke up for the most important part, the delivery, when a woman with the feathered stoner hair of all early eighties women breathed deep a couple of times, scrunched her face up, and pushed a squirmy purple extraterrestrial out of her vagina. The whole thing was wetter than I thought, and the baby bigger than I could have imagined, but it all took less than two minutes, and everyone was smiling and relaxed and possibly even high. And the mother didn't look so extra-special, and except for the mustache and the forearm tattoo, the father didn't look so different from Bashkim. The video was telling us that anyone could do this. And the book, too, said in many, many words — so many goddamned words, I barely skimmed a quarter of them — that it was no big deal. Some British doctor had figured out early in the century that it isn't childbirth that hurts, it's fear. We scare ourselves into feeling contraction pain. The doctor had a penis

251

and never felt so much as a menstrual cramp in his life, but he lived in a world alongside women, so I guess that meant he could know what they felt, right? He was the one who'd gone to medical school in England and I graduated middle of the class from a public high school in one of the crappiest cities in America, so who was I to question him?

I was excited to see Bashkim and tell him that we'd done it. The baby was beautiful, the doctor said it herself. We were actually doing okay for ourselves.

Yllka was outside of the Ross smoking a cigarette when I got to work. I tried to pretend I didn't see her, to save both of us the trouble, but it was hard to hide my ballooning body.

"Elsie," she said. She looked surprised at the sight of me, as if it was impossible that I could show up to my shift on time. She stubbed out her cigarette and straightened her skirt, which wasn't wrinkled in the first place.

"Hi," I said.

"What? Oh, hi, Elsie."

She looked back at the employee entrance. It seemed like she was waiting for somebody but nobody went in or came out.

"Chilly outside, huh?" I said.

"It's cold, yes. Did you get to your doctor's appointment?"

"Yes," I said. "Everything's fine. It's good, actually. Really good."

"That's good, it's good," she said. She started to head for the door, and I was disappointed that she didn't seem to want to know more, even though it was her and the Albanian wives who'd shamed me into seeing the doctor in the first place. Why didn't she want to know that she was right, and that I was stupid for having been afraid? That her precious little grandniece was beautiful, as verified by a bona fide blond doctor?

Yllka took a few steps and leaned against a car that didn't belong to her or, as far as I could tell, anyone she knew. She lit up another cigarette just seconds after stubbing out the first.

"You okay?" I asked.

She exhaled. She wasn't wearing a coat, but her shivering didn't seem like it came from the cold.

"I'm fine," she said.

"Okay, then. Just checking," I said and turned and headed for the door.

"I'm fine, Gjonni's fine. Twenty-five years in this country and we're fine. We started in

253

this country with nothing — with *less* than nothing — and now look at this." She waved her hand toward the neon lights and fake rock facade, and it was hard to tell if she was being sarcastic or for real.

I looked, but I didn't risk saying anything back, in case my answer was the wrong one.

"We went hungry for a long time so we could have this place. I mean, what did it matter, we were used to hunger. Big deal. It takes a lot of hunger to die from it. We knew that. You Americans don't know that. You think five minutes without a cheeseburger will kill you, the way some of these customers complain."

"I know, I'm usually the one they're complaining to," I said.

"Me? I would rather be a little hungry for a week and then buy a steak. Anyway." She ashed her cigarette. "I don't expect you Americans to know how to go without for five minutes, but these people." She shook her head. "We try to help them, you know? We try to set an example, but a week after they're here they want their cars and their swimming pools and their hearts' desires."

"Umm-hmm," I said.

"Fatmir in there, he was going to bring his wife over this month. They have a little baby, a little boy. And where's the money for the passage now? In some gypsy's pocket, that's where. Not even blown on a car. At least that he could sell back. Silly. Just so silly."

"I don't, like, really know," I said.

"*Oh, the money's coming, it's coming,* they say. From where? I want to know. You fall for that gypsy magic, you're even worse than the gypsies."

"What gypsies?"

"Not even gypsies, that's the worst part. Our own people. Our own people would do this to each other."

"Do what? I don't understand."

"Yes, exactly, you don't." She looked at me pityingly. "Aggie wrote to me. Bashkim had her sell their apartment. For what, to bring her over here, or at least to Greece with her parents? No, no, of course not. For more money for him to put into those stupid investments. Just like Fatmir, except Bashkim is in there feeling bad for Fatmir like everybody else, shaking his head, not realizing that when it's time for him to cash out, he'll be in the same position as Fatmir. 'No, no, no, Fatmir just made the wrong investments,' he says. My god, the skulls on these men."

It had been hours since I'd eaten, and Yllka was right, my American blood couldn't handle it. I was beginning to feel woozy.

"Where would Albanians have learned how to run a bank?" she said. "Albanians think they can put money into a bank and then the next month they have twice as much money, like it's magicians who run banks instead of regular people. This is how they think capitalism works. You put a little in, you get more and more out."

She was rambling on, and even lighting another cigarette didn't slow her down.

"So I say to Bashkim, 'Where do you think this money is coming from?' But he doesn't care, because the number in his account is going up, up, up. He sends Aggie all this money from his job here to put in the account, to invest, he says. But I say, 'What are you investing in? What is being built with this money? What is going to be built and sold so that you get your money back?' And he says, 'The government.' The government, he says! Albania's government! You believe the government now because it's a democracy, supposedly? Where did all of these democratic politicians come from, huh? They weren't shipped in from America. They were the same people in power before, now with a different name."

"Yllka," I said. "Slow down."

"How is Aggie supposed to live? She has no husband, no money, no apartment. Where is his heart?"

I winced when Yllka talked about Aggie like that, like a wife instead of an ex-wife-to-be.

"His heart is here," I said. "With me."

"Oh god," she said. "You're just as far gone as him."

"I'll talk to him. But he's not working this hard for nothing. He's obviously onto something."

"You really don't know this man, do you?"

"Of course I do. He's my," I said, but I couldn't think of the word to put at the end of that sentence.

"Do you know what Bashkim said when Gjonni and I picked him up from JFK a year ago? He said, 'The streets are black.' And we said, 'Of course the streets are black. The streets are paved,' thinking he was surprised that they weren't dirt. And he said, 'I thought the streets here were gold.' Do you understand that? He thought the streets here were made of *gold*. He thought that was true, not just an expression. A grown man believed that. We laughed so much at that time, but it turns out that wasn't funny after all."

I thought then that she must have been

confusing Bashkim for Adem or Fatmir. Bashkim wasn't any kind of naïve. That's one of the things that made me fall for him, that he already knew everything, or at least wasn't surprised by anything. That's how he got that swagger, the kind where he'd walk out to his car and start it so he could light a cigarette off the engine, when using the lighter that was always in his pocket would've been just fine. He'd pose against the hood like some kind of greaser, except the grease he modeled was all lard and vegetable oil instead of 10W-30.

And all of this was just occurring to me now, and I wondered who really was the naïve one.

"I'll talk to him," I said.

"Don't talk, just do," she said. "Talking is not going to put clothes on your baby. Just make sure you have something put aside. Promise me, Elsie. Promise."

"I promise," I said, but I said it the classic American way, which was to get someone to shut up. I didn't want to be the one making promises, I wanted to be the one hearing them.

Fatmir was manning the deep fryer as usual. He seemed more serious about his job that night, like he suspected Gjonni and Yllka would be watching him extrahard, working like he was paid by the cheese stick and could make back all the money he lost with a couple of good tables of pregaming middle schoolers en route to a Seven Minutes in Heaven party. But there weren't going to be any raises that night or in the near future, and if he had left out a coffee can for his own charity fundraiser, it would've stayed as empty as the one out front for MS. I thought about saying hello but didn't have the guts to pretend that everything was normal or, worse, to tell him everything would work out in the end. Instead I looked past him to Bashkim, who seemed calm enough from where I was standing, or rather the same as he always did, a little hunched over, lips pressed tight together to keep flies and his own sweat out while he worked the grill.

"Hey, babe," I said.

"Hi," he said, his lips opening up just enough to let the word out.

See, I thought, it can't be that bad. When he was in a real mood he wouldn't even bother to answer. He'd just look at me like he stepped right off the boat and forgot all of his English, like the Atlantic was still wedged between him and me.

"What's up?"

He shrugged. "Work," he said.

"As usual, right?"

"Always work."

"This kid's gonna pop out of me wearing orthopedic sneakers, I swear."

He shook his head. "No," he said.

"Well, the kid's got the feet for them, at least," I said. "I saw them at the doctor's office today. It was." I closed my eyes for a second and remembered her little dance, her slow, soft kicks. "It was pretty amazing."

He scraped charred bits of fat from the grill with his spatula. They dropped through the grates and caught fire and burned out almost immediately.

"I wish you would've been there," I said.

Scrape, scrape, sizzle.

"I mean, I know you had to work."

"You should not have to be working like this," he said.

I shrugged. "Everybody's gotta do it. No use complaining about it."

"I know how to work," Bashkim said.

"I know you do."

"I don't complain about it."

"I know."

"But you."

"But me what?"

"Look at you," he said. "You hang out of

260

that uniform. It doesn't even fit you anymore."

"Well, they don't make a maternity line of
waitress wear."

"It's shameful. Disgusting."

"Jesus," I said. Maybe I did prefer his
silent moods.

"You should not have to work like this,"
he said.

"It's not a big deal," I said.

"Your work should be at home. This is no
place for you."

"Well, it's where I am. I don't have much
choice in it, do I?"

He shook his head and pressed down on
the beef patties already overcooking on the
grill. "No, you don't have a choice. I have
decided. I don't want you here anymore."

"Bashkim," I said. I knew he was in a
mood and I was supposed to be careful
when he was in a mood, and if I thought
about it maybe I would've realized I was
more sad than pissed off that he didn't ask
a single question about the doctor, about
his own kid. But no matter what else I was
feeling, rage always won. It was like mixing
paints in art class: just the right amount of
red to blue made a pretty purple, and just
the right amount of white made it lavender,
but once you added black all you got was a

261

dark ugly gray.

"Go home. I'll tell Gjonni you can't work here anymore," he said.

"The fuck you will," I said.

He dropped the spatula. "The fuck I what?"

"The fuck you will. We don't have a choice, now do we? We don't have a pot to piss in."

He stepped closer to me. "You stop talking now."

"Fuck you! Don't touch me. If I'm so disgusting don't touch me."

That only made him grab on to my arm tighter. We had a crowd around us by this point, but neither one of us noticed it at that moment.

"What do you think you're doing with your money?" I said. "You're not some Wall Street whiz kid. You're not Gordon fucking Gekko. Why didn't you just drive out to Foxwoods if you wanted to throw all your money away? Why not just burn it for fuel?"

"Elsie," he said.

"We don't even have a real goddamned bed. We don't even have a crib or a diaper bag or any of the shit you need for a baby."

"You have to be quiet now," he said.

"You wanted this. You're the one who wanted this baby and now I'm going to be the one on the side of the street with a sign begging for money."

"Quiet," he said.

"And it's not just me. I bet you made your wife all the same kinds of promises you made me and I bet she's going to be out on the street, too, thanks to you. You think you're better than Fatmir? You think you're better than anyone? My god, you can't even take care of your damn self."

I never really believed it when people in accidents said they didn't remember a thing about what happened. It didn't seem possible to forget a thing like that. There were times I tried to forget entire passages of my life, banging my head against the wall to shake the bad things loose, but no matter what, I still remembered my mother sharing my twin bed with me for months after my father took off with their full-size one, and how I made my mother cry the last time I shat my pants because I was supposed to have been potty-trained for at least two years by then, and how I'd hit a kitten the first time I drove a car without supervision and drove away while it twitched because I was sure the suffering would kill me before it killed the cat. But honestly the moments before I opened my eyes and found the metal shelving and food service tins on top

of me are gone. I can imagine what Bashkim's eyes must have looked like before his
fists came down on me, but I can't remember them, and so I've always kind of
thought, even now, years after I was supposed to have learned better, that there was
something I must have misunderstood
about it all. Sometimes still I think that the
floor must have been extraslippery that
night, that I just fell and brought a mess
down on top of me. Sometimes I still think,
Well, Elsie, if it was Bashkim, think about it
from his perspective: you can be an extra-
superbitch.

I'm pretty sure that I never made a sound,
that it was Yllka who did all the yelling and
screaming when I came to, while Janice
pulled me up and checked me for fractures
and then brought me outside with a glass of
water when it was clear that nothing was
broken. She asked how my stomach felt and
I shrugged and she asked if I thought
something had happened to the baby and I
shook my head, and then she didn't ask any
more questions, just rubbed little circles on
my back and said, "I know, I know." I'd
never thought that much of Janice, but there
was something in the way she sat there that
made me think that she did know. Everybody except for me seemed to have already

learned it, whatever it was. Then Janice had to go back to her tables and to mine also, because Yllka forbade me to go back inside. For my own good, she said, not for Bashkim's.

So I don't remember everything about that night, but I did come out with something better than memory, which was a little bit of foresight. When I got home I pulled the leftover money Bashkim had given me for the doctor from my pocket and tucked it into a little flour tin someone had donated to us as a housewarming gift that had been sitting empty behind a box of potato flakes and a couple of cans of Campbell's chicken noodle. A rainy day was coming, it was almost certain, and I was going to need some shelter.

CHAPTER TEN:
LULJETA

You have to start taking Ahmet's phone calls before you can ask him for his car.

You learn more about him. His father runs a Subway franchise somewhere out on the West End. He expects Ahmet to work there and, eventually, take over, but Ahmet has different plans. He's majoring in business at UConn Waterbury, and he knows what a dead end a Subway life would be for him, that weird Subway smell infusing his entire wardrobe, the complaints of too little meat and too much shredded lettuce by customers in desperate need of an extra serving of vegetables. He's a modern guy, and his father is an old-fashioned guy, and he doesn't understand why his father would bring them all the way to America just to live the same old bleak Communist Subway lifestyle, with its beige turkey slices that lead to satiety but never pleasure.

"Nah, man, nah. Panera Bread, that's

where it's at. That's what I'ma get me," Ahmet says.

He speaks so naturally in such an American vernacular that the slight accent seems almost like an affect, but affects are generally adapted to impress people, whereas Ahmet's unplaceable one only confuses them. But Ahmet himself is not confusing. Ahmet himself is as transparent as the Sprite Zero that fills his ever-present Subway beverage canisters. He knows exactly what he wants and expresses it without reservation: first Panera in the ShopRite plaza on Chase; the second in Watertown next to the old two-screen cinema run by some distant relative of his; the steel-gray carbon-look vinyl skinz over the gas tank of his Kawasaki; and a nice girl. He's way into this hypothetical nice girl; not old-fashioned, not a subservient housewife like his mother, but *nice.* Someone who could run the books at his shops, like Yllka, but do it with a smile on her face, very unlike Yllka.

He talks about this nice girl, but meanwhile, he's spending more and more time with you. You aren't nice, no matter what ribbon you'd been handed back in kindergarten. You've shed the teacher's pet thing entirely over the past couple of weeks, acting surly and handing in assignments days late, and you're building up to skipping them altogether. What difference does it make, anyway? The $462 your mother managed to deposit in your college savings account won't pay for a semester at Western Connecticut State University any more than it would have paid for the same at NYU. Clearly that's how much investment has been made in your future: the equivalent of a new futon from Bob's Discount Furniture. It's about as much investment as had been made in your past, and only recently have you acquired the wherewithal for that to piss you way the hell off.

So Ahmet doesn't have a nice girl, or a good girl, or a smart girl, he has you, who every night falls asleep fantasizing about having punched Margarita right in the mouth, then coming home to tell your mother that you wish it had been her, with all her lies and silence and big talk about wanting what's best for you without ever once really planning for it. He has you, who won't even put out, not even a little bit, not even a kiss on the mouth.

That last part is what makes him think he has a nice girl. It never occurs to Ahmet that you would be willing to put out if he were a bearded denim model prone to bouts of depression that only you could talk him through. Ahmet is just a regular nice guy, one who deserves a nice girl with a moral code that truly forbids putting out, and you feel bad that what you really seek from him is not the day's surplus white chocolate chip macadamia nut cookies, which he offers via text at 10:01 P.M. every night, or the tight abs that he somehow finds time to work on at Gold's Gym between work and school and little not-nice-girl you. What you really have your eye on is his Civic hatchback, a compact, reliable thing whose backseat folds down into something approaching a sleeping cabin and whose efficient Japanese engine could get you to Texas with the $462 previously earmarked for a semester of medical sonographing textbooks.

"I need to do it. I need to meet my family. My *Albanian* family," you'd emphasized. You strategized this, knowing that even if Ahmet is the Panera to his father's Subway, he could never bring home someone without Albanian blood.

"Yes, yes, you should. It's wrong that you don't know them. I can't even imagine," he'd answered.

And after two short weeks, you announce that you are going. You are going to Texas, come hell or high water, dammit. You'll be leaving on Friday, coincidentally a week before his spring classes begin.

"What? How?" he asks. He appears genuinely hurt that you'd make a decision that large without consulting him, your fake short-term boyfriend.

"Greyhound, I guess. Or I'll hitchhike. It doesn't matter, I'm just going to go."

He slaps an open hand onto his forehead and holds it there, like he's holding a compress onto an open head wound. "Hitchhike? For serious? You? You want to be raped and murdered?"

"I don't *want* to be."

"That's just . . . It's just crazy. What does your mother say about this?"

"She says fine, what does she care?"

"Your mother says she doesn't care?" he asks, incredulous.

"She doesn't not care," you say. "It's just, like, I'm basically an adult, and of course she understands. Who wouldn't understand wanting to know your own brothers and sisters, your own flesh and blood? I mean, what's more important than family?" you say, and you don't even care that you're mostly just quoting the Kardashians.

Ahmet understands this, though, because he is the type who will shake down his sister's thug boyfriend if he keeps her out past 11:00 P.M.

270

"I just wish you wouldn't take the bus," he says. "You know there's crazy people on those things, right? Like, guys with swords that will take off your head?"

"I'd rather not take the bus, too," you say. "But."

"But what?"

"But I can't afford to fly, and I don't have a car."

At first he's silent. He shakes his head, takes a sip of his Sprite, leans back in the seat of the Civic in the Stop & Shop parking lot where you hold most of your dates.

"What if I come with you?" he says.

"What? No, I can't ask you to do that," you answer, and in fact, you asking him to escort you is not at all a part of the plan. Why can he not see that you just need to temporarily relieve him of the glut of motorized vehicles on his hands?

He throws his hands in the air. "I have my break from school, and maybe I miss a few days afterwards."

"But your job. Your father," you say.

"My sister will take over. She's grounded anyway, she won't be having any fun for a little while."

"No, that's crazy. I can't. You can't do that," you say, almost panicking now, because his plan is indeed more practical than yours.

"I don't want you to go alone. I can't believe your mother would want you to go alone. I mean, no." He shakes his head. "I won't let you do that. I'm coming. I've never been to Texas, anyway."

"You have no reason to go to Texas. You only go to Texas if you have a reason," you argue.

"My reason is to protect you. Your mother should want that, she shouldn't want you to go alone. I'm going to talk to her, actually. She's as crazy as the bus people if she lets you take a Greyhound to Texas."

"No! No," you say. You close your eyes and take a moment to think things through. On the one hand, you'd be sharing a few cubic feet for several days with a guy you had never even kissed. On the other hand, with two of you, there would be someone to help with the driving, and you could just pretend to sleep during your turns in the passenger seat. Plus he knows Yllka, so he has some connection to your family in some distant way, just like all Albanians seem to have some connection to all other Albanians in some distant way. He would be the adhesive between the odd American mutt and her purebred Albanian siblings. He could provide enough white chocolate chip macadamia nut cookies to get you through a couple thousand miles.

You exhale slowly. Ahmet wasn't a part of the plan, but then again, look how far you'd come so quickly by not thinking anything all the way through.

"Okay," you say. "But we're leaving on Friday. Ten A.M. sharp."

Does your mother really think it's fine that you're going to Texas? Does she really understand your need to be part of a family that isn't composed exclusively of her?

She doesn't think anything. She's as aware of your plan as you recently were of the existence of your siblings, which is to say, not at all. She knows something is up, because she's noticed that you've been talking to her less and less and to your phone more and more. When she asks, you tell her it's Teena on the other end, and you make sure to clear out your call log after every conversation. She knows; she's checked, just like she checks your text messages, for which you've kept only a strategic, boring few that reveal nothing other than the due date of your history paper (already passed) and a brief recap of the previous week's *Scandal,* which Teena had missed on account of her three-week anniversary with the new Burlington Coat Factory security guard. Ahmet exists only as a contact named Matt in your phone, and Yllka is renamed Yvonne, which just happens to be the name of the woman for whose drippy children you occasionally babysit. Everything checks out, but still, she knows you're up to something. You don't have proof, but you're sure that your mother has scoured your room looking for drug paraphernalia or condoms, and you wonder which would have been worse for her to find.

And what if she had been brave enough to ask you outright, and you had been brave enough to explain why you have to go? How would you have summarized it?

She lied to you. Your father wasn't a ghost in the Balkans, he was a man waiting to be discovered right here in your own native land. It doesn't matter why she lied, even if it was to protect you from whatever she thought you needed protection from. She made decisions for you that weren't hers to make. Yes, she made them on your behalf at a time when you had no capacity for language and freely shat all over yourself every few hours, but the number of words in your vocabulary is now an above-average seventeen thousand or so, thanks to the books you read for pleasure when television and even the entire Internet grow too boring, and you have been potty-trained for a good fifteen years. She's had plenty of time to come clean, and plenty of time to have convinced you that she made the right decision all those years ago. She could have explained to you that your father had managed to love you only while you were still an abstract thing, a thing that only loved back and cooed and did not repeatedly shit itself all night and then cry about it. She could have explained that he was a frightened man, and a frightened man, like a frightened dog, was a potentially dangerous thing. She could have said those things instead of repeating, if the topic ever came up, that your father was simply an asshole, the same term she applies to people who don't matter at all, like guys who cut her off in traffic and Bill O'Reilly.

But if she lied about where he was, who's to say she wasn't lying about what he was? What if he wasn't just some asshole, and you weren't better off without him?

To be fair, you acknowledge that you've been lying right back to your mother, and there's nothing in the Don't Lie kindergarten code that says it's okay to do it if it's been done to you first. And also, if you really, really think about it — if you choose not to lie even to yourself — you aren't sure if your anger can be distilled down to the fact that your mother has told you that it was an immigration paperwork snafu that kept your father away instead of the truth, which is that it was either her or him or some combination thereof. What you learned from Yllka, for example, doesn't explain all the nights you had quivered with rage in your bed before you even knew of the existence of the rest of your family. That rage has no clearly identified source or target. Maybe what you had gotten from Yllka isn't the origin of your rage but an end point, a bull's-eye.

And let's say you go through with this trip. Let's say you find yourself eating dinner with a brand-new family, leaving your mother to accompany Mamie to her nightly meetings in church basements and Skype with Greta when Greta could get a signal on a neighbor's unprotected wireless network. What makes you think that adding members to your family will somehow lead to conclusions instead of exponentially adding to the questions?

You think about those things in your bed the night before your departure, and there you are again, quivering and cold, full of rage and fear and a new ingredient in this toxic stew, something along the lines of a preemptive regret, which some wise old people might call foresight but which a seventeen-year-old would call superfreaking annoying. Maybe you are, after all, a shitty person who's just bored and doesn't care about spiting those who have loved and reared and sacrificed for you. You hope not — something a truly shitty person would likely not do — but you suppose you will find out when you depart in twelve or so hours.

"Don't come up," you tell Ahmet when he arrives Friday morning. "The neighbors will notice."

You think about the houses that sandwich the one you live in, a single-family commune of old people on one side and a triple-decker filled with four generations of the same Puerto Rican family on the other. All these years in the same place and you don't know anybody by name, except for Hector, with whom you've shared a bus stop since kindergarten but never a conversation. That's exactly the kind of thing that should've made getting into Ahmet's Honda easy.

What made it not easy was the one single

person who did give a shit. This morning she almost ruined everything by giving a shit, or rather leaving a shit in the form of a new blank journal on the table with your lunch, trying to make what she thought was just a random day special, like when you were younger and she'd get up extra early to get some of those Pillsbury cinnamon buns in the oven, leaving the extra white goo out for you to slurp up. She didn't bother to write a note to go along with the journal, because it's pretty clear what the gift is supposed to say. *Cheer up. Write out your feelings, especially if it means we won't have to talk about them later.*

Emotional blackmail, that's what the gift is. An emotional pacifier. It's cheap, and it's slightly effective, like generic cold medicine. It would've been much easier to leave even yesterday, before your mother went and pulled this goddamned journal crap. It's some corny Barnes & Noble clearance thing, the kind of uninspired Brass City Mall token one would expect from a Brass City Mallrat boyfriend on Valentine's Day, and you want to tear it to shreds for what it does to you, which is make you stop and wonder what exactly it is you think you're doing, driving off with a near stranger to find a perfect stranger who never in his life made a trip to the mall for you, who never in his life even stopped in to say good night.

This stupid journal, with its insulting asshole empty pages just waiting to be filled, telling you that there are stories you could find for it right here if you could only find your way in.

Your phone buzzes. *You coming? You need help?*

No, you tell yourself, I shouldn't *have* to leave this way. If she'd just given you some other choice.

Yes, and I don't need help, you respond. You don't know if you'll be going forward or sideways or backward, but it's time to make a move in some direction.

CHAPTER ELEVEN: ELSIE

A week after the argument with Bashkim at the Ross — that's what I called it, the argument, like we'd disagreed on what shape of pasta to buy, or whether the toilet paper should hang over or under — and I still hadn't seen or talked to him, both of us pretending we were the holdout, the strong one, waiting to hear our apologies. I'd been back to the apartment just to grab enough of my things to get me through a few days at Mamie's, where I showed up unannounced, and before she had a chance to ask me what I was doing there, I told her that the walls in our apartment were being painted and her little unborn grandchild shouldn't be exposed to the fumes.

"Huh," she answered, but didn't ask any questions.

On the second day she asked what color the walls were being painted, and I told her ecru, a color I'd heard of but couldn't define, realizing that if she ever stepped foot in there again she'd know straightaway that I was lying.

On the third day, she asked why my apartment being painted meant I couldn't go in to work, and I said I'd been feeling sick so I took a few days off.

"You put down a lot of beef Stroganoff for someone who doesn't feel good," she said.

I told her it was doctor's orders, iron and protein and all that.

On the fourth day, she stopped asking questions and was just happy to have someone around to keep her company while she drank, so she could convince herself it was a social habit.

"I miss having you here," Mamie said. The ice in her glass clinked like a meek little dinner bell, a come-and-get-it that she had already come and got. "It's too quiet around here now."

"I still live here," Greta said from the recliner.

"Yeah, of course you do, Greta, but you're such a goddamned mouse I don't even know when you're here and when you're not. You don't yap and burp and fart all over the house like Shamu over here," Mamie said.

"If you're trying to get me to stick around, you might try saying something nice every once in a while," I said.

"Oh come on, you know I'm just teasing. You're just really starting to pop. That kid of yours is gearing up to be a sumo wrestler."

"She's still wearing a smaller pants size than you," Greta said, and I smiled and realized that I missed having my sister around.

"You hear from any colleges yet, Greta?" I asked.

"Not yet," she said. "I don't know, I'm not getting my hopes up."

"It's not about hope for you. You're not just getting by on wishful thinking like the rest of us," I said.

"Don't speak for me. I don't do any wishful thinking," Mamie said.

"Of course not," I said, just because I didn't want to get into it with her. Mamie didn't do any wishful speaking, that was for sure, but of course it was some kind of secret wish that got her out of bed every morning. You'd never hear her talk about anything as pathetic as hope aloud, but she'd been known to spend her last ten dollars on a few scratch-off tickets while the milk in our refrigerator soured, and if she recouped two of those dollars she walked around glowing like Ed McMahon had just shown up on our front step with a bouquet of balloons and an oversize novelty check. Me and Bashkim weren't so different in that way, which was another thing I didn't want to bring up. Only Greta was really different from the rest of us, but it was in a way she couldn't help, and in a way that wasn't making her life any easier. But at least she had a plan. She saved every penny she earned, from the first dollar on a newspaper route she inherited when the last paperboy graduated to selling LSD, to babysitting the neighbor's future sociopath, to her current weekly paychecks bagging endless conveyor belts of canned corn and Giggle Noodle at ShopRite. The sum total couldn't have been near enough to pay for even a semester at the kind of college she wanted to attend, the kind of place with a quad and just enough black kids to put in a photograph on the brochure, but it had to be more than I'd ever seen in one account in my whole life.

I needed a plan. I needed to be more like Greta. It was too late for me to get a paper route or a scholarship or anything like that, but I decided then that there could be no more impulse trashy-magazine purchases at the checkout line at ShopRite, no more cans of black beans when a bag of dried ones would go twice as far for half as much. All I had to do was tighten the belt a little, and in about five more years, I might have enough put away to strike out on my own, and then there'd be no more tiptoeing around Bashkim or loitering at Mamie's. The kid would be almost old enough to chip in at that point. It could use its nimble little fingers to darn the socks I fumbled over.

"Fuck," I said.

"What?" Greta said.

"Watch your mouth," Mamie said.

I shook my head. "I need to find some new work. Something better than what I've been doing. These nickel-and-dime tips aren't going to cut it."

Greta nodded and smiled a little, and Mamie bit into her wine-slicked ice cube and spit the little broken slivers back into the glass.

"Good luck with that," Mamie said. "If you come across anyone handing out real jobs to people with no skills or experience, make sure you let me know."

"I'm going to talk to Uncle Eddie. He always seems to be able to hook somebody up with something."

"Entry-level factory jobs don't pay any better than the Ross," Mamie said. "Believe me, I've done 'em."

"Not at first, but at least you can move up. At least there's overtime."

"I think it sounds like a good idea," Greta said.

"Yeah, look at the lifestyle manufacturing work has afforded us," Mamie said. "Sitting in this place is like winning a Showcase Showdown."

"It affords you that box of wine you're hooked up to. It affords you cable TV."

"Wine's got grapes. It's vitamin C," Mamie said.

"A new job's a start," Greta said. "And it doesn't have to be the end if you don't want it to be."

"The two of you, I swear, you got everything figured out," Mamie said. She nearly spit out the last of her wine before she walked away to refill it, this time taking her glass into her bedroom so we couldn't bust her cozy little merlot bubble.

"So, uh, how's everything going?" Greta asked.

"Okay," I said.

"Still getting sick?"

"Nah, morning sickness is gone." There was another kind of sickness I was feeling, a ferocious heartburn I got when I thought about facing Bashkim again, or when I wondered why he hadn't even bothered to look for me here, the sole place in the world he knew I could go. But Greta was only asking about the kid, just like everyone else. She was asking about the thing that still had a chance of turning out okay.

"That's good," Greta said.

"Yeah, it's good. How about you? How are you doing?"

"What do you mean?"

"I mean how are you doing? What's up with you?"

"Oh," she said. "Fine, I guess. Pretty good."

"You look good," I said, and I wasn't even lying. Her cheeks had a little color to them, maybe because Mamie's thermostat was set perpetually at sixty-four, but maybe not. Maybe it was the glow of the light at the end of her tunnel. She was almost there. She was almost ready to tell the rest of us what else was out there.

"Oh," Greta said. She was blushing a little, and I realized what I said was probably the nicest compliment she'd gotten in years, maybe ever, and it made me want to cry.

"I'm sorry," I said.

"Sorry for what?"

I shrugged. "I guess I just mean I'm proud

286

of you."

Greta did me the favor of not asking what those things had to do with each other. She just wrapped her arms around her legs and said, into her knees, "Thanks."

We sat like that, curled up like conch shells, like we were waiting for someone, anyone, to put their ears to us.

"Things are hard," I said eventually, when the pasta maker infomercial faded into basic cable oblivion, replaced by the easy, soothing voices of a soft rock compilation.

"I'm sure they are," Greta said.

"I know you're sure. You told me that before all this even started."

"All what? Did something happen?"

"No," I said. It was an automatic response, to deny. "It's just the usual stuff. No money. We haven't even started putting together the baby's room yet. I don't even want to think about the hospital bill that's coming."

"Yeah, well, it's just a bill. They can't put you in prison for not paying them."

"They can't?"

"What? No. Not anymore, anyway. Not in this country."

"Oh," I said. "Then what are we all so afraid of?"

"I don't know, but it works. I'm afraid."

"Me too," I said.

Reunited and it feels so good, the infomercial sang.

"If you need anything, just like for now, I
could lend you some, like, money or something," Greta said.

"What? No, that's not what I meant. I
wasn't hinting at anything. I'm just saying
it's hard."

"I know, and it's not gonna get any easier
before the kid is born, so . . ."

"No."

"Why not?" She was getting defensive, or
maybe excited. "I have like six thousand
dollars in the bank just sitting there right
now."

Six thousand dollars. I tried to wrap my
head around that number. How the hell had
she managed that? I wondered if she was
sneaking off to Foxwoods on the weekends,
straddling three or four slot machines, but
then I realized she wouldn't risk losing. She
did it the old-fashioned way, the way I
didn't think actually worked: she'd earned
it.

"That's for school," I said. "For you."

"I don't need it until next year. You could
pay it back by then, right?"

"Yeah, of course, but —"

"But what? You can't put the baby on an
air mattress. You can't dress it in your hand-

me-downs."

"But you said you weren't going to help me," I said. "Back when this started."

She stared back at the TV screen. *Just call me angel of the morning, angel.* "It's not for you, it's for the baby."

Then it wasn't up to me to say yes or no, was it?

"Okay," I said. "If you really really want to. But you don't have to."

"Someone has to," she said.

She was so right that I didn't even have to confirm it. "Maybe just a thousand. Or two, tops. I'll start paying you back next week. I promise," I said.

I'd finally hit the age where I could legally work on heavy equipment, even if I couldn't legally go out for a beer afterward, so it was probably about time I did what my forebears crossed the ocean for and took a job at a factory. It was in our nature, the way royalty or sickle-cell anemia was for other blood-lines. The Ferruccis at Ferrucci Manufacturing respected that Great-Uncle Eddie had refused to join the union, which to him was Communist like Russia and full of either winos or whiners — it was hard to tell with his accent — and so they'd made him fore-man years before. In turn he'd acted like our family employment agency, scoring jobs for a bunch of cousins I wouldn't recognize in a police lineup.

Uncle Eddie had kissed me on the mouth when I stopped by the next day to ask him about any openings at Ferrucci. He was happier at that moment than he was when I made my first communion, and told me to show up at five.

"Third shift?" I asked.

"No, first, Elsie. Five A.M."

"Five A.M.?" I said. I usually went to bed closer to that hour than rose at it. "There's nothing that starts in the actual daytime?"

"Yes, for people who have earned it. Your cousin Steve was here two years before he could come in at seven. And I'm not gonna put you on the third shift, not with the kind of people who work overnight."

From what Mamie had told me, Steve was a cousin who'd actually been in a couple of police lineups. I figured if he could do this job then I could, too, and probably well enough to make it to shift boss before the end of the year.

"Fine," I said. "I'll be there."

I thought that at a real job there'd be some kind of application, an interview, a permed human resources lady named Sherri to fill out paperwork with before finally winding up on the floor, but somehow Uncle Eddie cut through that commie bullshit and I had a box of widgets and a metal folding chair ten minutes after walking into the shop the next day. I was an inspector, a job that sounded like it should come with a tan overcoat and tobacco pipe, but all it meant was that I had to look at the little metal ferrules Ferrucci manufactured and decide whether they were deformed or not. I didn't even know what a ferrule was until that day, and it turned out they were just little metal rings that wrap around other things to keep them from splitting. They didn't even get to be their own things, just tiny little parts of something better. Still, I was kind of excited. I thought about all the little round stickers I found on the inside of my clothes back when they were new: INSPECTED BY 54, INSPECTED BY 7, and it occurred to me that 54 was a person, and 7 was a person, and those people got their own stickers that made it from Indonesia or wherever they lived all the way to the Kmart in Waterbury, which made them seem a little famous, like they had their own little autographs that went out all over the world. The ferrules I'd be inspecting wouldn't get any stickers, but they'd at least have my fingerprints on them, and they could end up anywhere, on a pencil in Egypt or an electric guitar in California.

"Eddie said we're supposed to train you, but you don't look like a sea monkey so you could probably figure it out yourself," one of the three ladies at the table said when I sat down. "But just in case, I'll show you what you need to know. I'm Deena, by the way."

"Rini," said another.

"Margot," said another.

"Elsie," I said. Deena was a black lady with the ruddy sort of orangey red hair that came from years of abusing drugstore dye, probably buying whatever shade happened to be on clearance that day. The ladies next to her, Rini and Margot, both had sandy, fluffy perms and eyeliner just slightly more purple than the circles under their eyes. They were white, but they didn't look any more like Rosie the Riveter than Deena did. None of them had neat pin curls tucked beneath cotton kerchiefs, and they didn't wear blue jumpsuits like in World War II–era photos of factory women, back when ladies wore Pan-Cake makeup and lipstick even to work on heavy machinery, because who knew when a news camera might show up to make stars out of them? These ladies were all in dungarees and sweatshirts that their sons had probably outgrown, Giants or Raiders logos splashed across their chests, thin gold cross necklaces tucked safely away under the neckbands.

"How old are you, Elsie? You look like you could be one of my daughter's friends," Rini said.

"Almost twenty. I don't really have friends, though, so."

The three of them thought that was a hoot. Margot laughed so hard she sprayed her grape soda over a boxful of ferrules.

"You don't need friends when you got co-workers, lady. There's no time for anything else," Deena said.

"Seriously, I see more of you guys than I do my husband," said Rini.

"You're welcome for that," said Margot.

"All right, quiet down already. Let's not scare her off. Let's let the job itself do that," Deena said.

Deena wasn't just giving me credit when she said I could figure out the job on my own — either the threads on the ferrules were right or they weren't, they either screwed in or didn't, and there was a box for the *did*s and a box for the *didn't*s. So long as I could twist my wrist and remember which box was on the right and which on the left, I could be Helen Keller and pass my performance review.

"The trouble is, when they move you up onto one of them machines, they think you already learned everything you need to know by sitting here plugging screws into holes. No training, you know? That's why I'd rather just stay here at this table — my husband, Scotty, lost the tip of his thumb his first time running a lathe machine."

"My mom's missing half of two of her fingers," I said.

"My husband got the tip of his middle finger chopped off," Rini said. "Now when he flips someone off it's like he's missing a letter or something. ' 'Uck you!' "

"My husband got cut off from my vagina after he refused to recaulk the goddamn bathtub like I told him to three years ago," Margot said.

Turned out that all the brainpower you had left over from inspecting ferrules was funneled into hating men, and if their productivity on the job was near as high as their productivity in coming up with punch lines, those ladies would have been able to get a whole day's work done in three hours. I caught on quick. After a couple of generations the immigrant work ethic Uncle Eddie had stepped off the boat with had faded, and by the time lunch was over I was right

there with them telling jokes, the ones I'd
overheard back in high school at the neigh-
boring lunch tables that I wasn't invited to
sit at.

"So this guy is walking along the beach," I
said, "and sees this woman with no arms
and no legs crying in the sand. He says,
'What's the matter?' and she says, 'I've
never been hugged by a man before.' So he
picks her up in his arms and hugs her, but
when he puts her back down she's still crying. So he goes, 'Why are you still crying?'
and she goes, 'I've never been kissed by a
man before.' So he picks her up in his arms
and kisses her, but when he puts her back
down she's still crying. So he goes, 'Why
are you still crying?' and she goes, 'I've
never been fucked by a man before.' So he
picks her up and throws her into the ocean
and goes, 'There, you're fucked.'"

The ladies all laughed the way the kids at
the lunch table at Crosby High had, only
this time I wasn't waiting to be surrounded
in the locker room by them and kicked in
the crotch like a boy. Deena, Rini, and
Margot were Mamie's age, but their hearts
weren't near as hard as their helmeted
hairdos made them look. They all had guys
they called their kids' fathers and different
guys they called their husbands. They all

had a decade or two on me, but they didn't treat me like a snotty teen at the mall. For a minute I almost wondered what I was doing wrong with my life, because I was kind of having fun doing the thing in the world that was supposed to rob the most joy from you.

"Everything is going okay here, yeah?" Uncle Eddie said. Nobody heard or saw him coming over because we were hee-hawing over whatever Rini just said, everything just a little funnier than it should've been because of her French Canadian twang.

"Oh yeah, she's picking it up just fine," Deena said. "A chip off the ol' block."

"I hope she's better than the block she was chipped from. Her father was a sonofabitch," Uncle Eddie said and walked away, clicking the metal button of a pen behind his back over and over again, the metronome that kept all the machines on that floor running in perfect time.

"I'm surprised he'd hire you when you're pregnant, even if you are his niece," Deena said.

"How did you know I was pregnant?" I'd worn my baggiest T-shirt in — INSPECTED BY 39 — and was hoping I passed for just chubby.

She whipped a styrofoam peanut at my belly. "If that's all gas, I recommend laying

296

off the franks 'n' beans for a while."

"I didn't think I was showing that much," I said.

"You're showing enough."

"No ring on your finger," Margot said.

"I'm not married."

"You gonna get married?"

I shrugged. "Not anytime soon."

"Guy still in the picture? Not one of those cut-and-run types?"

It had been a good week since I'd seen Bashkim, but he was still in whatever picture I had in my mind. On the edges, maybe, a little blurry, but he was there.

"He's around," I said.

"I tell you, you girls need to be more particular about who you let in there," Rini said, shaking her head.

"It's not like he's some loser," I said. I surprised myself, sounding as defensive about Bashkim as he sounded about himself.

"Is he a winner? Because there's a big gray space between winner and loser and I don't think you should settle for it."

"All right, leave her alone already," Deena said. "Listen, they might look like washed-up old hags but they were young sluts once, too. They're only saying it because we've all been in your shoes."

"Yeah, maybe exactly those shoes," Rini said. "I think I donated them. You get them at the Goodwill?"

"Probably," I said.

"Hey, I got one for you," Deena said. "Why is a toilet better than a woman?"

"Why?" I said.

"Because a toilet doesn't keep calling you up after you use it. Another one: What do you tell a woman with two black eyes?"

"Nothing, you already told her twice," Margot answered.

"The one I heard goes, 'You don't listen!' " I said.

"How long does it take for a man to get dinner?" Rini said. "As long as it takes for him to take off his belt."

"Stop already," Deena said.

Rini didn't. "Why did the woman cross the road? That's not the point, what's the bitch doing out of the kitchen?"

"I don't like these," Margot said.

"Okay, what's the fastest way to a man's heart? Through his chest with a knife."

"Better."

"Why is it so hard to find a good-looking, sensitive man? Because those guys already have boyfriends."

"What do you call a woman who knows where her husband is every night? A widow,"

Margot added.

"Come on, Elsie, don't you know any more?" Rini asked.

I shrugged. "I'm newer at this than you," I said. "I know some dead baby jokes."

"Oh, Christ, don't you dare, not in your condition." Rini made the sign of the cross over her chest. "God will listen to those and it will come back to you somehow."

"So God doesn't listen to all the sexist jokes?"

"He doesn't have to. The baby isn't here yet, so it still stands a chance. Men and women together? Ha."

"You guys have listened to too much Jackie Mason," I said.

"We've listened to too much everything. Don't listen to us bitter old broads. Don't listen to your uncle Eddie, don't listen to your mother, don't listen to your husband or boyfriend or whatever he is. Take care of you and everybody else around you will be better off," Deena said.

"Oh, Dear Abby chiming in over here," Margot said.

"It's just a theory. Why don't one of you gals give it a try and see how it works out for you?"

"I'm perfectly happy," Rini said.

"Uh-huh."

"Me too, 'cause it's quitting time," Margot said.

"That's happiness, right. It's all about what you're not doing, it has nothing to do with what you are doing," Deena said.

"Somebody's ragging it today," Rini said.

Deena sighed. "Yeah, I guess I am. The monthly visitor, the curse. The curse of being able to let out for three days what I feel on all the rest of them."

I didn't want the day to end on that low note, so I pretended I didn't hear her over the hydraulic huff and puff of the machines all around us. "Good night, ladies," I said. "See you all tomorrow."

"Tomorrow, and for years and years after that," Rini said.

Deena slapped her hand down on the table. "Goddammit, I said be nice to the girl."

I wished I had Deena, Rini, and Margot as my cavalry after work, when, after too many days in the same recycled pair of underwear, there was no putting off going back to the apartment I hadn't even had a chance to get used to calling home. Bashkim wouldn't be there in the flesh, but he would be there in essence, his tank tops draped over the shower rod to dry, the smell of Brut in the

300

air like some musky macho tree in bloom. I was bracing myself so hard against him that I didn't even think about Yllka, at least until she intercepted me on the stairway on my way up.

"Elsie, you're home," she said.

Sometimes I felt like English was my second language, too, because coming up with the right words could be so damn hard. *Home* didn't seem quite right, but I was coming up blank otherwise. My things were in there, my pillow and the drool on my pillowcase, even Bashkim's scent, which he emitted but I was the recipient of. It was homelike. It was home enough.

"I need some stuff," I said.

"Oh," she said. "Are you not staying?"

"I'm not sure. I wasn't planning to," I said. It wasn't in the plan, but since when had I been known to stick with plans? Now that I was there, my legs were twitchy to get up those stairs, into a space that I'd half-paid for with money that I'd earned myself. It wasn't much to speak of, but it was all I could speak of. I was thirsty for tap water from my own foggy Burger King Star Wars collectible glasses, not the identical set at Mom's.

"Oh," she said again. When I started climbing the steps upstairs, she called out,

301

"He didn't mean to hurt you."

"Of course he did. That's what fists do," I said.

"I mean he didn't mean to hurt you forever."

"I don't know what that means."

"What I mean is." She sighed. "Does it still hurt?"

"Not really," I said. "Are you being literal?"

"Being what? No, I just mean, are you still sore?"

I paused a second. "I guess I'm fine."

"What I mean is that he was very angry and he meant it at the time, but that was just a little moment, and now he's feeling sorry all of the time."

"He hasn't said he's sorry. I haven't heard from him at all."

"He's scared. He thinks you're gone forever. It's hard for him to say sorry, but even harder for him to say he's scared."

"So you have to say it for him instead? Uh-uh. I don't accept that kind of apology."

I waited for her to remind me that it was my own big mouth that started the trouble in the first place, but Yllka just sighed and turned away. "Yes, well, that is your choice. I have to learn to stay out of these things," she said.

It was the last thing I expected to hear from Yllka, and I wondered if she'd gotten into her own trouble with Bashkim. She didn't look bruised anywhere, and I couldn't imagine Bashkim laying down any law with her. Probably she just didn't want to talk to me anymore. Probably she figured she shouldn't block my exit.

"Yeah, well. I'm going to go upstairs," I said.

"And you're not coming back to work?" she asked.

"No, I got another job," I said. "Tell Cheryl and Janice I said sorry for having to cover my sections, will you?" I didn't like those ladies at first, but in the end it turned out they weren't really that bad. They were like everyone else, broken things stuck back together with a kind of epoxy that ensured they would never be shattered again.

"You want me to say you're sorry for you?" she said. "No, that's the kind of thing I shouldn't do, you're right."

"Fine, I'll let them know myself sometime then."

"That would be nice," Yllka said.

"Okay," I said. "Bye." And we turned our backs to each other without waving, as if we both knew we weren't really saying goodbye.

Almost everything in the apartment was the same, maybe even a little cleaner than usual. I wondered if Bashkim was a better house-keeper than me, even though he never put his hand on a broom when I was around. It was probably just that he didn't get the chance to dirty anything up. He barely had a reason to have an apartment at all, as much as he worked, and yet he'd been so happy to move out of the boardinghouse and into his own place, so he must have been just as desperate as I was to make a little home for himself. It meant something to have somewhere to put up your own ugly string art with broken frames that would never hang totally straight. It felt good to be there again. At first I didn't want it to feel good, but then I figured I shouldn't ever chase away a good feeling, so I pulled up a chair to the kitchen table and let myself sit with it.

And then the good feeling faded, as good feelings do, and I remembered what I was there for. I grabbed a few of my things from the drawers and closet and shoved them into a couple of the plastic Pathmark shop-ping bags that seemed to procreate underneath the kitchen sink. When I had what I needed, enough clothes to get me through another week but not so many that I would never need to return, I started to head for the door, but suddenly a wave of fatigue hit that nearly crumpled my puffy, achy body in place.

"Christ," I said aloud. I thought for a second that I was blacking out, but then I realized that my eyes were just closed, and there was such relief that I thought how nice it must feel to be in a coma, never having to open your eyes again. I shuffled over to the mattress, so deflated by then that it was nothing more than a tarp between me and the dirty floor, and I lay down. Those early shifts were going to take some getting used to.

Bashkim tried to be quiet when he came in early the next morning. He cracked open the door, saw me there, and went back out into the kitchen to take off his shoes and pants. Then he lay down next to me without touching me, didn't even grab a blanket even though it was freezing in the room. I was awake for all of it, but I didn't say anything. When his breathing got deep and heavy, which meant he was asleep, I checked my watch and saw that it was time for me to get up, and I tried to return the favor by being as quiet as I could be, feeling blindly around for my shoes and pants, which I didn't remember taking off. His breathing halted for a second and then returned to normal, so I knew that he woke up despite my tiptoeing around, but he didn't bother trying to find anything to say, either. I tried to ignore the feeling I had, or convince myself that I was confusing it with another, more suitable feeling, but there was no denying it: I felt glad. And I felt sorry, sorry for being away all this time, sorry for making him so mad back at the diner. I'd been waiting and waiting to hear *sorry* from him but instead it got trapped inside of me and it was what I felt above all things, more than love, more than anger. Shit, I thought, because it meant I was still tethered to him. I had an obligation to see it through until I was not sorry, and I wondered if that was what responsibility to other people was all about, sticking around until you made up to them whatever it was you fucked up to begin with. I touched my belly, and the girls at work were right: I was huge, and I was tethered to this baby, literally of course, what with the umbilical cord and all, but also because I already had a lifetime of making up to do before she was even born.

I walked into the bathroom to wash up.

The sun was just beginning to break outside, but there was enough light that I could make something out in the other bedroom, a little rectangle that we kept meaning to set up for the baby but that until that point had been just a storage unit for dust bunnies. I turned on the light and when my eyes adjusted to it, I saw a white crib, hollow aluminum soldered at the joints to just support the weight of an infant. A few plush animals already peeked through the bars, a miniature irradiated zoo: lime-green orangutan, purple elephant, jaundice-yellow sea turtle. There was a changing table, too, the vinyl coating on the foam mat printed with wagon wheels and daisies. The colors weren't soothing baby colors, they were ferocious, oranges and yellows and greens and whites, but I felt the mattress and the blanket and they were soft, and I thought, Well, this is home, and it will have to do.

There were a few less things to buy with Greta's money, so I stashed the rest in the rainy day tin in the kitchen. It was possible I wouldn't need it at all, I thought. With my new job and Bashkim finally keeping some of his money at home, it was possible we might actually pull through.

Before I left for work I tiptoed back into our bedroom. I knew he wasn't asleep, and

307

I whispered to him, "I'm going to work," because I didn't want him to think that I was leaving again just to spite him, or that I'd come back in the first place for the same reason.

It took a few seconds for him to answer, as if he was trying to figure out whether he should still be pretending to be asleep. "I'm glad you're back," he eventually whispered back.

"Yeah," I answered.

"The baby, it's okay?"

"Yeah."

"This is good."

"Yeah," I said, one last time.

All the whispering didn't make sense, because there was no one else in there to be quiet for, but it seemed it was all we could muster at the moment. I'd blame it on the ungodly hour, when humans aren't meant to be awake, but I knew there wasn't going to be any more explanation coming from either one of us later, either. There was just me closing the bedroom door behind me and the reset button of a new day.

After two hours on the road, the exhilaration of having gotten more than a hundred miles from Waterbury begins to wear off. In its place, you're left with a muted panic that manifests as arrhythmia and diarrhea and that you cannot trace back to one specific root fear. At each of your frequent bathroom breaks, you think you pinpoint its origin: at the Woodrow Wilson rest area outside of Trenton, NJ, you're sure that it stems from your anxiety that you'll soon be sharing sleeping quarters with Ahmet, a guy whose Spotify stations consist exclusively of rap from the nineties, contemporary R & B favorites, and some electronic stuff that sounds like it comes from a windswept, apocalyptic future.

During hour three in Allentown, PA, you're certain that some particularly strong indoor draft has swept away the letter you'd written to your mother explaining that you'd left of your own volition, that you are safe, and that you are appalled at her lifelong deceptions, lack of ambition and imagination, and (though it didn't actually make it into the letter) her culinary reliance on aluminum flavor pouches. If she doesn't find and thus can't read what you'd written, you will feel compelled to answer at least one of the nine thousand calls or texts she'll soon be making to you, and the police to whom she will also make nine thousand phone calls will ping the cell towers along your route, and a fleet of barrel-chested highway patrolmen will be waiting for you at the next rest stop to deliver you back home.

By hour nine, in Roanoke, VA, you are so sure that your reception in Texas will be one of outrage to the point of violence that you nearly ask Ahmet to turn around. You see so clearly now that you'll be received like a poltergeist haunting your father in revenge for past transgressions. You'll be the creepy rag doll in horror movies who won't let that innocent family rest.

By hour thirteen, during some stretch of Tennessee that you can't be bothered to identify, you've grown as bored with panic as with Ahmet's chatter about UConn's chances for an NCAA title this season, and you find yourself disappointed at how much everything outside the window, even hundreds of miles from Waterbury, looks mostly like the place you just left. The exits grow farther and farther apart the farther you get from the Northeast Corridor, but the trees are the same trees, the cars are the same cars, the Exxons are still Exxons, and the McDonald's are still hawking the same meat-like patties to the same overweight, overworked moms and their overweight, hyperactive kids. At first you'd felt briefly excited upon entering the limits of minor cities you'd vaguely heard of, as if they were celebrities of which you were hoping to catch a glimpse, but if they were celebrities they were the depressing reality-show kind, with boring jobs and bad bleached hair and family members they were embarrassed by but not better than. Now, even Ahmet seems to be out of topics to try to talk to you about, and his chivalry is tested by your body's seeming inability to hold any food or beverage internally for more than twenty minutes.

"Maybe you shouldn't drink that Diet Coke right now," he suggests as he pulls away from a gas station where you'd flushed the last beverage and purchased a shiny new one.

"I need it to stay awake," you tell him.

"You don't need to stay awake. I'm the one driving," he says.

"But I want to stay awake. I just want to, like, see."

"It's too dark to see anything."

"Not that kind of seeing," you say.

"What kind of seeing?"

"I don't know," you say, in a tone meant to convey that if you have to explain it, he'll never understand, when the truth is you have no idea what you mean yourself.

Ahmet sighs. "You're a strange girl," he says quietly, only this time, he sounds slightly annoyed instead of charmed, as he had when he'd said the same statement during earlier phases of a courtship he hadn't known yet was doomed.

You're a strange girl. You're a strange girl, he'd said, several times over. But are you really a strange girl? The description doesn't seem quite right, the way that so-called synonyms never seem precise enough when you look up words in the thesaurus. You recognize, objectively, that your behavior over the past several weeks has been atypical, not just of you but of generally above-average-yet-unexceptional high-school-age girls from depressed-yet-still-first-world

312

New England cities. It is, perhaps, not what you'd call normal to manipulate a very nice, very wrong-for-you guy with a very innocent yet almost pathological crush to drive you across a large swath of the United States on short notice, only to — to what? What exactly do you plan to do with him once you get to Houston, hire him as your interpreter? Get back in his car and head right back to where you came from? You aren't even sure you are going back. You aren't even sure you could go back, or that there's any point. What would the point be, an early childhood degree from Western Connecticut State University? Sharing an apartment and cannolis with your mother for the rest of your life? At this point, you're not any more sure that your mother could forgive you than you are that you could forgive her. The kind of bitterness you'd share at your kitchen table would ruin every cannoli forevermore.

In any case, you don't feel strange. You feel like a run-of-the-mill shithead. By the time you check into whatever Bates Motel you manage to find when both you and Ahmet are too tired to go on, you've almost convinced yourself to accept this new role, and to adapt to this new transient world where you're attached to nothing and no one. Not long ago, you used to stare at the homeless people in your neighborhood park and try to imagine them as children, when they probably shared with their fellow second graders the same dreams of becoming astronauts or presidents or veterinarians. Could the homeless people even trace what kinds of decisions had led their second-grade peers to grow up to live regular lives of pump truck operators or daycare center workers or department managers at Target, while they themselves had gone on to sip from paper sacks filled with bottles of their own doom? Probably not. They adapted. They lived on, raged on, drank on, and in short order it all became normal.

Normal, inevitable, like your own fate. It is probably easiest to just accept that you are a turd, and parlay that self-loathing into something like a formidable narcotics addiction, so that each of the rest of your days is intensely and terribly purposeful. You are certain that you could score something instantly life-wrecking just outside the motel door. Instead, you remain in bed, tossing and turning, which means that Ahmet has remained as wide awake as you in the king-size bed you have no choice but to share, the motel having rented out all of its twin rooms to the versions of you that arrived earlier in the evening.

"I'm sorry," you whisper. If you're not yet capable of utter self-annihilation, you think that perhaps you should make one last attempt at decency.

He doesn't answer at first, while he mulls over whether or not to continue feigning sleep, but then answers, also in a whisper, "Sorry for what?"

"For keeping you awake," you say, now in a normal speaking volume. "And for peeing so much. And not buying your Whopper. I should've got lunch for you. I should get all the lunches from now on."

He rolls over on his side to face you. You recognize this as an intimate moment, and you work to correct the recoil your body instinctively makes, so that when he says, "It's okay, I can buy my own Whoppers," your mouths are actually not a foot from each other on your respective pillows, each breathing in the air the other breathes out. You can smell just vaguely the essence of that evening's dinner, which for him had been a carton of Muscle Milk and a sleeve of sunflower seeds, and it's just short of repulsive, just enough that you're able to hold your position and smile uselessly because it's too dark for you to be seen. You know that there's something wrong with you when pulling away comes so easy but lying still with someone sets off a panic, and you think that it probably isn't Ahmet's cheesy leather jacket or the startling amount of product he uses to maintain what looks to be fairly acquiescent hair that kept you from allowing him to ever touch you. It's been all you, babe. Your body — and, in fact, the brain that controls it, keeping its motions awkward and rigid and the skin perpetually goose-pimpled — is messed up, designed as a barrier to the outside world rather than a vessel with which to experience it. If humans are actually social creatures, as you'd been taught, then you are possibly not even human.

And yet maybe you could reprogram yourself to appear human, like the very best cyborgs of the future would one day be.

"Thank you for doing this for me," you say. "Driving with me and everything. It's crazy. I mean, it's crazy that you would just take off like this for me."

He doesn't disagree that it was crazy. You can tell that it's something he's been thinking about for a while, the first little seeds of regret beginning to sprout way back in Pennsylvania, making his attempts at conversation a little more stilted, so that the volume of the music had subtly crept up over the course of the hours in the car, until finally there was no point in even attempting to hold a conversation while it played. But it matters to him, what you just said, you can tell that, too. You aren't sure whether it makes you feel better or worse that it matters so much, but it makes you feel something, and you decide to run with that. You decide it's time to repay his generosity by giving him the thing for which he's been so patiently waiting. You reach out and find his hand, and it's cold and slightly jarring to feel it, because you were expecting something warm, the way you expect coffee to be warm no matter how long you've neglected the mug on the counter. He's jarred, too, because he jumps a little at your touch before relaxing into it, grabbing your hand back and holding just a little too hard.

"You needed someone," he says. "It's not right that you should be alone. I mean, that your mother doesn't even care that you left with a guy she doesn't even know? It's messed up. How does she know I'm not a murderer? How can a mother not care about that?"

By not knowing, you think, but that would ruin the moment you're trying to create. So far this isn't making you feel better, but you tell yourself that that's because you just aren't used to it. It's always uncomfortable to try something new: shoes, running long distances, speaking in a foreign language that relies on parts of the mouth not utilized by English speakers.

"I'm sorry," you say again.

"Why are you sorry? I'm sorry for you. I'm sorry that your people didn't care more about you."

"It's not like nobody cared at all," you say, though that was indeed what you had spent many sleepless nights convincing yourself of.

"The way your father just left? What kind of man would do that?"

"I don't know. That's what I'm trying to find out."

"Nothing could ever make me do that. Nothing."

"You don't know that."

"I do," he says. "I do."

"Well," you say.

"And your mother just let him go? Just like she let you go? I couldn't even tell my parents that I'm with you. I'm a twenty-year-old man and I had to tell them that I'm with friends in Myrtle Beach."

Your instinct is to defend your mother,

despite having been the one to convince him of the things he has just said about her. It is true that a week before, you had omitted certain representative facts that might have weakened your case to hit the highway. You never mentioned, for example, the celebratory pizza nights and that time she took you to the Beardsley Zoo on a Saturday because you'd been down with a stomach bug on the day of your third-grade field trip. You perhaps didn't mention that though you often felt more like a responsibility than like an object of affection, you were a responsibility your mother took seriously, when there were plenty of people like Margarita around to remind you that there was no responsibility that a truly negligent human would find too great to shirk. Yet you didn't feel like you were lying to Ahmet a week ago. You seem to remember feeling completely justified, just absolutely, 100 percent right.

The thread that carries between then and now is your inherent shittiness, and that's the thing, really, you've been trying to flee from.

You curl your shoulder to move in a little closer to Ahmet. "You're a good person," you say.

"So are you," he says.

"No, I'm not."

"Don't say that. Of course you are."

"Name one nice thing I've done for you," you say.

He's quiet.

"See?"

"You invited me on this trip," he says.

Christ, you think. Jesus fucking Christ.

You will your arm to reach for Ahmet's back, to pull him closer to you, since he seems not to understand that you want to pay his generosity back. His boner is instantaneous and, even to someone entirely inexperienced with boners, rather impressive. Still, his arms feel rigid under you, like those of an unwilling partner at a middle school dance. You scoot your body closer to his, until you're pressed together on your sides, two tectonic plates just beginning to move. His lips find yours and his tongue is also colder than you'd expected it to be, and it tastes of nothing despite its smell of several somethings. Still, it's not unpleasant. It's soft, and you like the feel of his breath on your neck when he pulls back for air. His hand begins moving up and down the length of your back, but his arm remains stiff, so you grasp it and squeeze, willing it to loosen up. You're doing this for him, after all. This isn't a thing that you want, except that your body does seem to begin moving on its own, pressing harder into his and — there's no other term for it known to you — grinding on him. You pull his top leg in between the two of yours and move over it, and without even meaning to, without having had to plan an exhibition of desire, you moan softly. Though you haven't even learned to masturbate successfully yet, the pressure there feels familiar, and you instinctively seek release.

"You're nice," you breathe into his ear, and he responds by releasing the tight grip he has on the flesh of your back, which makes you regret what you said. You liked the not-nice touch more than the soft circles he begins rubbing over your neck. Even his cock, as stiff as it is, feels like it's tentatively pressing into your belly. You curl your hand over it, first over his boxers, then under them. But first you take your shirt off, because you think that's what he would want. After all, you're doing this for him, you tell yourself. This is a gift to him, and he seems to not know how to unwrap it, so you have to do it yourself.

"Luljeta," he says, and you notice that he uses your real full name, which almost nobody does, and it sends a strange vibration down your spine and makes you grasp onto his cock harder.

"Ow," he says.

"Sorry," you say and let go of his cock altogether, though you quickly replace your hand with your mouth. That's when his tight grip on your shoulder returns, while his other hand grabs a handful of your hair and pulls hard enough that you wait to feel pain that never comes.

"Luljeta," he says, and then says it again, though he must know that you can't very well answer.

You moan something like "Hm?" with his dick still in your mouth.

He pulls your hair again, which makes you feel briefly like a marionette. It's your turn to say *ow,* but you manage to stifle it.

"You don't have to," he says.

You pull away from him just long enough to answer, "What?"

"You don't have to do this for me," he says.

Again you pull back. "I. I know. I want to."

He's silent, except for a deep quick breath, when you put him back in your mouth. Then he pulls on your hair again, then both of your shoulders, steering you away.

"Come up here," he says.

"Why?" you ask.

"I want to see you," he says.

"You don't like it?" you say.

"No, no, I do."

"Then what is it?"

He lets go an impressive lungful of air, a breath that could've gotten him deep under the surface in a free dive. "You don't have to do this," he says again.

"I want to," you repeat.

"I don't want you to."

"Oh," you say.

"I mean, like, I want it, but I don't want it from you."

His dick is still hard in your hand.

"I mean, I want it from you, but not like this."

You don't know what to do with your hand at that moment. You don't even recognize it as your hand.

"It's just, like," he says. "A girl's supposed to be in love first."

Penises are so ugly, you realize. They're skinned, weird baby animals.

"I like that you're a nice girl," he says.

"I told you I wasn't," you say. "I'm so not nice that I thought sucking your dick was being nice."

Finally he seems to understand, because he doesn't say anything after that.

You feel such a sudden, deep embarrassment that you have to wonder whether it's mere embarrassment or some new viral form of it. And as if you've come down with a virus, you begin shivering, and you pull away to your side of the bed and smooth the covers back over you. Still you feel cold, and apparently it's contagious, because you feel Ahmet all the way on the other side of the bed shivering, too. You lie there, huddled and contorting and rubbing your own limbs with your own hands, wishing you were made of wood so that the friction would start a fire.

CHAPTER THIRTEEN: ELSIE

Funny thing about getting accidentally knocked up, everyone tells you what a mistake you made and then goes out of their way to be nicer to you than they've ever been.

Yllka began bringing me tea when she intercepted me on the way up the steps, and I always sat with her and drank it even though what I really wanted was to crawl into bed and pick up where I'd left off at 4:15 A.M.

"It's çaj mali, mountain tea, it's good for the baby. It won't keep you up," she'd said.

The only thing keeping me up was Yllka herself, but I didn't say that. It was good to have her on my side, or more likely the baby's side, with me there just by proxy. Babies make people softer, at least while the babies are tucked away in wombs not crying or wanting for much. Homeless men downtown turned and smiled at me when I walked by. Mamie kept stumbling upon baby clothes at tag sales and buying them because she *might as well,* and Greta was doing the same with picture books and mobiles, and Yllka and Gjonni were forgetting to forward our gas and electric bills along to us.

"What is this?" Yllka asked the last time I stopped by with the rent check, as if she'd never seen one before.

"The rent," I said. "It's the first of the month, right?"

"Oh, that," she said and shook her head and whispered, though there was nobody around but us. "Just hang on to that for now."

So everything was fine, everything was settled, except, of course, for every part of my body, which was wound so tight that I trembled constantly and had to fill my cup only halfway with çaj mali so that it wouldn't splash over the rim when I tried to bring it to my lips. I couldn't tell people what Bashkim and I wouldn't even admit to each other: that things were fine because we saw each other never, him making it home to bed just as I was waking up, me getting home after he'd already left for work. Yllka must have known that, but still she said one day, after she refused the rent check, "I'm glad you two have worked things out."

"Umm-hmm," I said.

"He told her that they should divorce, you know," she said. "He told you that?"

Even though it was only half-full, I managed to knock the cup of tea completely over. "Yeah, of course," I said.

"He just can't leave her with nothing, you understand? Think about it from her perspective. All alone, her husband promising the world and then taking everything away from her all at once. And it's not like America, women can't just go out and make a life for themselves the way they can here. There a woman is for a family, and without a family she's nothing."

"I know," I said.

"You don't know. You can't. Nobody here can understand how deep that thinking runs. And now things are falling apart over there. It's almost worse now than it was before. At least with Hoxha you knew what kind of misery to expect. Why did she stay? Why, when she could have come here, where they could make some money and not worry from one day to the next if there will be bread to eat?"

It was true that our shelves here overflowed with bread. In this city alone there were a dozen grocery stores the size of small

Albanian villages with aisles dedicated to nothing but bread. There were outlets that sold the leftover bread on clearance, in the three-week state between fresh and moldy, and old people plucked up expired loaves by the fistful and threw the slices, chunk by chunk, into the ponds at Hamilton Park for the ducks to scavenge.

I also knew, because it was the white stuff I smeared my peanut butter on in the morning, that there would never be enough bread to satisfy the kinds of things human beings the world over were hungry for.

I said, "Yes, she shouldn't have chosen to starve."

"What was he to do? You can't just be married to someone on the other side of the world. She is so stubborn. She should have just come with him or divorced him there." Yllka looked at me, then reached for my hand. "I'm sorry. I know it's difficult for you to hear about her."

"Well, she exists."

"Yes, but not as his wife. Not anymore. It's just a matter of ending it properly."

"No, it's fine. I do think he owes her something," I said.

"Oh?"

"If he doesn't keep his promises to her, why would he keep his promises to me?"

"Right," Yllka said, but she was looking sideways at me, and she touched my hand I think to check if I was hot, because it must have sounded to her like I was talking through a fever.

Maybe the kid was making me softer, too, maybe it was just a hormonal shift, but it was true, I did feel a little bad for Aggie, stuck alone in all that mayhem, more loyal to her country than to her husband and totally let down by both. I'd found Bashkim's pictures of her and didn't retch even. Sitting in his sock drawer, underneath the fresh new pair he was saving for who knows what reason, was a plastic ziplock bag with a dozen or so snapshots undoubtedly taken on the kind of crap camera only a true Communist could get his hands on. Everything had a gauzy look to it, like the lens was smeared with Vaseline, but even still I could see that Aggie looked nothing like I thought she would. In my head she was middle-aged and heavyset and wore dark scarves over her head like in Time-Life photos of people who lived in villages instead of towns in countries whose names people never bothered to learn even when their social studies teachers made them memorize the entire world atlas. The real Aggie was young with eyes that weren't black just because of the shitty film stock, and she smiled in the same obligatory way that I did in elementary school photos. She wasn't beautiful, she wasn't hideous, she was just regular, except for an outdated eighties sweatshirt that put her a little on the dowdy side of plain. I wondered if Bashkim had called her beautiful when they met, and if that was a generous or a cruel thing to do to a person like her, and I remembered what Bashkim had said to me a year before.

I swear to Allah, you are the most beautiful girl I have ever seen.

If only I'd known at the time that Bashkim didn't believe in God.

I put the photos back in the bag and tucked the bag back into its little nest of socks, as if the photos would incubate into some kind of living thing.

Yllka was right that things were a mess back in the motherland. I knew that because Dan Rather corroborated it, telling us everything we needed to know about the state of Albania's people before Snuggle and Lean Cuisine took over and told us everything we needed to know about the state of ours. It was almost a good sign: Albania made the TV! It was a real place after all, not just a made-up locale where the generic villains in generic thrillers might have come from, and being around people straight from a CBS News set made me feel kind of like a celebrity, or at least like a groupie. But Albania's thirty seconds of fame didn't come in the form of feel-good filler at the end of the evening news. It was more like live footage of a phoenix with clipped wings, Tirana a city in black and white even when it was filmed in color. Thousands of people that looked just like Bashkim, just like Aggie, hell, just like me if I wore flowy overcoats and had been weaned on a diet of cigarettes and çaj mali, rioting, crying, setting Yugos on fire, while riot police looked on, probably sucking down unfiltereds underneath their face shields and wondering if their own investments were as bunk as those of the wailing throngs around them.

They called them banks, just like Bashkim did, but really they were pyramid schemes set up by their own countrymen who must've honed their crafts in places just ahead of the curve, like Russia, the mean, scary older cousin of all of Eastern Europe. I didn't understand how pyramid schemes worked, but I understood that they had nothing to do with the pharaohs and everything to do with people trying to make something out of the nothing they'd known their whole unhappy lives. Dan Rather didn't have to explain that part of it to me, that lust for anything other than bread and water, just the details of the operation, and he had to do that because my ambassador to it all, Bashkim, still hadn't said a peep about it. I didn't dare ask, and neither did Yllka. She said being in the kitchen at the Ross was like working at a funeral home, but I doubted that funeral home workers saw their own failure in the faces of the corpses they stared into every day, unlike Bashkim and Adem and Fatmir, who'd rather go days without talking than have to look each other in the eye at that point. And what did they really have to be ashamed of? Two million people just like Bashkim handed over their money on promises that it would triple or quadruple, everyone imagining what scents of air fresheners they would get for all the Mercedes they would buy. Everyone needs to feel like a winner sometimes, even me. I used to enter all the tickets I bought in my middle school penny auctions into the canisters for the prizes nobody else wanted, like weird homemade crocheted headbands and secondhand cop- ies of Lee Iacocca's autobiography, just to not feel empty-handed for a moment. And yet there they were on the TV, thousands of Bashkims marching around with the pockets of their slacks turned inside out, yelling at something the cameras never panned to. They looked like the Monopoly Man on the Chance card that sent you straight to jail, minus the top hat and the part where you get to fold up the board after you lose and shove the game back into the closet.

I understood it. They were embarrassed. They'd been duped. It was easy to recognize on other people, but it wore disguises when you looked in the mirror.

Later that week, when Bashkim came home early and sat down on the sofa next to me and touched my arm, I flinched, both because I wasn't used to him touching me anymore and because I knew he was going to tell me something he would need to apologize for.

"Things have gotten really bad," he said.

"I know," I said.

"We cannot afford to keep doing this."

"I know."

"She is going to have to come."

I touched my stomach, confused. Of course things had gotten bad, the two of us acting like boarders in the same house, barely talking, never mind preparing for her arrival, but of course she was going to have to come. I might have looked like an idiot to him but I understood the birds and the bees, and as much as I was scared to bring up the near future with him, seething as he was about the present, I was relieved to hear him acknowledge that we had to get back to planning for the baby. I was relieved, too, to hear him refer to the baby as a *she*. I hadn't even told him that I was sure what I was carrying was not the son he wanted, not wanting to add more disappointment to his quarry full of it.

"I know. Another month or so," I said.

He put his head in his hands. "Sooner. It has to be sooner."

"Bashkim," I said.

He didn't answer.

Again I was confused. So it was clear Bashkim hadn't learned anything about capitalism growing up, but did he also miss the lessons on basic human biology? You didn't even need school for that. You just needed some kids a few years older than you to take you out to a barn and draw some crude diagrams. If the kids were rotten and hormonal enough they might even try to demonstrate on you. I was pretty sure this was a universal lesson, since as far as I can tell, every civilization was built around the very concept.

"You know I can't do anything about that,

right?" I said.

"I don't expect for you to do anything about it," he said.

"She's coming when she's coming."

"She is on her way already."

"Yeah," I said. "I know. She's been on her way for a long time now. Eight months or so."

"No, just yesterday."

"What?"

"She left just yesterday. She is on the coast, waiting to get to Italy."

The baby had been kicking this whole time, but she hushed up then, too.

"What?" I said.

"Agnes," he said, using her formal name, as if he could make her into a distinguished guest, a diplomat who we were lucky enough to host.

"But that," I said and wasn't sure what to follow it up with, and anyway, I had to press my tongue to the roof of my mouth because I began to feel very sick, as if I'd been blindfolded and spun around and brought to a place that would be familiar if only the room would stop spinning.

"It has gotten very dangerous there. The government is gone. It is just riots and gangs in the streets, and she has nowhere to go, she has nowhere there to live."

The baby was kicking again. She had come back alive and was raging, but I was still just sitting there, trying to catch enough air to make me feel like I wasn't suffocating.

"Her parents are already in Greece, her brother is in Texas. She will go down there eventually, but first she has to come here so we can" — he paused — "take care of things."

"But you can't," I said.

"I will come right back. Nothing will change. It is just a duty."

"But you have a duty here," I said. I wasn't yelling, because I wasn't mad. I didn't understand enough to be mad. Surely he meant something else, and he was like those newscasts, getting lost in translation. I was sorry enough for Aggie that I didn't argue about the money he sent her when we were still sleeping on rubber, the changing table in the baby's room still empty of diapers, and the pantry empty of formula, but I felt sure that if she knew about me she'd feel sorry, too. All she had was nothing; we had a big something, a *someone,* who would be born with needs that couldn't be deferred the way the rest of us could train ourselves to do. There was hunger, and there was *hunger,* and all of us, I thought, had to know the difference.

"But you can't," I said again.

"I have to," he said again, a little sharper. "This is not about what I want, it is about what I have to do. It is too dangerous there, and I was stupid enough to marry her and she was stupid enough to stay behind and now it's time to stop being stupid."

"But you can't," I said.

"Stop saying that!"

So I thought for a second, because he was right, what I was saying wasn't making any sense. He could do whatever he said he was going to do, and I couldn't stop that.

"But I can't," I said instead.

"What do you mean, you 'can't'?"

"I can't do this," I said.

He still looked angry, but his voice was lower, and he unclenched his fists. "You can't do what?"

"I can't do this alone. I don't know how to do what comes next."

"You will not be alone," he said. "I told you I will be here. Your mother is here, your sister. Aggie is alone. You have plenty."

I shook my head.

"You have to grow up," he said. "We cannot have a house full of children."

The fault line inside of me had been active for a while, and all the constant little tremors had been shaking stuff loose. But the big one was coming, the one that would break me off and make me into an island, and it was only right of me: I had to warn him.

"Go," I said.

"Not yet."

"Go," I said. "Leave. Now. Forever. I don't care. I want you to."

"You are a child," he said.

"I hate you," I said. "Loser."

Then my cheek was cold. I put my palm to it and felt that it was wet, too. Bashkim's lips were still pursed, and I realized that he'd spit on me, as if I were some peasant who'd stolen his bread, not even worthy of the space in a jail. I wiped the spit off with my hands, smelled it to make sure it wasn't poison, and then, before I had a chance to think things through, or consider what the consequences of that kind of action would be, I let rage fill all the spaces in me where confusion and fear and regret had lived seconds before.

I flailed my arms in a rock-'em, sock-'em kind of way, like some primal martial art, but I couldn't make contact with anything, and it just made me wilder. The hate took my breath away. There was air around me but I couldn't get to it, just like I couldn't

338

get to any of the other necessary things that seemed to be all around me.

"You think I'm a loser? You don't know what losing is. I will show you what losing is," Bashkim screamed. He punched the wall beside me, my head just inches from the plaster spiderweb his fist left behind. Then he drew back his fist and aimed it just to the left, this time the bull's-eye drawn straight on me. I closed my eyes and braced for the impact, but I didn't cover my head with my arms or think about ducking or running away. I just stood there waiting to feel something, fight or flight or bone on bone, regret or cool blood or anything at all. When I couldn't bear the wait anymore, I opened my eyes and saw Bashkim on the other side of the room, fist still cocked, as if an invisible claw had pulled him away and pinned him to the wall.

There was no claw. It was just a knocking at the door, Gjonni's voice on the other side of it asking if everything was all right. I looked down at my belly. The baby was kicking so hard she made little flutters in my shirt, then landed one in the ribs that made me crumple in half. Bashkim was gasping, too, sympathy pains or something.

"Oh my god," he said. He ran to the door, but not to answer Gjonni. I heard his footsteps on the stairs, Gjonni calling after him, the sound of the Fiero turning over.

Even when my breathing returned to normal, it took a while before it felt quiet again, and then it wasn't quiet again because the phone was ringing, so I ripped it from the wall and told it to leave me the hell alone, screaming, *I don't want to listen to any of you anymore. I don't need any damn one of you.*

I didn't scream it loud enough. People kept trying to come through for me. The girls insisted on throwing a baby shower, and by *girls,* I mean almost every woman I'd so much as said hello to in the past year: Mamie and Greta, Yllka, Cheryl and Janice from the Ross, the inspectors at Ferrucci, even a few of the gruas, the wives of Bashkim's friends, who I'm sure Yllka threatened with deportation in order to get there. It was nice; it was lovely, *lovely,* a word I'd never used in earnest in my life, a word that sounded right only coming from a finishing school cadet. From me it sounded sarcastic, even though I didn't mean it to be.

"This is lovely," I said, and I meant it. It's just that I didn't round out the sentence with what I felt, which was lonelier than I'd ever been in my life, and that was saying something for a girl who'd spent all of her birthdays with only her mother, her kid sister, and sometimes, on the special ones, Fudgie the Whale. Everyone there knew what they were doing, and it wasn't celebrating the impending birth of my child, hoisting me above their shoulders for a job well done. They were picking up my and Bashkim's slack, finishing off the job we started but weren't seeing through to the end, and though I would never have described a single one of them as a gentle person, they were kind enough to disguise their rescue mission with the pastel-colored camouflage of streamers and cellophane. They'd already made up the crib with one of the half dozen sets of sheets Bashkim and I had neglected to buy, and then finished it off with a crib bumper that Bashkim and I had neglected to know was even a thing that we needed.

Mamie handed me a cup of punch and sipped from the second serving of her own.

"This is spiked," I said.

"I know," she answered.

"I can't drink booze."

"Oh, sure you can. That doesn't count toward the end."

My high school health teachers had never mentioned anything about the threat of fetal alcohol syndrome expiring in the third trimester, but nobody protested about the cup in my hand, so I took a sip, and then a few, and by the end of it I was able to muster the smile I wished I didn't have to fake.

The shower was at Yllka's, and people commented on how well that worked out, since we wouldn't have to drive all these presents back home, just drag them upstairs when everything was all over. Deena started handing me the presents that people had bothered to wrap, all of them tagged with two-inch cards printed with violets or rattles.

"Thanks, Dardata," I said, folding the little terry bath towel back into its box. "This is perfect."

She smiled a little, maybe even for real.

All of the things in miniature worked an opposite kind of spell on us. The tinier the object, the bigger the smile it put on a face. Somehow a plastic spoon was adorable because it was shrunken. The newborn-size diapers, each one the width of a fist, made everyone swoon.

"The shit isn't as cute, I promise you," Deena said, and everyone laughed but it wasn't clear if anyone agreed. Everyone volunteered to take a turn wiping the baby's butt when the time came, as if changing a diaper were some kind of privilege. Even the gruas were reaching out, taking turns placing their hands on my belly to feel the kicking. Greta took a turn, and tried her best not to smile when she felt the movement inside of me.

"What's the due date?" Rini asked.

"April first," I said.

"Ha, April Fools' Day," Mamie said. "Perfect."

"Do you have names picked out?" Dardata asked. She was looser by then, holding a cup of punch in one hand and the other shaking a rattle along to "Macarena," which made up about every third song on the mix tape she'd brought along.

Christ, babies needed names, too. Names and crib bumpers and spiked punch for the ninth month in utero.

I shrugged. "We're not sharing yet."

"Ugh, it drives me crazy when people keep everything a secret. Boy or girl, name, it's like you're the Sphinx," Dardata said, but she was smiling, because who doesn't like a riddle?

Mamie wasn't smiling. "Why don't we ask Daddy what the name is. Daddy?" she said. She was looking at the door, and so everyone's eyes followed hers, and there he was, leaning against the frame as if he were keeping it in place. Once he started to walk toward us, I saw it was the frame that had been keeping Bashkim upright, and without it his knees buckled a little.

If I had been standing, I would have crumpled.

"What's he doing here? Men aren't allowed at showers," Mamie said.

"He doesn't look good," Greta said.

"Mëmë," Bashkim said, after he stumbled over to Mamie and kissed her on the lips.

"You stink," she answered.

Even through all the punch in that room, I could make out the booze on Bashkim's breath. His stupid grin and weeble-wobble gait meant he'd poured down more than a few at the social club, which meant the rest of the wives in the room knew what they were in for when they got home. They sighed, all together, like the all-knowing chorus in a musical.

"Party's over, I guess," Dardata said and threw the rest of her drink down her throat.

"No, party is happening! Stay, stay," Bashkim said but didn't even look at her to see the glare she was giving him. The gruas gathered their purses, patted my stomach on the way out, looked at me as if to say not just *poor, poor you* but *poor, poor us.*

"Thank you, thank you for these beautiful

gifts," Bashkim said to them on their way out, in a voice like that of an emcee. "So beautiful, all of you ladies. So beautiful, Roza," he said to the old one, who shook his arm from her waist, whose scowling face and black mourning dress implied that she'd earned the right by then to be free from the clutches of any man, her husband or otherwise.

"And you, beautiful ladies," he said, going down the line, grabbing the faces of Rini and Margot and Deena. "So kind to have a party for my Elsie and my baby. So many nice people around here, so many kind people."

"I've never seen him like this," I said, in what was supposed to be an explanation or apology. It was true that I had never seen him like that, but I had seen the aftermath, when he'd wake up to down the half gallon of Gatorade he'd stocked in the refrigerator the night before and then walk into the shower with a lit cigarette, the wet ashes left behind in the tub like dead insects.

"What does that mean, 'like this'? I am happy. What is there not to be happy about? Good friends, good family. It is a dream come true, days like this."

"Did you just drive here in your condition?" Mamie asked, the pot to Bashkim's kettle.

"Oh, stop kidding, Mëmë, you know I am okay."

"Who's Mëmë? That's not my name."

"Mëmë, you know, mother," he said. "Like a mother to me."

"My name is Anna," Mamie said.

"You'll help us move some of this stuff to the apartment, eh?" Yllka asked, nodding to Rini, Margot, and Deena.

They scuttled upstairs. I grabbed a dirty tray so I could follow them up, but escape wasn't as easy for me.

"I feel better, to know that Elsie will not be alone," Bashkim said.

"What do you mean, 'will not be alone'? What, are you planning on leaving her already?" Mamie asked. It was a rhetorical question, an insult really, but Bashkim stumbled into the living room and fell onto the couch and didn't respond, and that terrified me, that he didn't seem to have a fight in him at all.

"Get your dirty feet off of Yllka's sofa," I said to him. He was coiled up like a snake, and I wanted to poke at him, to see if he posed a threat or not.

"It's gone," he said.

I didn't have to ask what was gone.

"Everything is gone," he said anyway.

"Quiet," I told him.

"What's gone? Besides his mind, I mean?" Mamie asked.

I shook my head. "Not now," I said.

"She is alone. There is nothing there for her," he said.

"And what's here for her?" I asked. "You?"

"What did you say to me?" Bashkim started to rise, but he lost momentum halfway up, and he collapsed onto his back, covering his face with his hands like a politician caught in a scandal, working his way through a crowd of photographers. Then he began sobbing, something I had never seen him do, something I didn't even know he was capable of. I remembered from the news the image that struck me the most: among all the women on the streets of Tirana wailing, among all the men stomping on abandoned riot gear, there was one man alone who was sobbing, his wife still and dazed beside him. There was a space around him, as if even in all of the sadness and outrage the crowds were afraid to touch him, as if he were contagious. The crowds knew what to do with an angry man, but not a broken one.

"I'm sorry, I'm sorry," he cried. I'd been waiting weeks for those words from him, but hearing them repulsed me, because they showed a kind of weakness we couldn't afford anymore.

"What is he talking about? Who's 'she'?" Mamie asked.

Bashkim switched over to Albanian, which to Mamie and Greta must have sounded like a made-up tongue, a man in need of an exorcism instead of a shower and some hot coffee. Yllka returned from downstairs, and Gjonni followed her seconds afterward, and we all stood around staring down at him on the sofa like we were at his wake.

"My god," Yllka said in English and then switched to Albanian, but by this point Bashkim had closed his eyes and stopped responding.

"Who's 'she'?" Mamie asked again.

"Agnes," I said. "Aggie."

"Who's Aggie?" Greta asked.

Yllka and Gjonni looked at each other and then at me and then back to Bashkim, not sure who to worry about the most. "Someone from back home," Gjonni said, shaking his head.

"Family from the old country," Yllka added.

"Like his sister? Who? What happened?" Greta asked.

Gjonni bent down and tapped his thumb

348

against Bashkim's cheek. "Ikim, ikim. Come, let's go upstairs. Let's go to your bed." Gjonni nodded at Yllka and they both prodded and pulled at Bashkim until he sat upright.

"There is tea made in the kitchen. Help yourselves," Yllka said, still playing host even with a monkey on her back, almost literally. "We will take care of him. You stay and talk."

Bashkim lifted his head as Yllka and Gjonni dragged him past us. "They will take care of me. You cannot take care of me," he said.

"Yllka, let me help," I said. I didn't know how I could help when I couldn't even look at him, but this was my mess to clean up after. All they should have had to worry about was tossing out the streamers and empty Solo cups.

"No!" Bashkim yelled. "You cannot help. You do not understand. Nuk jeni një prej nesh. Nuk jeni!"

"What's he saying?" I asked.

"Don't listen to him. He's not talking sense," Gjonni said.

"I want to know," I said.

"I want to know who Aggie is and what the hell is going on," Mamie said.

"There is just trouble back home and Bashkim is upset and had too much to drink

349

and that is it," Yllka said.

"Nuk kuptoni," Bashkim said to me.

"I don't understand," I answered.

"Yes, you don't understand!" he yelled, and he repeated it over and over as Yllka and Gjonni dragged him through the door. I heard his voice carry on over the shuffle of their feet on the stairs, until it was muffled halfway up the flight, and silenced altogether by the time they reached the top. I heard the door open and the screen door slap hard against the frame, more footsteps on the floor, and then a dull thud, followed by mumbled voices.

"What the hell is happening?" Mamie said. "Jesus, that was a goddamned show."

"Not now," I said. "Please."

"Is Aggie his sister?" Greta asked, almost pleading. "Why is he so upset? What happened?"

"Aggie is in Albania. The government has fallen, everybody's lost everything, there's chaos in the streets. It's dangerous, and she has to get out," I said. It sounded so simple, really. Too simple for everybody, including me, to be so confused.

"And she's his sister?" Greta asked again.

"No," I said. "His wife."

It was as if the silence had been written into this part of the script: it was, for a moment, absolute. No cars outside, no birds, no breeze, no more muffled voices from upstairs, no breathing. It wasn't peaceful, exactly, but it was reassuring. It seemed to say: You can always come back to this, to nothing.

"Holy great goddamned fucking shit," Mamie said, shattering that beautiful calm moment.

"No, Elsie, really?" Greta said.

"Really," I said. I was too tired to come up with a lie, and even an explanation seemed pointless by then. What was I supposed to say, that when I met Bashkim, his wife was a trinket in a life he'd left behind, like a high school trophy sitting in an attic? She was a ghost, a phantom limb, a bridge soon to be burned? How was I supposed to know that Bashkim's past wasn't a cold he could shake but a terminal condition? How was I supposed to know that everybody's was?

"You've really screwed things up, girly," Mamie said. Her voice was as rough as ever but she said it through tears. It was almost impossible to disappoint her, as low as her expectations were, but I was a prodigy at screwing things up. Not only had I let things fall apart, I'd demolished the raw materials before construction even began. Greta's hands were crawling all over her head, and Mamie wasn't even stopping her, because even if Greta pulled every last hair from her head there'd still be a good solid base to rebuild on. There were actual brains under there; everyone said it, even Mamie, and sometimes they said *brains* like it was a dirty word, but really it was because we were full of wonder at such a thing. Me, I was the Scarecrow, the Tin Man, and the Cowardly Lion rolled into one. I looked outside and wished for a twister to take me away, but it was just plain old afternoon sun out there.

"Could you leave me alone now?" I said, but I didn't need to ask. Mamie had already started gathering her things, including the presents she'd brought for the baby, but then she cussed under her breath and dropped them back on the table.

"That poor child," she said. "It never even had a chance." Then she walked outside, where Greta was already waiting for her, and they were probably halfway home by the time I thought of an answer to that.

"There is a chance," I said. It was just that the chance wasn't in that apartment, even with the new crib bumper and the pallets of adorable shitless diapers and the spiked punch, and it wasn't back at Mamie's house, with the cable TV and drips of

burgundy over every carpeted and uphol-
stered surface like the aftermath of a crime
scene. I had to get us out of there, me and
that kid, out to one of the mysterious
highway mile markers that chance had to
hide behind, out to where we had a shot at
something we needed more desperately than
plush rattles and microwaved breast milk. I
promise you, kid, I promise you. There is a
chance.

CHAPTER FOURTEEN:
LULJETA

Ahmet is a magician, a straight-up David Copperfield, whom he doesn't actually look unlike. You didn't sleep all night — not one second, not even long enough to daydream — and still he managed to slip unnoticed out of bed and get himself showered and dressed and looking like a brand-new man. He even looks a little taller than the one you got into the car with the day before, his head perhaps screwed on a little straighter, with one Nike firmly planted on the thin beige motel carpet and one foot literally out the door.

He sees you watching him and says, "I'm getting the car ready."

You think so long about how to say good morning that the moment passes altogether. He closes the motel door behind him and oddly it's then that the cold air from outside makes its way to the bed. An engine turns over outside and in five seconds flat

354

screeches out of the parking lot, and you know instantly that it's Ahmet's Honda, and that you are now truly alone in this shitty motel in whatever godforsaken red state you're in — you honestly can't remember. You wait for the panic to set in, but all you feel is the glorious warmth of the horrendous, scratchy floral coverlet, along with something that might actually be relief. What choice do you have now but to scrape together all of your remaining cash and book yourself a Greyhound as far north as two hundred dollars will take you? It's the only practical thing left to do, the only decision between you and a life lived at the seesaws of Tuscaloosa, Alabama's equivalent of Hamilton Park.

That's right, Tuscaloosa, Alabama. That's where you are, in a southern college town where people drive SUVs just to maximize the surface area for their crimson A car magnets.

The motel room door opens again, and Ahmet steps inside. "Car's warming up," he says. David Copperfield at it again: he was gone and now he's back, the phantom version of him already on the on-ramp to I-20, the nice guy version of him back in the motel room, unable to meet your eye. Really it was only wishful thinking that he had driven away, because you didn't want to have to stumble through this next part with him.

"Can you turn around?" you ask.

He does, without questioning why, and you scramble to find the T-shirt you never bothered to put back on the night before. You slip out of bed and dress in the previous day's clothes, right down to the socks that are still damp from the previous day's sweat. Dressing makes you feel more raw. You're colder the more you move, and you realize that the henley you put on is never going to keep you warm. You have gravely overestimated the temperature in the southern United States, and you made a serious mistake in not bringing along the winter coat that you had naïvely looked at as a relic of your old New England life. You hadn't even thought to check Weather.com before you left, one of the many oversights that you are finally acknowledging in a plan that is now too far under way to abandon. And you're hungry. Starving. In need of more than the leftover Gardetto's snack mix, especially since the premium rye crisps have already been vultured.

Your crummy motel shares a parking lot with a Walmart, a beacon of hope in an otherwise bleak strip mall. This is what the

Mormon settlers must have felt when they set out for the Pacific but instead reached the Great Salt Lake: it wasn't right, but it was right there.

"I have to go to Walmart," you tell Ahmet.

"What for?" he asks.

"Just some stuff."

He's antsy to leave. He doesn't bother to hide it, the way that the Ahmet from the day before would have. "Okay, but hurry up. I'll throw your stuff in the car and meet you there."

"Fine," you say. As you cross the parking lot, you stare at a lady standing outside of a minivan cum mobile home, and she stares right back at you. She's wearing a leather bomber jacket and gripping a mug of piping hot something with gloved hands, and you imagine how nice and warm it must be to be cloaked in that animal pelt. You bet it'd be worth killing something to be that warm.

Walking through the sliding doors into the Walmart feels like crossing over into the Emerald City, all warm and bright and swarming with people who've been hired just to tell you hello as you enter. So what if everything here is a placeholder, the thing you tell yourself you'll just get for now until you can get a better version of it someday.

You beeline for the women's section to try on a gray hoodie with a soft nubby lining, and it warms you all the way to your bones. Then you swap out the hoodie for a full-on peacoat and it's like getting a hug straight from God. It feels like armor, like there's nothing that could penetrate that thick skin, even the sharpest fillet knife that a sociopathic trucker keeps in the bunk area of his rig.

You somehow managed to ignore your bladder for seven whole hours, and you realize now how badly you have to go, so you ramble around looking for a bathroom, only the laundry aisle smells so good that you have to stop by for a minute and just take it in. You'd been in Walmart perhaps more frequently than any other structure aside from your apartment and school, yet you never before appreciated its splendor, never before noticed how many ways it offers solutions to things like cleaning yourself up, orange bottles and blue bottles and purple and white, liquids and powders and capsules and pods. And everything moves along in a way that makes sense: the next aisle over is for the body, shelves the length of your apartment back home, all filled with body washes that invigorate or relax, whatever you need that morning. There are washes for men that women can't resist and washes for women that women also can't resist. You'd gone your whole life not ever knowing what a mountain zephyr smells like, and all along it could have been right there in your armpits.

Before you know it you've accumulated more than you can comfortably hold in your hands, but what's that word your English teacher used once or twice? Serendipity! There's an abandoned cart with a brand-new litter box and the wadded-up paper from some breakfast sandwich waiting for you in the next aisle over. You drop your stuff in the carriage and pull out the litter box and the paper, but then you think that you might like to get a cat to keep you company in Texas, so back in the cart the litter box goes. The cat will be gray and white and named Bojangles after the breakfast sandwich wrapper, and Bo is going to need some kibble and a soft bed to sleep on, so off you go to fulfill his needs and then some, the spoiled little bastard he'll be.

By the time you feel the tap on your shoulder, you have an apartment for you and Bo fully furnished, and when you see Ahmet you think, Shit, don't tell me that I'm supposed to include him, too.

"What are you doing?" he says.

You look down at the cart and shrug. It's so obvious what you're doing that you don't feel the need to answer, but then again, it's impolite to condescend, and you're trying to turn over a new leaf. "Shopping," you answer.

He scans the stuff in the carriage, and by the way his lip curls over his tooth — just that one sharp canine tooth that sits too high in his gums, so it looks like it belongs in someone else's mouth — you know he's not happy about something, maybe the color of the cereal bowls you picked out. They're eggshell blue, delicate-looking but indestructible, more than sturdy enough to handle the Frosted Mini-Wheats you'd picked up in the cereal aisle, along with a couple boxes of Count Chocula for treat time.

"Are you kidding me?" he asks.

"I need some stuff for Texas," you say.

"A litter box? A Brita filter?"

You're beginning to take offense. A minute before they seemed like nice things to have, but he's making you doubt your taste.

"You're kidding. You're kidding me, right? This isn't your carriage."

Is it your carriage? Suddenly it doesn't look all that familiar. Eggshell-blue bowls? The real Luljeta would have chosen bone.

Luljeta would have chosen Shower Fresh deodorant over Mountain Fresh.

"This is a joke. You're just playing with me, right?" he asks.

You shake your head. He's right, this isn't your carriage. You are just playing with him.

"You did not just go crazy, right?"

"No," you say.

"You're not crazy. This stuff isn't yours."

"I'm tired," you say. "I am really tired."

He turns around and begins walking away. "Let's go," he says, and though that doesn't sound like the best idea you'd ever heard, it's better than anything you can come up with at the moment.

On the way back to the car, the woman from the minivan stares at you, her gloved right hand holding a cigarette and her left cocked up on her hip. You're pretty sure she smiles at you, and so you smile back. It's the least you could do for each other, these little acts of kindness in these little blacktop moments.

You were never a good sleeper. You'd stopped crying through the night at only a few months old, but that didn't mean that you slept through it. When you first learned to stand, you would immediately rise to your feet when your mother put you in the

361

crib, your hands on the bars as if in a prison, and often she would wake to find you standing in the very same position. She wondered if you'd moved from that position at all during the night, if you'd forgiven her abandonment of you long enough to rest for even an hour, but mostly she was grateful to you for letting her sleep if you weren't going to. Perhaps she should've been more concerned for your well-being than for her own, because she must have read somewhere that sleep was possibly more vital to the growing human body than food.

She'd told you about your sleepless infant nights as if in apology for the sleepless teenage ones you frequently experience now. She told you that you can somewhat compensate for lost sleep with fifteen-minute power naps, according to *Redbook* or some other women's mag that she browses through in the checkout line at the grocery store, but you suck at napping even more than at night sleep. Napping is the worst. It brings on the worst dreams, the sleep paralysis that you are not fully convinced comes from misfiring brain synapses instead of the paranormal, and so you avoid sleeping during the daytime when at all possible. Sometimes it isn't possible, like in the passenger seat of a car after a night of so little rest that it almost doesn't count as a night at all, when the long, tedious, rolling miles of I-20 have the effect of a narcotic. You feel yourself succumb and struggle to open your heavy eyelids, but when you do, you see cockroaches scurrying over the dashboard, clogging up the heater vents, a solid sheet of them, one throbbing red mass of cockroach. They drop under their own weight onto your feet and thighs, and you try to scream and flail but you're frozen. All you can muster is a little closed-throat moan that doesn't convey the terror you feel, that instead sounds like you smell something good in the oven, those crescent rolls from Christmas dinner.

"Hey," Ahmet says, shaking your forearm. "Are you all right? You're making weird sounds."

Weird sounds. That's the best you could do — it wasn't the scream you thought you needed, but it worked. The cockroaches scatter back to the little dream nests where they sit it out while you're awake. You blink your eyes a few times, then pry them open with your fingers.

"Can we get some coffee?" you ask.

"If we stop for coffee now we're going to have to stop three more times in the next hour so you can pee," he says.

"I'll get some adult diapers when we stop and just pee into those," you say.

"I wish you would do that," he says.

"I will," you say. It scares you a little that you're not really joking.

"What do you need coffee for, anyway? You're not even the one driving."

"I don't want to keep falling asleep."

Ahmet is white-knuckling the wheel. He's getting annoyed, and you don't blame him. You're still groggy, but conscious enough to realize how annoying you're being, annoying enough that you don't want to hear yourself talk, only you can't seem to stop babbling about cockroaches and the various forms of truck stop caffeine. You suddenly understand completely why NYU doesn't want you, and why your father didn't, and why some people want to punch you in the mouth, which knows only two modes: silent and this nonsense.

"You need sleep," Ahmet says. "You said yourself how tired you are. You almost had a nervous breakdown in Walmart."

"I don't want to sleep this kind of sleep. I'm having bad dreams."

"This whole thing is a bad dream," he says.

"What?"

"Nothing."

"I want to stop."

"Please just go to sleep."

"No, I want to stop. I don't want to do this anymore," you say. You didn't expect those words to leave your mouth, but hearing them makes you feel like Einstein stumbling onto some new physics theorem, an answer to something that's been sitting there all along, just waiting to be discovered. You want to stop. You want to stop! It sounds so perfect in your head that you repeat it again out loud. "I want to stop, Ahmet. Stop."

But Ahmet's foot is getting heavier on the go pedal, not the stop one.

"You don't have to do this anymore, either. I don't want you to do this for me."

"It's a little late for that. We're closer to Houston than to Waterbury."

"Just let me out," you say.

"Just calm down," he answers.

"I'm calm. Who's not calm? I just don't want to do this anymore."

He shakes his head in disbelief. You could have told him you were a genie and he wouldn't have been more confused. You could have told him that you were pregnant with his child and he wouldn't have been more disgusted.

"And what do you want to do instead?" he asks.

You shake your head.

"What is even wrong with you?"

"I don't know," you say. The question was meant to be hypothetical at best, insulting at worst, but you like the question. It makes you feel like some progress is being made: you both acknowledge that there's something wrong with you, which is strangely reassuring.

Ahmet doesn't seem to take comfort in it. Even with his hands firmly gripping the wheel, you can see that he's shaking, his Adam's apple moving ever so slightly up and down as he swallows what might be sobs, at least if you're willing to acknowledge that you could have caused another human being enough pain to cry. Sure, there's power in that, in making someone cry, there's that English-class *agency* word popping up in real-world practical applications again, and yet it doesn't feel awesome like it had back in the assistant principal's office, when it seemed like the key to forward momentum.

"I'm sorry," you say.

"Your mother has no idea where you are, right?"

"Can you please pull over? Will you please

stop the car?"

"You could just get up and leave? How do you do that? Don't you have any feelings?"

"I do," you say. "I feel sick. I think I'm going to throw up. Please pull over."

"Is that why you want to be with him? Because you're just like him?"

"Maybe," you say. "I might be. I don't know."

"It's cruel. You have been just cruel," he says, and he seems as confused by your cruelty as saddened by it. This boy refugee, who has seen neighbors kill neighbors, who had been born into a war and lost more than you had ever known by the time he had been potty-trained; this young handsome man, who has managed to find joy in Kawasakis and hope in Panera Bread; this person is confused and saddened by *you,* who, he is just realizing, has silently mocked him for his Kawasaki and Panera Bread, and used him not for his company but for his hatchback. He who had been born into cruelty and yet somehow had not been ruined by it, and in fact had rejected it so entirely that he didn't even recognize it in you when he met you, is now reminded that he should have never let his guard down, not even with someone whose face is as pretty as yours.

"There's a rest stop at the next exit," you say. "Please stop."

He does stop. He stops talking and, in half a mile, he stops the car. He stops looking at you quizzically when you grab your bag from the backseat, and when you come back to tell him that you'll be hitching a ride with a silver-headed woman who found you crying so pathetically that she felt obligated to offer you a ride in her camper with her and her old man, he doesn't try to talk you out of it. He tells you obligatorily that it's a bad idea, hands you a pair of brass knuckles from his glove box, and tells you to text him if you change your mind, but you know that he hopes you won't. You can see that he's already rebuilding, heading east back to the home he hadn't chosen but had enough sense to treasure.

CHAPTER FIFTEEN: ELSIE

I came home from work and went to collapse onto the air mattress and found instead an actual mattress with an actual box spring sitting on an actual metal bed frame. It wasn't made up — that was women's work — but the sheets were ready at the foot, and a new comforter was waiting to be plucked from its plastic sack and made to live up to its name. It did, briefly. It was such a beautiful innerspring-and-latex oasis that I didn't care if it turned out to be some rent-to-own wonder that might be repoed in the middle of the night. I just enveloped the mattress in the scratchy sheets, pulled the blanket up to my chin, and let myself be comforted straight into a deep, deep sleep. I woke up because I was starving, and the hunger was infiltrating my dream, in which I was standing in line at a Chinese restaurant but never able to quite make it to the buffet. I cried and flailed, but I never got my hands on any of the crab rangoons I needed to stay alive.

When I woke, Bashkim was looking at me like a prowler caught in the act.

"Do you like the bed?" he asked.

"It looks like I do," I said. "What are you doing home?"

He walked over and sat down by my feet, knowing that I wouldn't be able to reach him with my fists in my condition. He was expecting a fit in response to whatever it was he was about to say, but that just went to show that he hadn't been paying attention to me at all. I was past rage, or rather it was past me. I couldn't even strive for rage anymore. I mostly got out of bed because I had to pee and also because, really, I had no other choice. There were mouths to be fed, time cards to be punched. Sitting upright was the goal.

"You needed this. You should not be sleeping on the floor anymore."

"Mary slept on the floor."

"Who?"

"The mother of Christ, our lord and savior."

Bashkim rubbed his temples. "You are not her."

"I know."

"Not even a little bit her."

"Yeah."

"Listen, I will be away for a little while."

There was no reason for him to flinch the way he did. I knew it was coming.

"How long?" I asked.

He shrugged. "I don't know, maybe two, three weeks."

I sank down deeper into the pillows. They were new, too, thick stuffed things that kept my neck at an unnatural angle. After all my lobbying and whining for a real mattress, the damn thing was harder on me than the floor was.

"We haven't decided on a name for the baby," I said, some kind of halfhearted attempt at protest.

"The baby is not here yet."

"Yeah, but you're supposed to decide ahead of time."

Bashkim pulled a cigarette from his shirt pocket, looked at it and then at me, and put it away again. "I like Jak. J-A-K. It looks Albanian and American both."

"What do you like for a girl?"

"I have not thought about for a girl."

"You should," I said. "Just in case."

He might as well have been on the plane somewhere over the Atlantic already, as far away as he looked to me. He cracked his knuckles one by one, each of them at a slightly different pitch, as if someone were lightly tapping the toy xylophone in the baby's room. "My mother was named Luljeta," he said. "It is a nice name."

"Was she a good person?" I asked.

"She lived through hell, and you could see it. But yes, she was a good person," he said.

"Okay," I said. "We'll see."

"I will be back for the birth, though. Hold on as long as you can," he said.

I almost laughed at how naïve he sounded then, and I almost cried for the same reason, but instead I just closed my eyes and opened them only once more that night, when he woke me to tell me goodbye.

He didn't say goodbye, actually. What he said was "I'm sorry." He grabbed my hand so tight it hurt and said it again. "I'm sorry. I am."

I'm the one who said goodbye.

The next time I got out of bed it wasn't to pee or eat or get ready for work. I sleep-walked to the kitchen, but when I came to I knew exactly what I was looking for, just like I knew, before I even reached my hand into the empty tin, that Greta's cash loan, that fat paper knot that represented every favor I had ever called in, every hope I dared still hope, was already gone, on its way to the Balkans, and that I was right there at the bottom of that pyramid scheme Dan Rather had talked about on the evening news.

It was a lot of weight to support, and my legs shook until they gave way altogether.

On the floor I wept, but it felt like a performance, like I thought someone was watching me and I had to grieve the right way or I'd fail that test, too. I understood, in theory, that my paddle was way, way down the shit stream, tumbling over a shit waterfall, caught up in a violent shit eddy. I understood, in theory, that the person I was planning to escape from had escaped me instead, just like Greta's money had escaped me. Every promise I had made to her, every promise I had made to the kid, every promise I never even bothered to make in my head or aloud, were all broken before my water was. But it was all happening an hour before my alarm clock was set to go off, so I thought that maybe none of this actually counted, since the day's sandglass hadn't really been turned over yet. So I did the only thing I could think to do: I picked myself up and went back to bed. I told myself I'd come up with a plan later, *later* being that dangling carrot a few ticks ahead in time, that little future heaven where all my greatest plans are made and deployed.

A pain tore through my middle and I curled into myself and wriggled.

"Jesus Christ," I said aloud. I thought for a minute: My god, I'm in labor, but I remembered the British doctor who said that labor doesn't hurt, fear does. I'd been afraid for months without ever feeling these kinds of spasms, so it had to be something else. The new mattress, I thought. Bashkim had bought one made of nails and they punctured my vertebrae as I slept. The alarm clock was still twenty minutes away from ringing, but I cursed it as if it was what had woken me instead of the pain. I could barely move. I needed some Advil desperately but we'd run out earlier that week, between my back pain and Bashkim's endless headaches — headache, really, a singular one that stretched on forever. We still hadn't fixed the phone that I'd ripped out, and it was too early to call anyone, and who would I call to run my errands for me anyway? Another spasm hit, and then I had to shit, too. The pain in my back had made me forget about the rest of my body, but eventually I recognized the familiar pressure on my lower gut. I thought that if I could just get myself to the bathroom and rid myself of it, I could flush the pain away, too. The pain wasn't part of me, it was a phantasm and could be exorcised, I thought. It could be shat out.

I rolled to my side. The pain bit back, gnashing at whatever parts of my insides it could reach. My spleen, it felt like. Or my liver. I never could remember what went where. The baby had taken over my whole middle and pushed all the organs aside anyway.

I clutched my thighs. My sweatpants were soaked through. The comforter was too warm, my body rejecting it after months of acclimating to the cold.

I wanted Bashkim. Or Mamie. Or neither. Pull yourself together, Elsie, you don't need Bashkim or your mother to shit. I used the wall as a brace to pull myself to my feet and looked back down at the demon bed, surprised it had even been able to support my weight, the thousand pounds of it I had to be carrying. But I was on my feet now, well on my way. I slid across the floor as slow and smooth as I could, but the pain still washed over my back in steady, hard waves. After what felt like a decade, I was closer to the door, and then in another year or two I was at the door, and then I was down the hall, at the bathroom. When I made it inside, I wanted to plant a flag down, declare it mine.

I closed the door behind me and dropped onto the toilet so hard I expected it to shatter into a million porcelain pebbles, but it just rocked a little on its bolts and took on my weight. I waited. The pressure was building but nothing was moving. I waited.

Something was moving. I gasped because something was moving fast and hard inside of me. My insides were about to drop out of me. I put my hand to my crotch to hold it in, but I was too late. My insides were right there, pushing hard and ready to fall.

It wasn't my guts. It was a hard stone. I'd swallowed a boulder and it was going to pass.

It wasn't a boulder. It was the head of my daughter, trying to peek into the spacious world outside her tiny walls.

"No," I told her. I held her back. This wasn't going to happen now. I'd carried her around for so long like Atlas carried his globe, an eternal punishment. Eternal. One that would last forever. I wasn't ready for it to end. I wasn't ready for her, not ever. "No," I said again, softly. I didn't have enough air in my lungs to pump out a louder sound. I moaned and sat still. If I didn't move, the baby wouldn't, either. I'd sit here forever. I'd take my meals here. I'd invite Greta for Christmas.

She moved again. She'd gotten a taste of air and didn't want to go back. Or she wanted to stay in there but the walls were closing in on her. I had to convince her to stay inside, where it was warm. I had to help her out or she'd be crushed.

I had to do nothing. She called the shots. She pounded on the walls of my stomach like she was ringing a brass knocker. Let me in. No, actually, let me out.

Fine, I told her. Fine. Just let me up and I'll call a cab. I'll get downstairs and Yllka will walk us out the door.

Here's fine, she said. I'm not picky. Look who I'm being born to. You think I have airs?

It doesn't have anything to do with that. I don't know how to do this. I didn't go to nursing school. I barely made it through high school.

You watched that episode of *Nova*, what's the one? "The Miracle of Life"? Didn't you read a book or something?

I skimmed. And it didn't look like this. *The Miracle of Life,* all the illustrations, none of them looked like this.

Anyway, what's to know? Mammals do it all the time. Remember when the neighbor's cat had kitties, right?

Tippy? The whole litter died.

There's no point in arguing, I'm coming whether you like it or not.

She pushed hard but I held her back. I wouldn't be able to for much longer, though. I felt her dropping lower, swimming to the edge.

She was going to come. All along I'd known that without ever once believing it. Other people's babies were things swaddled in soft blankets like little puff pastries in pastel wrappers, but I thought of my baby as something that lived inside of me and ate my food and made me ache from the inside out. She'd seemed content enough in there. I would've been happy to trade places with her.

It's hard out here, you know, I told her.

It's no great shakes in here, she said.

"Ah," I said aloud. She was pushing again. "Okay," I said. "Okay okay okay."

I slid to the edge of the toilet seat and walked my hands down the side of the sink and the wall behind me until I was on the ground. The chill of the linoleum sent a fresh volt of pain through my spine, but after a minute the cold felt good against my back. The wetness on the floor made it feel colder and better. I turned to see if the tank was leaking, but I saw instead that it came from me.

Was that my water breaking? I asked.

No, that already happened, the daughter said. What you're lying in is piss.

It's water. The floor is dirty. That's why it looks yellow.

It's piss.

I shuffled a few inches on my back toward the towel rack. I must've looked like a cockroach turned over on its side. I pulled the towels to the floor and stretched one flat, then lay on top of it. I balled the other one up and wedged it under my neck. They were Yllka's towels, which she'd lent us. She washed them in the sink once a week with bleach and dish detergent and the fibers reeked of both. She was going to kill me.

Should I call Yllka for help?

How's she going to help?

She could call someone.

Call who?

An ambulance.

You're not having a heart attack, you're having a baby. You want a doctor to charge you thousands for something that's going to happen with or without him?

Yes. I don't want to be alone.

You're not alone.

"Shit," I said. "Ah." She pushed again.

God, are you coming or what?

It's a tight squeeze. Settle down, I'm doing the best I can.

"Yllka," I gasped. It was pathetic. On TV women screamed and flailed and kicked their husbands. I couldn't stand up or let out a proper yell.

"Yllka." I tried again. It was loud enough this time to bounce off the shower walls and land back in my ear. "Yllka."

I heard nothing else, no stairs creaking under the pumps Yllka wore from sunup until bedtime.

Don't worry about it. She'd only make this whole thing harder. Too many hands in the bathroom. She might even kick us out onto the street if she saw the mess this is going to make.

She'll help us. I need help. I'm not going to be able to do this once you're a crying wiggling monkey in my arms.

Another wave of pain washed over my back. I rolled onto my side and pulled my knees in toward my chin.

Quit it, I said. I can't take this.

I'm not doing it, you are, she said.

I'm not. I'm trying to stop it.

You started it and the only thing that's going to stop it is the end. Hang in there.

I can't.

You can.

We lay in silence for a while, spasms shaking my back into convulsions every few minutes. It was cold. I was sweating. I wanted to shackle myself to the radiator and burn myself like Joan of Arc. I was guilty. Let me face my maker.

Stop being so dramatic, she said. You're not going to die. It hurts for me, too.

It does?

I'm in a vise here.

I'm sorry. I'll try.

I'll try, too.

We both pushed but nothing happened besides a fresh batch of new hurt.

"Ow," I said. I was crying. Crying from sheer physical pain, which I hadn't done since I was ten or eleven. I thought it would be a refreshing change but it wasn't.

I'm not ready yet, I told her.

I could see now that the lines that swirled through the ceiling tile weren't solid but tiny little dots that looked like ants marching in perfectly ribboned rows. I thought I saw them moving, marching, but it was probably my own shivering that wobbled the dots into movement. I preferred the ants. They seemed like company, like a squad there to cheer me on.

Can we try again? she asked after a few

minutes.

I didn't answer at first.

Can we?

I opened my mouth and let out a sob. A thin line of snot trailed straight into my lips.

I'm disgusting, I said.

You're having a baby. It's messy. Can we try?

Yes.

I pushed again. I wailed, a cry vibrating my clenched lips.

It felt like she'd shifted in there, but she still lay inside of me.

I thought you said you were coming, I said.

I am coming, she said. I'm trying. I can't fit through.

There's only one way out.

No shit. I'm looking right at it.

Don't get snotty.

I'm sorry. It's a habit.

You're not even born yet. How can you have habits?

What can I say? I'm my mother's daughter.

Under my hand, my stomach felt hard and rough as a rock ledge at a quarry. She was all turned around in there. She was kicking and twirling.

I breathed in deep through my nose and

hissed the air out through my teeth like I'd seen pregnant ladies do in the movies. This whole performance was an imitation. They should've put a warning on those films: Don't try this at home.

Are you ready? I asked.

Yeah. You?

I shook my head. I don't know, I said.

Close enough, she said. Let's go.

I couldn't catch her. She slid onto the towel like she'd ridden a hot metal slide into the sand, as smooth and fast as that. She was veiled in pink but she was purple underneath. The trip had bruised her entire tiny body, or the vise inside had. She vibrated like a car engine that wouldn't turn over. I waited to hear the noise, the sparks connecting and the engine roaring to life, but she was silent. The baby opened her mouth and screamed silently. I looked into it but it wasn't a cavern like I expected. I remembered about the jelly inside, that I had to clear it from her nose and throat. I slid my pinkie into her mouth and wiped the jelly away and it was a cork released from a bottle, her voice spilling from her lips like champagne bubbles. Her cries pierced but didn't carry far. It only looked as if they would be strong enough to tear down the walls around us, convulsive and angry but without the volume to match the rage. She shook so hard. She must've been cold but I didn't hold her, I didn't wrap her up. I watched her, her legs and arms wiry and frantic. I didn't know how to pick her up. I'd never held a baby, not since Uncle Eddie had told me to be careful with my newborn cousin. He said an infant's head was soft and would cave in if you touched it the wrong way. The baby looked as if she would just slip right out of my hands. I would crush her if I held her wrong. She'd disintegrate in my arms.

But she cried so hard. I knew that kind of cry, that she'd take the chance of being pulverized if I'd just keep her warm. I grabbed the towel that my head had rested on and brought it to her. I wiped her down and began to wrap her but I couldn't. She was still tied to the placenta, the cord still held us together. Sometimes the doctors asked the daddies if they wanted to cut it, but there were no doctors or daddies around. I scanned the sink. Nothing, just my toothbrush with its splayed bristles and a thin mound of pale green soap melted onto the enamel. I remembered a straight blade in the medicine cabinet that Bashkim kept for close shaves. I tried to stand but I wouldn't be able to get to my feet without dragging and hanging the baby, so I picked her up. Just like that, one arm bracing her back and head while the other hand pushed our bodies upright. I held the wall, then the sink for support. I saw a brief reflection of the two of us in the mirror and it calmed me a little. We looked okay together, both wet red messes, but okay.

I reached in and grabbed the blade and laid us back down over the towels, me upright with my legs spread wide and her placed in between them. She shivered when I put her down and began crying. I told her I'd hold her again but we needed to do this other thing first, this thing that was important for I don't know what reason. I pulled the cord taut and laid it across my palm, a thick veiny root that looked alive on its own, and sliced into it with the blade. I didn't feel anything. I wondered if the baby did, if this was a thing that belonged to her or to me, but she didn't flail as I cut, either. I sliced until the cord slipped away from my hand in two pieces, the longer one still on my side, six inches of it dangling from the baby's belly.

"Okay now. Shh, shh," I told her. I wrapped the thin towel around her a few times, a sloppy cocoon that swallowed her entire body and strapped her limbs to her own core. She cried for another minute, her eyes closed. I tucked her into my chest and we shivered together, her cries dying down as my own breathing slowed.

We lay still for what I guess was an hour, the two of us, on that bathroom floor. I passed the placenta after a while, and it hurt like a second delivery, only this time all it brought was a purple, veiny, deflated balloon left behind after the party ended. It looked like its own living thing, or at least its own once-living thing, something I should have buried and held a service for. I rolled it up in the towel I'd been lying on and threw it in the trash bin.

I wanted to lie still forever but I couldn't. The baby moaned once in a while and I was afraid she'd cry again, this time not for warmth but for something I didn't have for her, food or comfort. I knew I had food in me somewhere but I didn't know how to get it out. Something had already leaked from my nipples but it didn't look like milk, more like the cloudy white pools that formed off the banks of the Naugatuck River, something that could never sustain life, something that might even kill it off. I had to move eventually. I had to move now, get to Yllka and to the hospital. The baby looked healthy but how the hell was I supposed to know? To me babies looked like a different species altogether, not tiny versions of our own. Nurses would know what to do. They could show me, those clean pink women dressed in white like angels, their hair smelling like shampoo always. I was a girl whose hair smelled of nothing ever. I was a girl who turned something fine into something scratched and broken, even when I swore I didn't do anything wrong. Every CD I ever owned had scratches pitted in the grooves as soon as I'd released them from their cases. It was a birthright, a reverse Midas touch.

But look at me, even without the nurses — I held not just a baby but an advertisement for babies. Who wouldn't want one of these? Those Punnett squares from biology class, the baby was living proof of the bottom right-hand box, all recessive and perfect. Even under the waxy coat and dried blood, she looked nothing like me, nothing like any human I'd seen before. Every step I'd taken so far was a stumble, and yet look what I produced, a genetic fluke, something so better than any of its sources that it was a miracle as grand as the Virgin's, or else evolution taking place before my very eyes.

"Ready?" I asked her, but she didn't answer. I guess somewhere along the journey she'd lost the words.

CHAPTER SIXTEEN: LULJETA

You were so close. You almost made it. That's what you think once you make it inside Houston city limits, five hours and fifty-seven minutes after you parted with Ahmet at a rest stop west of Jackson, Mississippi.

Noreen — that's the camper lady's name, Noreen, and her husband is Jeb, actually Jeb, which you didn't think was possible, because nobody's name is actually Jeb, that's just what people like you call people like Jeb when you think they're not listening — Noreen put you in the sleeper of their Winnebago and mostly left you alone, just looking over now and again to make sure you weren't shooting up or dead.

Later, though, Noreen started asking more questions. First your name, then your age, then if you were running away. You told her Samantha, eighteen, and that it isn't running away if you're a grown-up. She asked where from and where to, and you told her Massachusetts and California, respectively, after a stop in Houston to visit a second cousin who up until then you'd only ever known as a Facebook friend. Your cousin was a music producer for some local R & B artists. You didn't seem to have much in common except blood, but blood was thicker than water, as the saying went.

"And tar is thicker than blood. What's that got to do with anything?" Noreen asked.

"It's just an expression," you answered.

"It's a dumb one. What were you doing with that kid? He your boyfriend?" she asked.

You told her you met him online, and you were just sharing a ride to save gas money.

"That's dangerous. Meeting up with somebody you met online is dangerous," she said. "In fact, anybody you don't know, consider 'em dangerous."

"My cousin's riding with me out to California," you said.

"Good," she said. "We're not stepping foot inside that hellhole."

You had no reason to lie to Noreen, other than taking her advice about treating everyone as a potential threat. But Noreen and Jeb are harmless, disproving their own point. They're helpful, even. They bring you

all the way to the address you had memo-
rized — your second cousin's, right —
which is generous of them. On the way, they
fed you half of an Italian grinder, which they
called a sub, they let you recharge your
phone, they put some crappy straight-to-
DVD romcom on the television, and they
did it all without even once acting like they
were doing something nice or being particularly kind in demeanor. They just did it, as
if that was the thing you did with people
you picked up in a rest stop on the side of
the road. You think of all the trashy names
you would've had for them had you passed
their camper on the highway, what you
would've said about their bumper sticker,
which managed to be pro-gun, anti-
abortion, and anti-Obama in less than six
words total, and it doesn't reconcile with
the people you're looking at, who are not
actually total shitheads. You aren't sure
whether the bumper stickers are false advertising, then, or not advertising at all. That
complicates things, suddenly, within the
four walls of that moving house and especially outside of it. Just how the hell are you
supposed to know these things about people
if not by the signs they carry?

Before you part, Noreen asks, "You got
money?" You nod, and she says, "That's

good, 'cuz I don't." You smile at her joke but she doesn't, and you realize she isn't joking.

"I could give you some money for gas," you say, crinkling the last twenty in your pocket against your thigh, not really ready to let it go.

"Eh, keep it, Samantha. We were going to be driving this way with you or without you," she says. You thank her and that's that. That's how fast a story can start and end. And then you're at the end of a street that you'd traveled nearly two thousand miles to find, and you wonder if stories ever really start or end.

You don't know why you weren't expecting what you see. You imagined your father's family in one of those big cul-de-sac behemoths with a pull-around driveway, a wrap-around porch, and an interior that had never met a beige it didn't like. After all, he's a businessman, a pizza scion, maybe not quite Papa John but an entrepreneur nonetheless. He escaped both Communism and the gray-and-rust part of New England that didn't have Sherwin-Williams paint colors named after its towns, so he has to be a man of some means in order to make it as far as he has. But you quadruple-check the address, and there is no pull-around driveway, or a second or third floor, or a wraparound porch, or a porch at all, unless you count the three concrete slabs that lead to the front door. It isn't that it's awful. It isn't as bad as Greta's place, it doesn't share walls or floors with anyone like at your place, there are no discarded Reeboks tangled up in the telephone wires outside. It isn't awful because it isn't anything, just a little rectangle like the one Mamie lives in, something that looks like what second graders draw when signifying *house*. It has four walls covered in yellow vinyl siding with black shutters and a chain-link fence, which keeps a yappy little Bichon Frise in and strangers like you out.

Strangers like you. That's what you are, as the barking little dog warns its masters inside.

This is the part where you're supposed to hesitate. Everything before this point has been rising action, and this is either the climax or the point where everything falls apart. For it being one of the oldest stories in the book — at least the YA books you so loved when you were far more young than adult, those pages of wayward parents and lonely, precocious, tough-as-nails daughters who talk like teenage girls never talk — you have no foresight into how this will end. It's here that either you will be initiated into an entirely new family, which will mean you'll be loved and hurt and protected and betrayed exponentially more than you have ever experienced; or you will learn for certain that you're a thing to be shunned and rejected, unlovable by vampire or werewolf, your own father and siblings, and, if you go ahead and complete the betrayal by knocking on the door, even your own mother, once and for all. You know that the apprehension a reasonable person would have felt two weeks ago, when the seeds of this maniacal idea had been planted, should surely be occurring to you now.

But dear god, do you have to pee, and you really want that nippy asshole Bichon Frise off your ankles. So you knock three times, before you have a chance to think any better of it, and the hesitation that follows isn't on your side of the door. You hear some low talking, and some louder talking, and then a series of dead bolts being unlocked. There's the sound of something stuck, a metal jiggling or something, but as the door opens you realize that the sound isn't a sound but a feeling, and that the feeling is that of your heart shaking loose in your chest. Standing before you is a woman with her hand over her own heart, so whatever condition you've suddenly been afflicted with is obviously contagious. Neither of you says a word, but she opens the door wider to let you in, and two small children rush over to the woman's side.

"It's her," the younger one, a girl, says. She's about eight years old, her thick hair in a side ponytail, and she looks at you with a mixture of fascination and fear, the way that kids look at things they've been told about but have not yet seen, like a body at a wake. The girl's brother, who's just a little taller than the girl, keeps a safer distance, his black eyes fixed on you like on a television screen. From somewhere away from the door and the huddled mass of human that's accumulated there, someone calls out, "Hi." The source is a buzz-cut kid in a black sweatshirt, his posture as bad as yours. It must be Adnan, that oldest son, that legitimate firstborn.

There's someone sitting next to him at the table, too, her hands wrapped around a teacup that has to be close to shattering under her grip.

"Mom?" you ask. It comes out as a question because despite what you're seeing, it's impossible that she's there. But then again, it seems impossible that you're there, too.

CHAPTER SEVENTEEN: ELSIE

I couldn't tell if it was nerves or childbirth that unsteadied my legs as I walked the staircase, but I took the steps one at a time as I climbed down, first one foot on the plank and then the next one landing right beside it, the way toddlers do. My free hand clung to the rail for support until I changed my mind and held the baby to my chest with both hands instead of one, then switched back again, not knowing which would keep us safer. Eighteen steps later and we were on the landing, both of us okay for now, even though I worried about crushing her in my arms, which were holding her too tightly. I tried to loosen my clutch around her but I couldn't. I was too afraid of losing her. Even off the stairs, I walked a pace at a time, one foot meeting the other ahead of it like a bride walking down the aisle. A bride in heather-gray sweats, dyed pink with blood.

The radio was on, a stream of talk radio raging about war or taxes or traffic, something to get Yllka's heart pumping before the Turkish coffee kicked in. It was barely dawn, and I imagined the shuffle of her slippers over the linoleum floor. I knocked once, but didn't hear any footsteps move toward me, so I knocked again, and again, until finally I opened the door and let myself in.

"Yllka," I said.

She whipped around and dropped the bucket of sudsy water she was holding in her hands. "Punë muti!" she shrieked and pressed a wet hand against her heart. "Elsie, you scared me," she said. She squinted through the fuzzy bangs covering her eyes, then pushed them out of the way. "Elsie? Elsie, Elsie," she repeated and dropped the sponge that was in her other hand.

Yllka looked at us, me and the baby, hand to her mouth, eyes wide with horror. Suds dripped from her fingertips as if she bled cleanliness, and could just wash over us with it, but she held her arms close to her, cradling herself.

"I didn't know she was coming," I said.

"Oh my god," she said.

"I didn't know until it was too late. I couldn't move."

"You . . . Oh, Elsie . . . You didn't know she was coming? Oh, oh, oh." She touched a fingertip to the baby, to my shoulder, feeling us out, making sure we weren't a bad dream. "Oh, this is bad, Elsie. How could you not know? Oh, never mind, you need to go to a hospital. Oh, oh, oh. Oh god, and Bashkim! Sit, go sit down!"

"We should go," I said.

"Go? Where do you want to go?"

"The hospital."

"Yes, of course the hospital. Here," she said, as if about to hand me something, but instead dropped down into the seat beside me, colected herself, and when she rose, she was again the woman I was anxious and terrified to come to.

"Okay, you have cleaned the mouth?" she asked. "She has cried? You have fed her?"

"She has cried. I haven't fed her. She's been asleep," I said.

"She's moving, though? She's breathing?"

I could feel her warm shallow breath against the nook of my arm, where she was cradled, stretching a limb sometimes, and opening her mouth like a bass out of water, silently gasping for something. "She's breathing," I said.

"And you?"

"I'm breathing, too."

"No, I mean, are you all right? Are you still bleeding? Do you feel ill, or in pain?"

I hadn't noticed either until she asked, and then I felt both, immediately and entirely.

"I'm sore. I feel weak," I said. My heart began racing, the pain and weakness so great that I worked up a sweat feeling them.

"Okay." Yllka grabbed her purse from the kitchen table. "We are going to the hospital. Hand me the baby."

I held her tighter. "What? No, I can't let her go," I said. I was keeping her safe, and she was doing the same for me. Remove her from my chest, and who knew what kind of wound would open up.

"You are weak, it is dangerous to walk. I will carry her, you will hold on to me and walk very, very slowly, one step at a time. In the car you will hold her again."

"Maybe we should wait for Gjonni," I said.

"Gjonni? What does he know about childbirth? I know childbirth more than every man on the block added together. We go now."

I didn't answer. Yllka tapped my shoulder and pulled the baby from my arms. At once I began shivering, and the baby crying. She had come out but she wasn't meant to be separate from me yet. She wasn't meant to be her own thing. I was freezing without her, and she was hungry and upset.

"See, she doesn't like it. Let me have her back," I said.

"Babies cry, they will always cry. Stand up, Elsie, we must go."

I was crying, too. I felt the tears and hic-cups finally, not sure how long they'd been there.

"Come," Yllka said, softer this time. "It will all be fine, everything is okay, we just have to take this first step."

"I'm scared," I said.

"Scared is fine. You're a mother now, you will get used to it. Come."

I stood, and Yllka coached me down the stairs, got me down one at a time, followed so close behind me that her knees brushed against my back on the way. She was right about a lot of things, but wrong about one: we didn't have to take just this first step. There were many more to follow, and each was harder than the last. My back slumped more with every stride across the blacktop to the car, as if my head weighed more than the rest of me combined, and my knees buckled under the weight of all of it to-gether. Yllka braced me with one arm, held tight to the baby with the other, and guided me to the garage, and when I was safe in the car, buckled up and everything, she handed me my daughter.

I always thought that when life ended there'd be a procession of dead grandparents and great-aunts and -uncles to greet me. Maybe even my father, if he'd managed to crash the pearly gates, and if he was more interested in seeing me in the afterlife than he had been in the regular one. We'd stand in puffs of dry-ice smoke like Alice Cooper onstage and I'd manage to keep my white robe free from coffee stains and ring around the collar, because, after all, this was heaven and anything was possible. Instead, in this heaven, all I saw was white light, and I didn't feel the peace that people suffered through entire lives just to get to. I felt groggy, that's all. Maybe heaven was like smoking pot: it seemed to make other people really happy, but all it did for me was make me sleepy and too dumb to speak.

"Hey, look who's awake," someone said.

The white light was an overhead fluorescent lamp, and it was burning my eyes. I rolled my head over to follow the voice. I couldn't really move yet. Mamie was standing near the bed, cradling something, but every time I blinked I saw bright light in her arms where the baby should be.

"They cleaned her up and brought her in," Mamie said. "She's healthy, they said. She's sleeping as much as you."

I closed my eyes again, but the light followed me.

"She's beautiful," someone else said. It was Greta, standing somewhere beside me. I couldn't lift up my head to follow the sound of her voice. "So tiny! She's only six pounds."

They had the wrong baby, then. The one I had carried and borne weighed at least a hundred. I wanted to tell them to call the nurse so they could get the right one from the crib, but my mouth was too dry for my lips to come together and form the words. I sensed a headache but the pain receptors weren't firing all the way.

"Maa," I said instead.

"Yeah, that's who you are now. Ma," Mamie said. "And I'm Grandma. Twenty years away from a senior citizen discount and I'm Grandma. At least I won't be too arthritic to run after her when she starts crawling."

"I'm in love with her," Greta said. "I can't believe it. She's perfect."

I wanted to see for myself, but my eyes wouldn't focus, and then they wouldn't even stay open. Given where she came from, it wasn't possible that she was perfect, but maybe she could be like a mutation, the kind that starts off an accident but ends up being the first of a stronger, better something.

The next time I opened my eyes the fog was gone. There was no mistaking the room for heaven anymore. Too many fluorescent lights and mechanized blips. Too many bright colors, Mylar balloons, bouquets of pink carnations and baby's breath. The television was on and the door was open. The whole world could go in and out of the room as it pleased, except for me. I was tethered to the Craftmatic by a rubber tube jammed into my arm.

"She is alive after all," Gjonni said. Yllka was holding the baby while Gjonni held a thick ugly cigar between his lips. Yllka was grasping my hand with her free one, rubbing little circles into my skin with her thumb.

"A beautiful girl, beautiful," Gjonni said. "Who needs a son with a daughter like this?"

"Nobody needs a son," Yllka said. "What a stupid thing to say."

"You will have a son next time," Gjonni said.

"There is no next time," I said.

"Every woman says that after her first child. 'Never again.' The whole world would have died off if women could remember the pain of childbirth," Gjonni said.

"I remember the pain of childbirth," Yllka said.

"I remember," I said. "There's no next time. Can I hold her?"

"Of course you can," Yllka said, but she looked reluctant to give the baby up. "Do you want to lie with Mama, Luljeta? Are you ready to eat?"

"What did you call her?" I said.

"What do you mean?" Yllka asked. She eyed the sac of fluids being funneled into my arm suspiciously, like she was wondering how much morphine, exactly, it was necessary to give someone who had just undergone the most routine of all procedures in the history of mammals.

"It's just saline. They're just giving me ibuprofen now. Can I hold her?" I asked again.

Yllka bobbed my daughter a few more times before she placed her into my arms. "Back to Mama, Luljeta," she said.

"You said it again," I said. "Luljeta."

"Yes," Yllka said. "Of course. It's her name."

404

"Says who? Who named her?" I asked.

Yllka looked at Gjonni, and then to the button on the wall that would call the nurse. "You named her, love," she said. She spoke gently, as if she were still talking to the baby.

"I did? When?"

"I don't know, Elsie, we weren't here for that. Isn't that the name you wanted? It's a beautiful name. It means 'flower of life.' "

"It's what Bashkim wanted," I said.

"Oh," Yllka said. "Well, it's good that he had a say, since he couldn't be here."

"He could have been here. He just wasn't," I said.

"Oh, don't say that, Elsie. He couldn't help it. He had to leave, you know that."

"She's just tired. And the drugs," Gjonni said to Yllka, as if I weren't in the room at all.

I looked away from them both, down to my daughter, Luljeta, as if we were alone in another room after all. She was my daughter. It felt strange to think it at first; I wasn't used to putting those words together, and they sounded foreign to me, like her name, so I said them over and over again until they started to feel natural on my tongue.

"My daughter. Luljeta. Luljeta. My daughter," I said.

"It's a beautiful name," Yllka said again.

She was pleading a little, trying to convince me to keep it instead of trading it in for something I wouldn't constantly have to explain. But she didn't have to convince me. The name fit, there wasn't another name in any language that would suit her more. I wondered how Bashkim had known that and I resented him for it, that this was my daughter and she was more of a mystery to me than she was to anyone else. I was holding her for the first time since I'd given birth to her and I resented that, too, that she'd been taken from my arms so quickly. They thought I couldn't be trusted. They thought I was like one of those mama pandas at the zoo who give birth to tiny babies and then crush them to death by holding on too tightly. Or they thought I was the opposite: the mama panda at the zoo who takes one look at its young and walks away in search of more apples and biscuits from the zookeepers, its instincts obliterated by its own selfish wanting.

Luljeta opened her tiny mouth and began crying, and I understood it. I knew what she was asking for. "She's hungry," I said.

"Should I get a nurse to bring some formula?" Yllka asked.

I shook my head. "She doesn't need formula."

"Have you nursed her yet?" Yllka asked. "It's not always as easy as it should be."

"I don't think it should be easy. I just think I should do it," I said.

"Okay, but don't be afraid to ask for help. There are lots of people who can help," she said.

I nodded, but I didn't want her help, or Gjonni's, or Mamie's or Greta's, or even Bashkim's. "Can I be alone now, please?" I said.

"Of course," Yllka said, and she came over and kissed Luljeta on the head, and then she and Gjonni took turns kissing me on the cheek, and then I was alone with my daughter.

"Here, here," I whispered to Luljeta, but she kept crying, refusing to latch on. I moved her from one arm to the other, from one breast to the other, but she writhed no matter how I held her, until a nurse popped her head in.

"Everything all right in here?" she asked.

"Yes," I said. "She's just being fussy."

I bobbed her up and down in my arms, and I kissed her tiny fuzzy head, just barely grazing it with my lips, afraid that the fontanel might collapse if I pressed too hard. She kept crying until I joined her, my hospital gown sopping with tears and milk that was sustaining nothing.

"You're going to have to trust me," I told her. "It's just the two of us, you know."

Eventually she quieted down, and eventually she latched on and drank until she was full. We both fell asleep and when she awoke she was startled, as if she'd forgotten who I was, and when I tried to feed her, I had to convince her to trust me all over again. It went on like that until we were released from the hospital, and even sometimes in those first days back home. She was a suspicious little thing, cynical by nature. She'd cry and she'd follow me with her barely open little eyes and wrap her tiny little fingers around one of mine as if she thought I would let her go. I didn't blame her; what had I done in all those months leading up to her arrival to convince her I had her best interests in mind? I'd have to spend the whole rest of our lives convincing her I cared about her well-being, I thought, but that was okay. Eventually she would believe me.

CHAPTER EIGHTEEN:
LULJETA

Your audience is rapt. Adnan at the table, his kid brother and sister, all of them watching you and your mother, waiting for the silence to break. Only Aggie looks away from the soap opera playing out in her dining nook, a rectangle carved away in a corner of the living room, where an actual prime-time soap opera plays on a flat-screen television that balances precariously on the dirt-brown shag carpet. She walks into the kitchen and begins opening drawers and cabinets, clanking things around, obviously looking for nothing in particular except for perhaps a way out.

For what feels like minutes you try to ask, *How?*, even though you must realize that you'd left a trail of bread crumbs all the way to Texas. Ahmet probably called her last night, or he called Yllka, who called her, and your mother drove straight to Bradley International and booked a direct flight with the ticket agent, which she probably didn't realize isn't really how one purchases airline tickets. She probably paid thousands and was too distraught on the plane to eat the surprisingly delicious Delta cookies or watch the second-run coach-class movies. It would have been her first time ever on an airplane. Her first time, as she'd described it to you more than once, was supposed to have been en route to the Bahamas, to an all-inclusive where she would spend a week once you'd left her for college. She was supposed to sip from fishbowls of banana daiquiris instead of shrunken Solo cups of diluted orange juice. You were supposed to be in a dorm room in Manhattan, perfecting your cat-eye lining technique and reading *Les Misérables* in the original French, which you'd somehow mastered in a semester despite having taken Spanish for six years without ever being able to so much as correctly order a burrito.

Instead, look at the two of you, not looking at each other.

The other kids look, waiting for some kind of action. This dining room soap opera had started promisingly, teasing fraught confrontations and ticking time bombs, but now seems to be fizzling into some atmospheric, broody drama that overutilizes silence and shadow. They're just kids, and haven't yet mastered things like theme and subtext. And even if they weren't kids, you haven't provided enough context for anyone to make sense of you. You don't even make sense to your mother, who appears neither angry nor relieved to have traced you to a carpeted living room rather than the stainless steel gurney in some coroner's cold medical building, which was the worst-case scenario she both refused to entertain and could not keep from entertaining. She looks embarrassed, as if she were the one who had brought this mess on.

And hadn't she, in a sense? Her lies and cover-ups, her clumsy maneuvering of the marionette strings that she nonetheless refused to relinquish, that was what had pushed you out. You were pushed, you remind yourself. Right? Right.

Or wait. Were you pulled? Wasn't there also a pull involved? Wasn't there something you were forgetting?

There's also a pressure involved. Not in the room so much as in your own body. The pressure is so real that it's physical, and then you realize that it is indeed physical, and is coming from your bladder. It's painful, yet it's a relief, because you know the solution to this problem, and it gives you some kind of hope that maybe you could stumble on some other answers, too. "Bathroom?" you ask no one in particular, and the little girl answers, or rather silently grabs your hand and marches you down the hall, like a teacher dragging a naughty student to the dunce corner. You step into the room she leads you to and lock the door behind you. There's no window. You won't be getting out of this one.

The question will be coming soon — *Why?* — and you have to come up with an answer. You think, maybe, that you have been too good for too long, and the pressure of acting good when you are so obviously not finally became combustive. You've been good because you'd been promised some reward at the end of it all: college, let's say, the reason for and solution to everything, but that dangling carrot has been snatched away from you in one two-hundred-word email, a rejection driven home with a punch to the head. And then you realized that the prize wasn't ever really a prize anyway, but rather a door that opened up to a long, hard road to some other destination unknown, and it was like you lost something and had to retrace your steps all the way back to when you last remembered having it. Before you knew it, you were all the way back at the beginning.

It sounds good, and it briefly makes sense in your head. But then it doesn't make sense, because how is this your beginning? The people out there are your family, kind of, but except for your mother, it feels so wrong to use that word. They aren't your origin. This isn't your home. You look around and none of this is familiar to you, not the pink carpet in the bathroom or the lavender-scented everything or the men's yellow Bic classic razor with soap and dark stubble découpaged onto blades that are rusted into the same hue of sunset orange you and Ahmet had chased down I-20 only yesterday.

But wait a second.

That hair belongs to your father. You're in his house, sitting on the same toilet on which he sits, possibly staring at the same spot of dirty caulk he stares at when wondering how he, too, had fucked things up so impossibly.

That's it. You've been in his house for ten minutes now, you've caught the electric rabbit you'd been chasing, and yet you've forgotten to even conjure his name.

You flush and don't bother to run the faucet water to pretend that you're washing your hands. "Where's my father?" you ask before you reach the end of the hall. "Bash-kim?" you say, when you arrive back in the dining area, in case they don't understand what you mean by *father,* but nobody responds, other than to glance at each other or stare at you blankly.

"Is he here? Is he mad?" you ask.

Finally Adnan shakes his head.

"He's not mad?" you ask.

"He's not here," Adnan says. "He's dead."

"You don't have to say it like that," the younger boy says.

"Dead?" you repeat. "Like, dead?" you ask their mother, who responds by getting up to put water in the kettle for more tea. The little girl clings to her side, though she seems a little too old to do that kind of thing.

"She doesn't speak English too good," Adnan says.

"Dead," the woman repeats anyway.

Your mother hasn't said a word the whole time, not since you walked through the door, and you don't know why the woman is bothering to make more tea because your mother hasn't taken so much as a sip of hers. She's so mad she can't even look at you, and suddenly you're so sorry that you can't look away. All of this was for nothing. This intangible thing that you've been chasing because you decided the tangible things you started from were worthless, and this is the final nothing. All you've accomplished was getting two thousand miles closer to someone who would always be a million miles away.

The end.

But really?

Maybe not. What now? Do you quit, or cry, or leave, or keep running, or what? You can't just end things by being sorry. That's not an ending, it's just a feeling, but it's the one that consumes everything else.

Fuck. I'm sorry, I'm sorry, I'm sorry, you think, but you don't have the guts to say something so puny out loud. Instead you look over at your mother and hope she sees it on you, or that she can pierce into your skull and let it out that way. You want to tattoo it across your forearm so people will know it when you wave to them in greeting: Oh, that's the girl who's sorry.

"I'm so, so sorry," your mother says, and you're shocked that it worked, that you managed to convey it strongly enough simply through breathing that she can read it off of you. Except she's crying, and slowly you realize that she's not translating what you're thinking but saying what she is. You don't understand it. Why is she crying, why is she the one saying she's sorry, when you're the one who fucked up her life and these people's lives and Ahmet's life and maybe even whatever life an already dead man had left behind? But even if you don't understand it, you're grateful that she's able to say it, because it feels good to hear. It makes you think that maybe you don't understand much of anything at all, which feels awful and a little hopeful at the same time.

CHAPTER NINETEEN: ELSIE

The helium *It's a Girl!* balloons that danced in the kitchen for days began to droop, skirting the room like trapped birds looking for the way out. There were people around constantly at first — Mamie, Yllka, Greta, Deena, Rini, Margot, Dardata, the rest of the wives whose names I still hadn't figured out — and then, because they needed to preserve their vacation days for their vacations and their sick days for their sicknesses, they started dropping by just for a few minutes after work, and then just calling to see how we were doing, and then telling me just to call them if I needed anything. Gjonni had fixed the phone, wouldn't let that kind of disaster happen again, though it couldn't actually happen again, not to me, anyway. *Don't be shy, call!* they said, but I didn't call, and it wasn't because I was shy. I was grateful and didn't want to ask for more from them. I had to figure out how to do things for myself, and not just for myself, but for you. I needed food because you needed food, so I filled out the paperwork for WIC and vowed that your milk wouldn't always be reconstituted nonfat powder that nobody could swallow without some added cocoa and sugar. Who'd have known that by the time I could buy us cartons of the actual stuff at Stop & Shop you wouldn't even want milk anymore? It's for the babies of the animals that gave birth to them, you say now. You say, That milk is not meant for me.

I gave you my milk as long as I could, but because of all of the other things you needed, eventually it had to come from somewhere else. Once I went back to work at Ferrucci you spent your days with Aunt Greta, and she gave you bottles I prepared, half asleep, while listening to Led Zeppelin on the lowest volume that still carried sound. Once Greta left for New York and my milk dried up — I wasn't pumping enough, they said, or wasn't hydrating enough, or was thinking too much about it, or worrying too much about everything — the ladies at the daycare fed you formula the state provided, along with the child-care vouchers that paid their salaries when the low-income mothers of Connecticut couldn't.

How's that line go? *I have always depended on the kindness of strangers.* All those kind strangers grumbling about us come payday, when a few of their cents trickled down to us by way of food stamps and Section 8 credits. I do thank them now, even when I grumble the same way when I look at my paychecks, and I have to remind myself about all those years. Funny when you have to remind yourself about things that, not long ago, consumed your every thought.

Yllka didn't understand why I wanted to move out, especially not to the townhouse apartments the developers called a village, which everybody knew was code for "the projects." She forbade it entirely, even stood at the bottom of the steps refusing to budge on the day that Deena's husband came with his pickup to help move our stuff. She cried and tried to get Mamie to talk some sense into me, but Mamie just threw up her arms and said, "Do you think she's ever listened to anything I've said?" I'm sure she also said something like *I hope someday you have a daughter just like you,* and I probably rolled my eyes about it, that oldest of curses that, it turns out, is also the only one you need to be afraid of.

Yllka was right: the apartment in their building was nicer, quieter, and free for as long as I needed it to be. Yllka and Gjonni offered that to me, but I paid them the last month's rent by returning the crib and the changing table Bashkim had bought before he left. I could change you on a towel on the floor, and you could sleep with me until I saved up enough for something from a tag sale or a classified ad.

I never did get another crib, by the way. We shared a bed until you refused, and then you moved straight to the twin mattress you sleep on still, in the triple-decker we moved into when I no longer had to look to others to subsidize the place we call home.

Yllka asked me, before I drove off in the passenger seat of the pickup that day, you on my lap with the seatbelt around both of us as if we were still one thing, what she was supposed to tell Bashkim when he came back.

"Don't tell him anything. He'll know," I said.

He already knew. I hadn't told Yllka, but Bashkim had called two weeks after we were released from the hospital. Somehow Yllka and Gjonni had gotten a message to him, which seemed impossible, because nobody even knew what country he was in at that point, if he was even in a country at that point. As far as I knew he'd drowned in the Adriatic on the ship of refugees that sank off the coast of Italy, or he was trampled by an angry mob in Tirana, or he never made it back to Albania in the first place, and was in some kind of UN holding purgatory where they kept people who were citizens of nowhere. I pretended I didn't care, but I kept an eye out for any article in the World section of the newspaper that might have some information. If there was any news on what was happening in Albania, it was usually an inch of copy nestled between ads for discount produce and discount three-piece suits, but usually there was nothing, and never was Bashkim mentioned by name. Of course he wasn't. He was a man who barely registered from a country that was more a punch line than a place. If he died, where would the obituary even run?

I alternated between wishing him dead and wishing him back. I alternated between wishing him back so that I could seek vengeance and wishing him back so that I might, maybe one time out of ten, not have to be the one who woke up to feed you, because I thought I could take being strangled, robbed, and drawn and quartered more than I could take one more sleepless night of nursing, terror, and filling out forms to apply for charity hospital bed funds. I alternated between forgiveness and apology and unadulterated hate. I alternated between thinking I could do it all alone and thinking I could do nothing at all.

Yllka and Gjonni were people who could get stuff done. They'd managed to get the message I never asked them to send through to Bashkim, wherever he was. They sent word by carrier pigeon or something, message in a bottle, smoke signal. He called one afternoon as I tried to nurse you, tried to convince you, once again, that the well was safe. I picked up the phone, and right away I could hear every single one of the miles between us. Our voices were thin after traveling the long line of string beneath the ocean, and the constant echo and delay made it feel like we were having parallel conversations with ourselves instead of a single conversation with each other.

"You had the baby," he said. There was no hello.

"Yes," I said.

There was static on the line, which covered what I imagined was a sigh.

"You couldn't wait?"

The delay on my answer to that was so

long that the words never came through at all.

"It's a girl," he said, finally.

"Yes," I said.

"Luljeta."

"Yes."

More static, a cover for the silence that was obviously lurking beneath it.

"Where are you?" I asked.

"In Greece for now."

"With Aggie?"

"Yes."

"Everyone is safe?"

"No, not everyone. It is still bad there."

"I didn't mean everyone, I meant you."

"Oh. Then yes. We are safe."

"Okay."

Silence.

"I don't know how long I will be here," he said, finally.

"Okay," I said.

"I have to take care of some things while I'm here. It just makes sense."

"Okay."

"Okay?"

"Yes."

Static.

"Are you okay?" he said.

"We're fine."

" 'We'?"

"Me and Lulu. That's what I've been calling her."

"Oh," he said. "That's good."

Static.

"I'm sorry I was not there," he said.

"I'm not."

"I'm sorry for the money. I will pay you back."

"It wasn't my money."

"It wasn't my money, either, but I needed it. It's not that much. I will pay it back."

"Send it straight to my sister. It already did what it was supposed to do. It got you away from me."

"You are mad," he said.

"Yes, but that's beside the point."

"We will talk about it later."

"No we won't."

"You are very mad."

"Yes, but it doesn't matter."

"I should go," he said. "This is very expensive."

"I don't want you back, is what I mean."

"What?"

"When you come back here, I mean. If you come back. I don't want you back with us."

The line was getting really bad. Maybe he couldn't make out what I said. Maybe that had been it the whole time, not that he didn't care but that he didn't understand, because I was expecting more fight from him, a threat, a plea, something that would give me the bravery to follow through. But all he said, after a pause, was "I have to go."

"Okay. Bye," I said. I didn't wait for a response to that. I just hung up and waited for the phone to ring again. When it didn't, I took it off the hook so I didn't have to hear it not ringing.

For seventeen years now, the phone's been off the hook.

I'm supposed to say that I did whatever I had to do to keep you safe, but the truth is, it wasn't all my decision. In a sense I got what I asked for, in that I didn't have to do everything alone. He helped make the decision. He didn't call back. If he had, it might have been possible that he would have convinced me to stay in that apartment waiting for him to return. He might have convinced me that loneliness was a bigger threat than hunger or terror, that giving up on him meant giving up on everything, which meant that everything was hopeless, a feeling I would have passed on to you through my milk, a bigger threat to you than any virus or food allergy or secondhand Rossi you could've been exposed to through me. He could've taught you to say hello, goodbye, and sorry in a whole different language. He could've taught you the value of a dollar, that the things we think constitute suffering don't even qualify for an inch of space in the newspaper, and what kinds of guys to stay far, far away from.

But he didn't call back, so that was that. By the time I heard from Janice, who still to this day slings food at the Ross, that he eventually made his way back to the States, it didn't matter. We no longer lived in the same world, never mind the same country.

You latched on that night and drank like you'd just discovered it was necessary for survival. I was glad. Everyone talks about hunger as primal, as if having it and knowing how to manage it are the same, but sometimes even instinct fails us. It was okay, though. It didn't have to come easy. Don't ever listen to the person who tells you that it will.

The younger son is Tarik, the daughter is Mirlinda. They're your brother and sister, like Adnan is your brother, but none of you use those words to describe each other. Their mother is Agnes, and she's dressed head to toe in black like the middle-aged manager of a Hot Topic, though even you, who have not even buried a pet, know that she's simply donning the universal uniform of mourners. The dress isn't what sells it, though. Agnes exudes mourning. It's all over her face like a rash. Her eyes are dark and always wet and her face is cast downward as if gravity has always worked extra-hard on her, and not just since the death of her husband. Sometimes she says something that Adnan translates for you and sometimes she says things that Adnan keeps to himself, but mostly she fiddles with things on the counter or in the cabinets, tidying things that were never messy, dropping fresh sugar cubes onto a dish that's already spilling sugar cubes. She looks as if she'd been caught eavesdropping, even though she doesn't understand most of what you're saying and even though you and your mother are the intruders in her home, making her bear witness to a scene she never asked to be a spectator to. You're the one who should be contrite, who should offer condolences and atonements in equal measure, and maybe later, once you aren't so god-damned tired, once you're back at home thinking about all of this from your own familiar bed, you'll be able to muster it. But your bed is far away, so for the time being you sit in someone else's uncomfortable chair and let yourself be a quiet spectacle. It's already gotten old to Tarik and Mirlinda, who've gone off to the living room to play some game on some half-shattered electronic device. To them, even math homework would be more fun than the sorry group that took over their kitchen. Sometimes Mirlinda slides back in to take a look at you and whisper something into her mother's ear, but she disappears quickly, which is fine, because you have no idea what to say to a kid sister anyway.

"Shy," Agnes says, and it's hard to discern if she's talking about Mirlinda or herself.

428

You learn that you're three months too late. A year ago your father began coughing. Nine months ago he began coughing blood, six months ago he was whittled down to ninety-eight pounds, and not long after that it was clear to everyone but himself that he would die of the always fatal combination of lung cancer and denial. Adnan tells you he smoked Marlboro Reds until almost the day he died, oxygen tubes and all, and while he exhaled he talked about buying out the pizza joint he ran for his brother-in-law once he was back on his feet.

"He could blow perfect smoke rings. A lion could jump through them," your mother says.

Adnan looks embarrassed by that, that a stranger would know that kind of private information about his father. He's polite, a good enough kid, it seems, but he's not yet old enough to hide how much he wishes he didn't have to be there, translating and explaining things even the older ones among you can't find the right words for in your native tongues. He shrugs his shoulders almost constantly as he talks, as if trying to shake off someone's grip from them.

"Did you guys even know about me?" you ask.

Adnan shakes his head. "He never said

anything about, like, other kids."

Your mother looks down at her hands. "It's not that I didn't want you to exist to him," she says.

"Then what did you want?" you ask.

"I don't know," she says. "I need some time to think about that."

"Seventeen years hasn't been enough time?"

"No, not really," she says. "I was doing other things." She takes a deep breath and says, "But I'll try, okay? I'll try. I know that's not what you want to hear, but I have to figure out how to make it make sense."

Adnan squints his eyes, like he's trying to make out some tiny figure off on the horizon. "There was this time, though, with Mirlinda. I forgot about that," he says. "Mirlinda walked in and he just started crying, and he was like, 'You're here, you're here.' He was all drugged up and stuff, so we didn't think too much about it, you know? But maybe, I don't know, that could've been something."

You nod. Maybe it was something, maybe it wasn't. You'll never really know, as you had never known, and so it isn't as devastating for you to hear as you think it should be. Maybe it's even a privilege of some kind, that someday you'll get to decide for yourself what it meant. You can tell the story and make it beautiful or sad or stupid or pathetic, and who will possibly ever challenge it? You have a great big blank that you can fill in however you see fit. These kids, meanwhile, are left with the memory of a man in a father mask that fell off once he was dead. You're the oldest of them and should feel an instinct to protect your siblings from that kind of pain, or reserve it for yourself to dish out when you feel like you have to put them back in line, but you have no idea how to be a big sister. It would be nice, you think, to not be an only child, but you're thinking you'll probably have to settle for this in-between thing, not an only and not part of a whole.

You stay longer than uninvited guests should. It seems like there should be more to say, but each one of you expects the other to be the one responsible for it. Nobody save for a single housefly touches the crackers Aggie spread out on a dish a couple of hours ago, and you think that you should send her something when you're home, one of those epic gift baskets from the Italian shop, to make up for the tea and snacks and time she wasted on you.

"Can we go?" you ask. You realize how rude that must sound, but nobody seems offended. Everybody, in fact, seems relieved.

"Yes, yes, yes, we can go," your mother says. She stands up and picks up the plate of crackers like she's going to help put it away, and then realizes she doesn't know what to do with it and sets it back down. She wipes a few crumbs on the table into her open palm and then, not knowing what to do with the crumbs either, balls up her hand into a fist and shoves it in her pocket. Nobody else notices, but you notice, and you aren't sure why, out of everything that happened that night, this is the thing to break your heart.

At the door you all look at each other, wondering what's the most appropriate send-off, handshakes or embraces or a nothing that would reverberate all the way back to Connecticut.

"Okay, then. Mirupafshim," your mother says, and Aggie even smiles a little, with the kind of smile she could muster, a smile coated with grief.

"Mirupafshim," Aggie says.

"And sorry," your mother says, but Aggie doesn't respond to that word the same way.

In the car, a rented subcompact ten years newer than her car at home, you ask her what that word she said meant.

"*Mirupafshim?* It means goodbye," she says.

"How did you know that?"

"There are a few Albanians at work," she says. Then she sighs. "And I don't know, it's just one of the things I remember from back then."

Robbie is at the motel waiting for you. You open the door and scream when you see his six-foot-three figure draped over the floral coverlet, lit up from the light of the TV, until you make out the black plastic eyeglasses and the amber bottle of some craft beer or another on the nightstand.

"Oh my god," you gasp. "Sorry, I didn't know you were here."

"I can go somewhere else for a while if you want me to," he says.

"I meant to say something on the drive over, but it slipped my mind," your mother says. "Robbie offered to come, and you know, I didn't want to be alone."

Of course she didn't. She's never been alone. She's always had you following her around, asking stuff from her, needing stuff from her, telling her that you didn't need anything from her. Or maybe that means she's always been alone, since it doesn't really seem like togetherness if you never get anything back from the person you're with. Either way, you know that you should thank him for being there, and you know that he's one more person to add to the list of apologies due. He's taking time off from his job, paying for all this nonsense, and he gives enough of a shit about your mother that you know he never even thought twice about those things.

"You should stay" is what you manage to get out. And "I feel really, really stupid." He nods, and with all his education you hope he's able to read the subtext, at least until you're able to find some better words.

Your mother doesn't ask any of the questions you've been trying to prepare answers to. Everybody's too tired. You're going to need a full recharge before you can even begin to work this out, but the motel parking lot is lit like high noon, which is confusing to your bodies and makes it hard to sleep. It's a cheap motel, but not that cheap. This whole thing is costing a fortune, the plane tickets and car rental and motels, the fast food and data usage surcharges. You've fallen into deep, deep debt, and tomorrow you'll have to begin climbing out of it.

But that's tomorrow, not tonight.

Robbie volunteers to take the cot, so you and your mother are together in the queen bed, each of you feeling every restless twitch as the other tries to fall asleep. Even so, there's no confusing the feeling when you settle under the covers. It's relief, a little break from all that happened and whatever's going to come next.

ACKNOWLEDGMENTS

Huge gratitude to my agent, Julie Barer, for never saying *good enough,* especially when those were the words I most wanted to hear. Also for her mondo patience, because getting me past *good enough* took as long as getting a child from the womb to the first grade.

To my supereditor, Andrea Walker, for her advocacy and enthusiasm from the very beginning, for laughing in the right places, for gently pointing out the wrong places, and for hopefully sporting a Hartford Whalers beanie. The publicity and marketing superstars who got this book into so many hands deserve more drinks than I could possibly ply them with: Jennifer Garza, Andrea DeWerd, Avideh Bashirrad, and Emma Thomasch. Thanks also to many others on the Random House team, including Andy Ward, Susan Kamil, Leigh Marchant, Emma Caruso, Jennifer Rodriguez, Toni

Hetzel, and many others working behind the scenes whose names I wish I knew. Further props to Nicole Cunningham at The Book Group for keeping this machine well-oiled.

To a few critical early readers, who also happen to be dear friends and brilliant stars themselves, and whose input and insights helped this manuscript find its way from desktop clutter to real-life book: Jennine Capó Crucet, Gwendolyn Knapp, and Christopher Rhodes. Your suggestions were invaluable and you were far nicer about them than you had to be.

Big thanks to the Djerassi Resident Artists Program for providing shelter, food, a surrogate dog, and the company of damn cool humans during a critical revision period. Particular shout-out to Lunch Club and Barn Burn members Mark Conway, Brittany Powell, Chris Robinson, and Susanna Sonnenberg. Everything I've written since 2008 owes its existence in some way to the Bread Loaf Writers Conference, where I met so many people I wanted to impress that I had no choice but to become a better writer and sharper dresser. Thanks to the faculty and students in the creative writing department at UNCW, where the characters of Elsie and Bashkim were first born.

Many, many other friends provided inspiration, support, respite, fantastically inappropriate jokes, meals, beds on which to crash, and a reason to keep going, among them Patricia Engel, Ru Freeman, Susan McCarty, Matt Kirkpatrick, Dawn Lonsinger, Jacob Paul, Esther Lee, Davy Gibbs, Lauren Knowlton, Jessie and Thomas Wilcox, Bob Glass, Gabrielle Lucille Fuentes, Jason Labbe, Steve May, Tim Parrish, and others whom I'm being an idiot for not thinking of as I write this. The fact that there are enough amazing people in my life for me to not be able to come up with all of their names in one sitting is something for which I'm profoundly grateful.

To Timothy O'Keefe: thank you for letting me work and making me want to. Thank you for the noise that comes between the quiet. Thank you for the manhattans, the pad see ew, for walking the dogs, and for not getting mad when I ask you if you've done the things around the house that of course you've already done. Thanks to the rest of the O'Keefe family both for making someone like Tim and for being as gracious, generous, and kind as you are.

Finally, I owe the biggest debt to Mom, Chuck, Kyjtim, Michael, Sarah, Kim, and Kristen (and now their spouses and kiddos).

We may not all share the same blood, but we shared things that I think made us even more of a family: a single bathroom for the eight of us and a fleet of Dodge K-cars. You taught me how to laugh at adversity and just about everything else. Without you, I wouldn't have bothered with any of this.

ABOUT THE AUTHOR

Xhenet Aliu's debut fiction collection, *Domesticated Wild Things, and Other Stories,* won the Prairie Schooner Book Prize in Fiction. Her stories and essays have appeared in *Glimmer Train, The Barcelona Review, American Short Fiction,* and elsewhere. She holds an MFA from the University of North Carolina Wilmington and an MLIS from The University of Alabama. A native of Waterbury, Connecticut, she was born to an Albanian father and a Lithuanian American mother. She now lives in Athens, Georgia, and works as an academic librarian.

xhenetaliu.com

The employees of Thorndike Press hope you have enjoyed this Large Print book. All our Thorndike, Wheeler, and Kennebec Large Print titles are designed for easy reading, and all our books are made to last. Other Thorndike Press Large Print books are available at your library, through selected bookstores, or directly from us.

For information about titles, please call:
(800) 223-1244

or visit our website at:
gale.com/thorndike

To share your comments, please write:
Publisher
Thorndike Press
10 Water St., Suite 310
Waterville, ME 04901